THE QUEST OF ALL AGES

The Quest Of All Ages

Maha Devi Li Ra La

Book 1 of the
Within The Ocean Of Eternal Love
Series

An Ananda Bliss Consciousness Book

Ananda Bliss Consciousness Inc

www.anandablissconsciousness.com
www.mahadevi-lirala.com

Book and Cover Design Copyright © 2015 Gabriele Brigitte Klonek

Book and Cover Design by Maha Devi Li Ra La

ISBN: 978-1-910518-17-5

Printed and Copyrighted in the United States of America

British Library Cataloguing in Publication Data

Maha Devi Li Ra La

The Quest Of All Ages

Book 1 of the

'Within The Ocean Of Eternal Love' Series

First Edition 2015

To true Love which gives us Wings

And lets us ascend to the Heavens of

Unity and Bliss Consciousness

Preface

This is a spiritual fantasy novel about the power of true love and the Divine qualities it conjures from the depths of our souls. The story is fictional and loosely based on historical facts. By no means does the authoress claim historical accuracy. Nevertheless, an attempt was made to draw on the historical facts of the time period around 270 B.C. to support the storyline and characters of this novel. The story originates in Magna Graecia, Greek colonies located on the Italian Peninsula, and evolves through defining scenes taking place in additional locations and cultures, including Ancient Greece, Macedonia, and the Roman and Phoenician Empires, as well as the World Oceans.

The Within The Ocean Of Eternal Love book series is a vibrant epic tale that resurrects many of Ancient Greece's most powerful and enigmatic Gods and Goddesses to either support or wreak havoc on mankind, depending on their unique traits and inclinations. Underwater Realms of exotic beauty and sunken marvels of a glorious past from long ago invite the reader to explore the oceanic depths alongside the protagonists, to rejoice in pleasant mer-folk company and sweat under the pressures of larger-than-life challenges that test the heroes and heroines to the core.

Fairies and elves enlivening the mystical forests add to the fairy tale and fantasy character of the novel; enchanting scenes of great spiritual meaning open the reader's mind to higher truths and realities. This is not a story that can easily be categorized; it is an epic tale of the kind that will still be read and appreciated a hundred years from now, for it is timeless in its message, and transforming and uplifting in its wonderfully deep impact on our souls. Let yourself be entertained by the absorbing, suspenseful adventures the heroes and heroines go through, and come out the winner in the end, as true epics always reward you with a satisfying ending that is equal to the protagonists' persistence and investment in their own self-transformation and personal growth.

CHAPTER 1

Indirali, the princess daughter of the King and Queen of the kingdom of Lucania, is to be engaged and married to Hecto, the prince son of the neighboring kingdom of Campania, from the city of Neapolis. Theirs is a union of sacrifice and vote of good faith, symbolizing the unification of two bordering kingdoms that have been at the brink of war for quite some time now. An unfortunate chain reaction of several compounding misfortunes has thrown both kingdoms into fatal poverty and overwhelming societal anguish. Let down by their Gods, the people of Magna Graecia find themselves divided and caught in a downward spiral of animosity and hardship. Poseidon, the God of the Underwater World, has gotten fed up with the prevailing corruption and moral decline of many kingdoms within his dominion, and has begun a campaign of his own to facilitate the downfall of these once stellar cultures and societies that have long begun to engage in the spiritual Winter season of diminishing Divine values and life expressions. Knowing that the spiritual Winter season, or Iron Age, is the most decadent and death-oriented of all four existing seasons, with a continuing increase of violence and killing modalities of all kinds spreading throughout the world, the Gods seem to have turned their backs on most of humanity, leaving them to fend for themselves in the many battles of their lower-self willpower and arrogance. Only the lower Gods seem to still possess an interest in mankind, aggravating the unstable, volatile atmospheres with their negatively charged superhuman energies to affect the kind of societal imbalances that allow misery, suffering, and hardship of all kinds to grow and thrive. War between many different tribes and nations has weakened the collective spirit of the land, with Greek colonists of Magna Graecia now trying to preserve their cultural heritage and identity against the Romans, who are fast becoming the superior imperialist force that threatens to end the autonomy and independence of any city-state on the Italian peninsula. Enlisting the help of reputable, heroic Greek war kings, the Greek colonists and their allies, the Lucanians and Samnites, have been trying to thwart the usurping influence of the new superpower of Rome, lest all the different tribes and diverse cultures cease to exist and merely one single empire, controlled and censored by the senators of Rome, reigns the whole peninsula, forcing everyone to adopt their ways and bow down before their Gods.

But instead of being able to call and count on their own Gods of Ancient for help, the allies experience added hardship when trying to cross the ocean waters because Poseidon, the mighty Sea God, considers himself a facilitator of the demise of mankind, unless one man would stand out with his righteousness, courage, and alignment with Divine Will. But such a hero has evidently not risen above the mass-average levels for many decades now, and so Poseidon continues to ravage the ocean waters as if wanting to teach every decadent or natural law-violating soul a lesson or two. With ferociousness only comparable to the power wielding of Aries, the God of War himself, Poseidon cast a spell of destruction upon the sea and everyone who dares to cross it. Trade with kingdoms and countries across the ocean has become impossible, as most ships get caught in Poseidon's wrath and suffer their demise in harrowing vortexes of insurmountable water waves, tossed around by high winds and thundering storms and losing their sight and direction within massive downpours of highly condensed, monsoon-like rain that threatens to knock anyone unconscious who dares to resist it. Many have lost their lives in the infinite depth of the sea, and many once wealthy men have lost their ships and fortunes to the absorbing grip of the Water God. The ocean has become a field of unrest and turmoil, an impossible area to cross anymore, preventing humans from trading their precious goods with one another. Even the Strait of Messina has become a deathtrap that devours the lives of many heroic oversea-trades merchants and their crews, leaving their homelands segregated and separated from the rest of Magna Graecia and from the prosperous Greek colonies of the island of Sicily, a territory occupied by the Phoenician and Carthaginian empire that rules and trades their extensive commerce along the Tyrrhenian Sea. But because of Poseidon's curse, access to these more affluent regions has become sparse and extremely difficult, forcing the Italiot Greeks to live and contend without the delicious citrus fruits and olives of the southern regions and without all the exotic and basic goods from Siricusa and Messina, all coveted produce the northern kingdoms had grown accustomed to over time.

A big void has begun to spread, and the morale of all societies concerned has dropped to an all-time low. The leaders of many coastal regions feel besieged with the pressures of unfulfilled demands from the mostly swampy or mountainous inland regions. A long time ago, the tribe of Samnites living along the coastline was driven from the fertile land by the early Greek colonists into the more barren and hardly accessible mountain ranges, turning their people angry and helpless over many years of growing destitution, and even more so now under the squashing rulership of Rome, towards which superpower many smaller tribes are turning for help in defending themselves against the angry, trespassing Samnites. Three gruesomely long and harrowing wars did the Samnites wage against Rome until they finally gave up and were granted a limited sphere of existence under Roman dominion. Their fate, and that of many other such desperate inland tribes, depends heavily on trading their simple goods for the more abundant cornucopia of goods coming from the sun-drenched regions of the southern islands if they want to experience any sense of prosperity and comfort at all. Envy towards inhabitants of the more fertile flatlands of the sunnier, lush coastal or island regions and despair about everyone's own increasing destitution have tribes, city-states, and kingdoms turning against each other, ignorantly trying to squeeze the life juice out of their neighbors since their own efforts for satisfying their collective or kingdoms' needs have failed terribly, thus attesting to a growing misalignment with the Gods of their ancestors.

Posidonia, the governmental seat of the King and Queen of Lucania, was once a flourishing and prosperous city founded by Greek colonists from the South Italian city of Sybaris, a city that itself knew no comparison to its own opulent wealth, splendor, and prosperity until it was stomped into the ground by the city of Croton, to be no more and to only leave behind a wealth of memories and legends about its grandeur and fabled luxury for all the Greek colonists to remember it by, and whose Hellenistic roots were thus lost to the citizens of Posidonia. With the Roman forces now trying to conquer and subdue most parts of the Italian peninsula, and with many tribes already allied with the Romans, including Lucania's northern neighbor of Campania, the King of Lucania fears a similar fate might soon befall his city as has already happened to Sybaris, their founding city, would he not consider the volatile situation wisely and align himself with those who arrogantly try to squash the last vestiges and remnants of Hellenistic heritage from the souls and culture of the Greek Italiots. With an air of superiority and according to their imperialistic motives, the Romans have recently suggested a different name for Posidonia, namely Paestum, as a symbol of their conquest and a name closer to their language. But for as long as the present king rules the kingdom of Lucania, he intends to keep the name their Greek ancestors bestowed upon the city, hoping that a peaceful attitude towards Rome will allow him to keep his kingdom safe and unaltered by the imperialist force.

Even though many Samnites have joined their kingdom over the last centuries and decades, thus comprising the citizenship of Lucania along with the Greek colonists, it is through the latter that much elevating culture has been added to the kingdom, and it was deemed wise under the precarious circumstances for the people to choose a king from among the well-educated Greek colonists. Thus Nikodemos ascended the throne and performed his best in regard to maintaining peace and trying to incentivize the economy until at last he handed the crown to his son and successor, the now present king of Lucania, Eurylochos. The situation throughout the Italian peninsula, however, and within Lucania itself, has not improved over all these years but has instead continued to deteriorate, leaving Eurylochos wondering how on earth he will ever be able to turn the tide of his kingdom's identity loss around when all the world is gradually consenting to follow the Roman direction on, literally, all the many roads this eager-beaver imperialist force is carving out of the ground for their armies faster than any tribe can prepare itself for their subduing impact. Instead, the constant threat of the many warring factions all around the borders of Lucania and the burden of the curse of the Sea God Poseidon that, on top of everything else, is severely impeding the trade and commerce of Lucania with the surrounding regions, near and far, have all contributed to a despondent attitude amongst the people, and among the royal court members as well. Within the palace, the grandeur and prosperity of the ancient city still tries to live on, with many lofty buildings and beautiful gardens decorating the grounds, light-reflecting marble temples rising towards the Heavens boasting tall pillars aesthetically adorned with cascades of everblooming flowers of all kinds, and delicate orange blossoms and opulent rose bushes of all colors perfuming the atmospheres with waves of refined scents, dazzling the senses of anyone who has the fortune to find access to this human sanctuary in a world of war and decay. Outside of Posidonia's palace walls, however, a less beautiful picture shows, as in their daily lives many citizens feel the consequences of a faltering economy and long-standing, exhausting deploys of military defense forces, resulting in a growing uncertainty about their future, leaving parents to worry about their children who may never grow up to know the carefreeness and glory their ancestors once knew.

King Eurylochos loves his daughter Indirali dearly. He would have liked to see her married to a man of her choice and true love. But the times seem impossibly dire, with the first of his own people beginning to die in the streets of hunger and starvation, and his front-line soldiers threatening to collapse from the increasing military pressures of the surrounding forces. His only son, Indirali's brother Athos, is stationed with his army at the northeastern border of the kingdom, trying to prevail in keeping his father's kingdom safe from an increasing threat of intruding forces from Apulia. King Eurylochos would prefer to have his son and heir to the throne safe with him in the palace, but the times demand extra cautionary measures, and reliable, loyal, and competent military leaders are not easy to come by these days. Still, he misses his son and hopes every day that the threats will lift soon, and he will see him alive and well again. In the meantime, he has plans for Indirali as well, basically using her as a bargaining chip to secure much needed peace between the kingdoms. Out of despair and to also indirectly signal to Rome his desire for peace and cooperation, he agreed to a political alliance with one of the neighboring kingdoms, Campania, an ally of Rome itself, to have Hecto, the royal heir of Neapolis, and his daughter married to each other as an act of good will and wise statesmanship, aiming to lend strength and power to both kingdoms' welfare and defense. His heart, however, has begun to bleed for the misfortune of his beloved daughter to never be able to experience the deep and everlasting love he feels for her mother, Penelope, his wife of many years. Every time he looks at his wife's beautiful face, losing himself in the infinite love of her deep, unfathomable eyes, he feels tears forming in his own eyes, as if to lament the great sacrifice and misfortune he has to expose his darling daughter to, wondering what difficult situation the questionable justice of the Gods has thrown his family into, and whether there is any reason for hope left anymore, or whether this is the end of the family's blessings as they have known so far, a love so pure it has kept the king going throughout all the arising difficulties of his kingdom. Indirali herself has grown increasingly silent and distant since hearing the dreaded news. Hecto is known as a politically ambitious, eager-for-war kind of young man, and Indirali couldn't care less for these kinds of attributes in a man who is to become her husband. Contrary to his inclinations, Indirali loves peace, kindness, wisdom, and beauty — all the Divine qualities of the highest Gods — before any base human interests and pursuits. The thought to have to share her life with someone eager to fight and amass power seems to only trigger her fears and dismay. And so she has begun to withdraw from life, as if it is nearing its end anyway, nothing left to look forward to, nothing worth directing all the tremendous amounts of love towards that she is able to feel and conjure from the infinite depths of her soul.

A messenger has just arrived to announce the courtship visit of Hecto and his entourage at the Lucanian palace within the fortnight, as the Prince is coming to woo his future wife with all the proper pomp, accessories, and gifts that seem standard procedure at an occasion like this. The palace has been thrown into a whirl, with servants and ministers roaming around as if in an ant nest, each pursuing some meaningful task or another, trying to meet the varied demands of such a once in a lifetime visit, attentively obeying the orders of their king to the letter. Indirali has locked herself into her chambers, her maidservant Hedna kneeling at her feet trying to ease the Princess's heart pain with the love flowing through her fingers into a healing reflex massage of Indirali's delicate feet. The Princess sits near the big window overlooking the beautiful park-like garden below and in front of her, dreamily watching the gentle stirrings of Nature as the willow tree near the pond softly sways in the fresh spring breeze and the ducks float on the still waters, occasionally diving for some food or cleaning their feathers, and then bursting into a standing position that prompts several of them to start taking flight across the pond, lifting themselves into the sky like all the other free birds who are able to just leave the ground whenever they choose. Indirali's eyes begin to fill with tears as she contemplates the notion of her freedom. The only freedom she is given is the one of silent endurance and inner withdrawal from everything she is unable to bear and approve. Hers is the fate of so many women whose sole duty in life is to stand behind their men whether they feel like it or not. Death seems like a sweet liberation from this undesirable condition, she concludes, if only her death wouldn't hurt her parents so much whom she loves so dearly.

Deeply touched by the pain she feels in her Mistress's soul, Hedna suggests an outing into Nature to a beautiful spot near the ocean secludedly tucked away from the public's eye behind some big rocks planted in the ocean. Hedna heard about this spot from her cousin who likes to explore the hidden landscapes of Lucania's beautifully wild Nature, and she was made aware that this spot exudes a bewildering magic uncommon to most other places this person has come across.

Indirali gazes at the sky, her heart longing for an answer to her impossible situation, a miracle that could have the power to turn her destiny around and allow her to feel the same true love in her heart that she has been witnessing all her life between her loving, devoted parents. Silently she agrees to the outing, and the two women dress up for this explorative occasion.

Chapter 2

*T*he night is falling, but the two women ride their horses with the passion of haunted souls trying to escape their fateful destiny. Their velvet cloaks flutter in the wind, and their hair whirls around their heads in a wild and untamed fashion. Indirali knows that her days of playful ease and lightness are numbered, and she is intent on making the most of this moment. Her loyal maidservant always at her side, she rides the horse as if her life depends on it. And her stallion is all games, enjoying the ride as much as his mastress, leading the way through the misty landscapes as if under a magic spell of sorts.

Finally, they near the bay area that is supposed to harbor the idyllic spot Hedna's cousin revealed to her with an air of mystery in his voice. The women dismount from their horses and begin to look for signs of the place described to them. They wander in the moonlit evening with their horses trotting by their side, trying to discern the landscape to make out the environments they are getting into. And after walking for a while, they find a certain landmark mentioned to them, from which mark they now know how to find their way into the elusive cave that supposedly leads to a pool surrounded by big boulders and the open sea on the other side. The women fasten the reigns of their horses to a tree and set out on their nightly adventure by foot.

After another hour of walking and climbing, they arrive at a small canyon that leads directly to the pool. Their eyes open with wonder, as they perceive the beauty of this magical feeling place. With saturated green grass surrounding the pool and beautifully smelling scents coming off the many varieties of flower bushes all around, a huge waterfall rains down from several high boulders, splashing playfully into the pool and spraying its mist all around. The moonlight falls onto the water and reflects itself in trillions of sparkles and glittering water drops, veiling this beautiful place in the magic only known to the Gods, or so it seems. With a sigh of relief, Indirali lets herself sink onto the grassy green ground,

jasmine flowers raining down on her as she slightly touches a branch, and begins
to bathe in the wondrous rays of healing this mystical place seems to exude from
the moment they both laid eyes on it. Gratitude and an air of freedom immediately
begin to stream from her and upon her, as if Goddess Aphrodite Herself awaited
her arrival, greeting her with Her unconditionally loving, big heart that has the
power to overcome and drown out any and all sorrows from a fragile human
heart like hers. And for the first time in a long time, Indirali feels the urge to cry
and to open her heart again to let the beauty of the moment sink deeply into her
soul.

And then something truly magical and out of this world happens, something
so unforeseen and unpredicted that it takes Indirali several moments to accustom
her eyes to the transparent image she detects within the waterfall in front of her.
The face and figure of an infinitely handsome young man seem to float within the
waterfall, serenely gazing back at her as if utterly mesmerized with what he sees.
Their eyes meet, and an inner dance of joy begins to take shape, a joy so pure
and elevating that it possesses the power to knock Indirali out of her normal
conscious awareness, right into the transcendence of an elevated state of being.
Both of their soul essences begin to intertwine as their immediate love begins
to unravel in a flurry of images from their common past in other lifetimes than
this. Indirali feels breathless as she endures the intensity of the moment, ready
to soon sink with him into a blissful equilibrium of their extended soul essence.
The handsome young man opens up with a serene smile, overwhelming Indirali
even more with the unbearable sweetness of his magnetic presence, drawing
her deeper and deeper into his loving spell that drives Indirali's mind into the
escape of sweet surrender and devotion. How is this moment possible? How can
such ecstatic feelings of love exist, she asks herself again and again as the mutual
gaze persists beyond time and space. Both souls seem to fall forever through
the corridors of time and space as they remember the fortunate moments they
spend together within eternity and beyond. So deep and pure is their love that it
seems impossible to part from it and reorient oneself in the here and now.

Then the handsome young man takes a step forward, exposing his stately figure outside of the waterfall. But how blown away is Indirali when she sees his full body. Instead of legs, he demonstrates a fishlike tail that keeps him dancing on the water as if it was a cloud that carries his body weight with ease. Indirali winces as she realizes she is in love with a merman, with a being so mysterious and out of this world that she has a hard time all of a sudden believing what she sees and feels. And then a cloud of denial sets in, enveloping and shrouding her elevation like it was a thing of the past. How could any of this be? She is promised to another man for marriage, and everything about it is set in stone. And this being she just felt fascinated by must merely be a figment of her imagination, driven into manifestation by the pain she has held repressed for quite some time now. A sobering shudder tears her even further out of her wellbeing. The harsh reality of her situation catches up with her fully as she withdraws her gaze and essence from this beautiful, handsome male appearance. Her soul fills with the well-known grief and sadness she has grown accustomed to over the last agonizing months. Tears well up in her being, and the longing for death overtakes her again even more so now that she has tasted a hint of eternal true love for the first time in her young life. She knows this torturous state of being all too well — longing for something way out of her reach — and doesn't want to fall prey to it anymore. She would like to end it all here and now by throwing herself into the absorbing waves of the infinitely vast ocean, merging with All That Is, becoming One with a greater force than her self-diminished state and life. And when she looks up again, wondering whether the appearance is still in place, she finds, to her confirmation about the inevitability of her disastrous situation, that the handsome merman is starting to fade, with an expression of utter disappointment on his face that causes Indirali to fall into an agony and despair deeper than ever previously felt. A beautiful dream has just disappeared, and life will never be the same again. She got reminded of how eternal true love feels like, and now the difference in comparison with the objecting feelings she harbors towards Hecto seems overwhelmingly drastic and impossible to ever overcome. The sea of melancholy in her soul threatens to lose itself in the vast essence of the physical ocean, annihilating her essence and remnant joy for life like it is water itself returning back to its original expanded and boundless state.

CHAPTER 3

*F*rom that day on, Indirali retreats into an inner world of mystery and longing. All the hustle and bustle around her in the palace leaves her unfazed. The excitement everyone exudes just makes her want to withdraw even more to those inner shores that lure her with the promise of an otherworldly solution to all her problems. It is clear to her that a positive answer to her inner dilemma is not going to come from her environment; if at all, the festivities will continue and culminate in her imprisonment as a wife to an ambitious war hero. How different did she feel by the waterfall a few days back; her longing must have conjured up a divinely beautiful manly figure, a representation of her unfulfilled dreams and deepest longings. Or was it really an illusion? Maybe she didn't just imagine it. Maybe the merman actually was in the waterfall, and she has been reprimanding and denying herself this absolutely stunning reality out of an old habit of punishing herself for even thinking she could find her fortune somewhere other than what seems to be predestined for her by the needs of her father's kingdom. How can she be sure? And how can she find out? An unknown restlessness takes her over, making her pace from one end of her room to the other. Hedna observes her Mistress's inner dilemma, unable to think of anything more to distract her. All her recent attempts to make the Princess feel better about her life have failed miserably. No pleasure seems alluring enough, no activity interesting. She even shuns her other maidservants who before delighted her in lighthearted games and adventurous outings of all kinds. The Princess has changed a lot, and Hedna is at a loss as to what to offer to her beloved Mistress anymore. Silently she kneels on the floor, demurely watching the scurrying feet of the Princess hurrying back and forth next to her, patiently waiting for a clue from her lips that would prompt her into action and allow her to help ease her Mistress's discomfort.

"Have you seen him as well?" Indirali blurts out, hoping for confirmation of her innermost hope.

"Seen who, my Lady?"

"The beautiful man in the waterfall … the other day, at the waterfall …" The Princess's voice exudes fragility and vulnerability.

"I'm afraid I haven't," Hedna admits humbly, trying to not disappoint her Mistress more than she can bear.

"But I have seen him, with my own eyes. He looked at me from within the waterfall, gazing at me with this enormous, unconditional love …"

Hedna nods her head as if to agree with her vision.

"We have known each other for an eternity it seems," the Princess continues. "He must have felt it as well, I know he did. … If he exists …" She lowers her eyes.

"I'm sure he did," Hedna affirms. But then it strikes her: "How can he have stood there in the waterfall all this time and not drown from the massive downpour?"

"Because he is a merman, you dummy. Mermen can breathe and live in the water for as long as they please." The thought makes her laugh out loud for a moment as a strange sense of relief begins to spread in her. It feels good to share her recent experience with her confidante; it somehow makes the whole thing more real to her. And that is exactly what she wants, for the merman to be real and alive, and as much in love with her as she is with him, strangely enough, since they evidently don't seem to share the same worlds with one another.

"Do you want to see him again, my Lady?" Hedna asks with some curiosity. Because for whatever reason, the vision of this merman seems to have aroused the Princess's life spirits again, and Hedna, as good and loyal a maidservant as she is to her Mistress, will do anything in her power to bring the Princess back to her old, jubilant self.

"Maybe …" Indirali ponders, "maybe … yes!" And all of a sudden she stands still. An inner light seems to have ignited in her, and suddenly she knows that she owes it to herself to find out whether this merman really exists, or whether her yearning mind just made him up as a sort of comforting escape from her reality. She cannot, with a pure conscience, go into this unwanted marriage without getting to the bottom of her recently experienced love relationship with this mysterious merman.

And so, with her mind made up, Indirali resolves to ride out one more time with her maidservant to this magical spot at the ocean that seems to hold the key to her ultimate happiness.

CHAPTER 4

*E*arly the next morning, Indirali and Hedna storm out into the wild, their horses racing with each other in leaps and bounds according to the mysterious joy they feel radiating from their riders. The air is fresh, and the sun is gradually rising at the horizon, bathing the meadow valley in a golden tone of vibrant energy and warmth. Indirali's heart is leaping with happiness as she thinks about hopefully meeting this mysterious lover of hers again. Oh, how beautiful life is when you are in love, she thinks. How radiantly, exuberantly magical and beautiful! All the horror of her recent days is washed out of her, and an all-absorbing, joyous anticipation spreads like the rolling waves of an infinite ocean of bliss and life. Nothing can stand in her way right now; she challenges the Gods themselves to a duel of wits, reminding them of their true merciful nature that allows a Happy Ending for all those who ask it of them.

Around midday the two women finally reach the secluded pool area. It looks different by daylight, but nevertheless breathtakingly beautiful, with the ocean waves gently rolling in from the side. The waterfall thunders down from the high rocks, and the greenery around the water looks as fresh and healing as Indirali remembers it from her first visit. Everything is strikingly pristine, but where is he? Indirali takes a few steps into the water — her silken dress beginning to float — and looks around, feverishly panning the vistas to all sides. And the longer she looks, the more discouraged and foolish she feels. So delicate are the deepest feelings of love that they make you feel like a fool right away when it is believed that these feelings are not reciprocated. Beaten, Indirali lowers her eyes, tears immediately rolling down her cheeks. How can she have been so wrong, how can she have dreamed such a beautiful dream and felt such ecstatic feelings without there being any truth to it? How much more pain and defeat is she to bear before the Gods will have mercy on her soul and set her free? Such are her desperate thoughts and feelings when, all of a sudden, she hears her maidservant's excited scream as she points to a place near the ocean entrance, where, on a medium-sized rock, three mermen comfortably rest and smilingly watch the young women who have just joined their playground.

Indirali wipes away her tears as she tries to discern the mermen figures against the bright sunlight. She squints her eyes, and then sees him slowly approaching her, the same handsome merman with whom she had the romantic encounter that sent her hurling into the depths of her most secret hopes, desires, and dreams.

"Hi!" he greets her with a smile. "I'm Loriolan. Nice to meet you!" He swims up to her and playfully dances around her. Indirali smiles back, happily trying to catch his sight as he curiously circles around her.

"Indirali," she introduces herself, "nice to meet you, too. Or so it seems ..." She laughs in response to his attempts to fathom her from all sides and angles.

"We met the other day, didn't we?" he probes, wanting to make sure he has the right girl in front of him.

She nods, and he finally comes to a standstill in front of her. Both share another one of those deliciously intimate looks before they each break out into exuberant laughter and joy. They have found each other again, and neither of them intends to let go of the other this time around.

"Where are you from, Indirali?" Loriolan inquires.

"I'm from the palace of Lucania. And you?"

"My father reigns over this part of the Undersea-World, Ocean-King Hadores." He smiles broadly: "A fierce and fear-inducing old fella." He swims a few yards towards his friends and waves for them to come over to the women. "I brought my buddies with me to help pass the time while I was waiting for you to come back. Here, let me introduce you to them." And as the two other mermen come into close vicinity, he introduces them by their names. One of them who goes by the name Chekilian looks like a young teenage merman, and the other is his older teenage brother, Torilander. Indirali introduces them to Hedna, and Hedna immediately fills everyone in that Indirali is her Mistress, the Princess Indirali of Lucania.

Loriolan whistles admiringly and then offers Indirali his arm, inviting her to a playful swim around the rock. And out of the blue, the mermen throw a golden ball into the air, laughingly competing with each other for catching it. They seem to have such heartfelt fun that the young women immediately feel right at home with them, trusting the mermen as if they are beloved old friends.

The sun caresses her face as Indirali allows herself to be carried by Loriolan's strong arm into the moving sea, ecstatically happy to be by his side, feeling their essences merge once more and onward into the vastness of the ocean itself. Oh, sweetest surrender and inexplicable bliss! Moment in eternity where all sorrows cease and only indescribable joy and happiness exist! If it were up to her, she would dwell in this moment forever, never to live beyond the here and now again! Inner music of celestial beauty resounds in her ears according to the melodious waves of the ocean. Indirali smiles as Loriolan smiles at her. The inner sunlike presence of their united being radiates with enormous strength and power, turning their world into the most blissful Heaven mortals could ever dream of.

The water feels like velvet, flattering her figure and spraying her beautiful face with the mists of love pure. Loriolan offered himself to her and keeps sweeping her off her feet in an endless seeming journey of their souls through the landscapes of love, peace, and ecstatic fulfillment. Indirali can't help but keep smiling: an inner radiance wants to shine and expand beyond all boundaries known. Loriolan seems to feel the same, because his smile keeps getting brighter and sweeter all the time as well; it's as if their souls are intent on stepping together into the infinite blaze of the sun, ready to become the light of all lights, the very essence of a life of absolute fulfillment and absolute true love! With a prayer in her heart of deepest gratitude, Indirali thanks the Gods for listening and answering her request for a Happy Ending in regard to her longing for truest and deepest love. It exists after all, and she stands corrected in the eyes of the Almighty. With humility, she acknowledges the Gods' infinite mercy and wisdom that have brought her to this place and allowed her to meet her soulmate in these most unusual of circumstances. Indirali is thrilled at the Divine organizing power that completely changed her life around in the blink of an eye. She still can't believe her fortune! Over and over she gazes at Loriolan's handsome face, wanting to make sure that this is not just a dream but also the most beautiful of realities a human heart and soul could ever conjure up.

Meanwhile, the two brother mermen have invited Hedna to join them in the water. She gingerly takes a few steps in, carefully keeping her long skirt held up, trying to slowly adjust to the cool water. The brothers shout their encouragement and try to interest her in giving in to a playful mood. She begins to smile under their cheers and finally just lets her dress drop into the water. Then she takes a dunk and emerges smilingly with drops running from her face. The two mermen are utterly fascinated; they have not seen a beautiful girl like her behave in these unfamiliar ways, treating the water as if it were an unknown element that has to be understood and conquered slowly. But soon Hedna joins their life-enjoying play and exuberant laughter.

How nice to have found a new friend from the human realm, they think. And how nice it is to teach her a trick or two about getting around in the water in the most enjoyable, smooth, and efficient ways! The three of them soon lose themselves in playfulness and innocent, loving interactions of all kinds. The ball flies high and far, and everyone has a great time trying to catch it and continue the flow of throwing it to the next person. Hedna has not had so much fun in a long time. Sometimes, when a big wave threatens to overcome her, Torilander is right by her side to give her a welcome prop, making sure she stays on the surface of the water and not under. Hedna smiles gratefully at him, and a mysterious bond is struck between them, where their eye contact slowly moves into the realm of deep inner attraction. But Hedna knows not to give in to these strangely beautiful feelings, because her first loyalty belongs to her Mistress to whom she owes her life and love. And so she keeps it on the innocent, playful level with Torilander, and he obliges willingly. At least for now!

At some point, the group unites at a little cave near the shore, talking about this and that and finding out a lot about each other's lives and preferences. Indirali and Hedna thus learn that the mer-beings exist on a slightly higher reality level than that of earth humans, a level of more refined life force vibrations that allow them to live within the water, but not be restricted by it as much. They are a race of Nature spirits that inhabits a higher-frequency world that still intersects with the human world to some degree, but is slowly retreating to higher-frequency dimensions under the impact of greater negativity oozing from the human world, and has, therefore, become rather invisible to most humans since the perceptual range of senses of the human race as a whole has deteriorated and become quite limited over the last millennia. They can be seen, however, by humans who are more sensitive and loving than the average human, and by almost any human should a mer-being succumb to lower frequency emotions like fear or anger, depending on whatever crisis situation a mer-being would be exposed to for any reason. The mermen say that any mer-being prays that such a calamity should never befall them, because once entrapped in the vicious cycle of fear and anger, it is hard to escape such a situation and not fall completely prey to the lower-self urges a predator kind of human being exerts on them. Indirali and Hedna agree wholeheartedly and are happy to realize they have the privilege of being able to communicate with them so freely and joyfully. And so they all keep merrily chatting about their lives, eager to convey as many notable facts about themselves to each other as they can spontaneously come up with. One thing Indirali, however, carefully tries to avoid talking about is her present dilemma in regard to her marital fate. This topic would only spoil the peaceful atmosphere and destroy the harmony and happiness everyone feels, and stands in contrast to to the lightness of the moment. And so the little group keeps chattering to their heart's content, laughing and joking, and enjoying every moment of their first get-together. But then the women notice that night has fallen and that the King and Queen must surely start to wonder where their daughter might be out so late. As much as it pains everyone to say good-bye, the group finally parts ways, but only under the promise to meet again the following day.

CHAPTER 5

An inner smile stays with Indirali throughout the night and morning. Nothing seems the same anymore; it's as if a magic veil is buffering her from the ominous happenings within the palace. Indirali floats on a cloud of happiness, greeting those she previously ignored, and uplifting the servants all around her with her cheery attitude and laughter. It is a good thing that the King and Queen are busy with an official matter; otherwise, they would notice the tremendous change in their daughter's emotional state and would certainly question her about it. Indirali is happy that she can escape unnoticed by her parents, off again to the magical pool, back to Loriolan, back to her love and all the beautiful things that spring from it. Only Hedna shares her most sweetest of secrets, sworn to her Mistress by her lifelong loyalty and love for her.

When they arrive at the pool, the three mermen are already waiting for them. They've brought a boat along and invite the two women for a ride across the ocean, pulled by them with a seaweed-leash. Indirali laughs with joy as the mermen alternate with the pulling, making the women drift atop the waves as if their boat were as light as a nutshell. Dolphins join in the fun ride and entertain everyone with their squeaking laughter and buoyant jumps. Indirali feels an overwhelming relief from the fear and anguish about her sinister future. Everything in her wants to completely be consumed by this most magnificent moment; she wants to lose herself so much in the lightness and carefree momentum of it all that she keeps drowning out any inner promptings to remember her looming imminent fate at home and just keeps thrusting herself towards Loriolan and his oceanic world with all the enthusiasm for life that she has. The ocean seems so welcoming and peaceful, completely different than the reports of the mariners have portrayed it. She feels the presence of angels, the sun welcomes her with its warming and healing rays, and God seems to whisper into her ear: "All is well, my child! Just trust your inner guidance, and you will have what you truly, deeply want and desire! Follow your joy and happiness, and don't allow the world to compromise you in any way. All is well, always was, always will be! You are loved, and love is all there is!" Tears of joy form in her eyes as the mermen pull the boat towards the sun, and Indirali feels like merging with the magnificence of the Divine Presence.

Several days go by, and the group meets regularly; their love for each other inspires them to various beautiful adventures whereby the ocean becomes this fathomless jewel that discloses its many treasures to the unsuspecting eye. Loriolan, Torilander, and Chekilian bring gifts from the depth of the sea to adorn their lady friends — pearls, sea stars, corals, and even jewelry from sunken ships of long ago, all to support their intent of pleasing and uplifting their beloved new friends who seem so mysterious to them as well, being humans and all. Indirali and Hedna, in turn, bring gifts from the Earth: fruits, instruments, and toys of various kinds. The mermen are easily fascinated by their treasures, and love to be playful, always finding ways to convey their gratitude, love, and admiration for the women in funny, witty, and respectful ways. Indirali feels increasingly drawn into their world perspective of infinite pleasure and savors every building momentum of the love she shares with Loriolan. This beautifully fulfilling dance of true and Divine Love could have lasted forever if it were up to this blessed little group of cross-world friends, but unfortunately the outside world shoves itself in the way, reminding them that certain immovable obstacles exist that threaten to destroy the delicate harmony and balance of these new friends, obstacles that mercilessly demand attention if the soul doesn't want to get squashed under the weight and burden of their consequences!

King Eurylochos has been noticing a pleasant change of attitude in his daughter for quite some days now. His deep concern for her, however, in a strange way, forbids him to question the real reason behind her cheeriness, afraid that the answer might not coincide with the necessities of the time and with the fact that she will be married and carried off to a kingdom that his kingdom has been in a lingering quarrel with for way too long. He just wants her to be happy, no matter what, and if she seems to have found her inner happiness despite the looming wedding, then he is going to be the last person to destroy the illusions she might have about her future husband. However, fate wants it otherwise! At the breakfast table, the King and Queen notice the impatience of their daughter to get up and leave. They also become aware that they haven't seen their child around the palace much lately, and since today is the day of the tailor needing to measure and fit the engagement dress, they insist Indirali stay around and not storm away as she has done the last few days. In fact, their curiosity is aroused as to where Indirali is going off to every day, as no one in the palace seems to really know where she spends the majority of her days lately. And even though the parents want their child to still spend as much time as possible roaming around freely in Nature, enjoying the last bits of her freedom and independence, a growing sense of concern begins to overshadow them, reminding them that the time for a life of etiquette and palace routines is approaching quickly for their beloved daughter, and that it would be wise to insist she prepare herself for what is to come, and become a dutiful wife unto Hecto.

And so they don't let Indirali get away so easily this time. They insist she explain herself, and all of a sudden, her cheeriness becomes a source of great concern for them. Indirali casts her eyes down as she confides to them her secret, trying to explain that she might just have met her true soulmate and love for life, a stunning merman who happens to be of royal descent, the son and heir to the throne of the Underwater King, Hadores. She wants them to understand how much Loriolan means to her and that she cannot imagine life without him anymore. Pale, and shocked to the core, King Eurylochos addresses his daughter with consternation and threats in his voice. He reels from the news, and the mounting pressures of his state affairs add to his intolerance with which he orders her to not see this merman anymore. Queen Penelope adds her softening influence as she tries to dissuade her daughter from such foolish attempts as to unite with a member of the water races, a futile undertaking at the least and one that would just render her disappointed and unfulfilled when it comes to producing an heir to the throne. And even just on the mere obvious level, what future could she possibly have with someone who lives in the water all the time, whereas she lives on land. Both parents won't have any of this anymore, and all the whining and pleading of Indirali leave them stone cold, so deep is their sense of betrayal by their beloved only daughter.

Indirali is shocked as well. Quietly she withdraws to her chambers and throws herself crying onto her canopy bed. Hedna is beside herself with worry about her Mistress's fate and wellbeing. Silently she sits beside the bed on the floor, waiting for Indirali to quiet down. But Indirali doesn't want to calm herself; she doesn't want to give in to compromise, not now after she experienced how true love feels like. If only her brother would be here right now to comfort her. He always manages to lift her spirits. She misses him terribly and wonders whether she will ever see him alive again. Why does life need to be so complicated and difficult? Why must her brother expose himself to potential death just so the kingdom can be safe, and why is she not allowed to decide for herself whom she wants to love for the rest of her life? With bitterness in her voice, she asserts her right of freedom from imposed restrictions and predestined marital bondage to a man she is sure she will detest because of who he is and what his ambitions are. She already knows that they both are very dissimilar and that life beside such a man would mean lifelong misery for her and thus equal the end of her life the way she loves it and is used to.

"How come those adults get to make such an important, long-lasting decision for me?" she asks. "Why can my parents have true love, and then destroy my chance of happiness? How unjust of them!"

"I guess your parents feel forced to sell you off as a means to keep peace between the kingdoms," Hedna injects softly, trying to bridge the gap that just opened between royal parents and daughter.

"Why?" Indirali shouts out in anguish. "Why me?" She continues to weep bitterly.

Hedna begins to stroke Indirali, trying to give her some comfort and ease.

"I have to get to him!" Indirali sits up straight, and a faint smile flickers across her face. If anyone can help her, it is Loriolan, her love! She trusts him more than anyone in the world. She needs to confide to him the full extent of her disastrous story. They have to come up with a solution, they just have to!

And with utmost resolution, she steals herself out of her chambers, Hedna close behind her, past the well-meaning guards who pretend to look the other way when she sneaks by them, allowing her to break free from the palace and out into Nature that welcomes her with open arms.

Chapter 6

$\mathcal{L}$oriolan has been waiting for his beloved, ready to adorn her with the most exquisite little sea stars he could find in the sea beds below the water for her long, flowing, beautiful dark-brown hair. With utmost care and love, he places the little stars onto her locks, smiling warmly at her so as to convey his deep feelings with every star he illumines and lets shine on her lovely countenance. Then he takes a few steps back and begins to play the lyre she has given him as a present. His voice spirals in mesmerizing circles of admiration and love, lifting the serenading hymn of her beauty to the realms of the celestial and pure, magnetizing his beloved to the common rhythms of their united beingness. Indirali feels his caressing attention and feels lifted to those realms beyond any daily cares and worries that are accessible only to the unconditionally loving and innocent at heart. She revels in the beauty of his words and melodies until the ecstasy prompts her to feel the impossibility of their ultimate unification, hitting against an inner wall of sorts that sends her hurling right back into the pits of suffering and pain. Reminded of the strain of her situation and knowing that Loriolan is actually farther away from being her ultimate lover than this detested Hecto is, she lets herself fall into a heart-wrenching melancholy that knows no escape. Her eyes begin to glaze under her stagnant tears as she silently gazes back at Loriolan, who puts all his heart and soul into his beautiful music and singing.

Loriolan is smitten by her pristine beauty; he looks at her as if placing his sight on an image of the Divine Itself, her star-strewn hair the infinite cosmos, and the misty spray of the waterfall enveloping her statuesque beauty like the nebulae surrounding the inner core of the galaxy. His heart spirals along an infinite array of tonalities that express the bottomless and unbounded nature of his exquisite love feelings for her. He feels he could fall endlessly into her inner universe and be hopelessly lost if she would not catch him with her merciful, nourishing love and passion. Such are his elevated and boundless feelings when he begins to all of a sudden notice the sadness in her being, a pool of hopelessness so vast and deep that it possesses the power to pull them both down into the bottomless pit of utmost despair and pain. Shocked, he lets the lyre sink and looks at Indirali with puzzlement.

"What is it, my dearest angel? Have I offended you in any way?"

Indirali is unable to answer. The tears feel as if they are choking the air out of her. Everything seems to turn and spin, now that Loriolan has caught up with her inner pain. Where to begin, and how can such deeply painful truth be revealed to him, an angel himself, so full of purity, innocence, and the sweetest love for her? Indirali's stomach feels upset from resisting the thought of what she has to disclose now.

Loriolan takes a look at the rest of the group, who quietly dwell at a nearby rock formation. Why are they not swimming and chatting? Where is the playful spirit he has seen everyone display in the last few days since their fortunate encounter? Everything seems odd and strange, really very unusual and alienating. And then it strikes him that as soon as the women arrived, Hedna took his two buddies aside, and they have been sitting at the rocks ever since. He notices that their heads are down, and a strange vibe of hopelessness seems to exude from them as well, the kind Indirali is now expressing herself. What conspiracy of potential misfortune is smoldering in the atmosphere? He looks at Indirali again, only now her tears are running down her cheeks as if having torn down an inner dam, and she seems to be reeling from pain, crying her heart out in an anguish that could have triggered the mercy of the Gods. Loriolan hurries to her side, compassionately putting his arms around her and lovingly comforting her while stroking her face and hair.

After her outbreak of tears slowly subsides, she begins to tell him the whole story of how she is the pawn in a political scheme of truce and how her parents feel helpless in the sight of their kingdom's potential ruin and war, how her brother is caught in this unfortunate game himself, with the family not knowing when he will come back and whether at all. So deep is the well of her pent-up pain and stress and so at home and safe does she feel in Loriolan's presence that she lets her feelings and thoughts run freely, emptying all the bitter and desolate truths from her subconscious pockets so she might feel reconnected with life and her love again.

Loriolan is stunned. It seems his breath is coming to a standstill under the harrowing news she conveys to him. How can this be? How can such an ominous force all of a sudden come between them? How can she have known all along and not tell him sooner? Or more accurately, how could he have deceived himself about the fate of a human in relation to himself and the Underwater Kingdom he is to inherit from his father and which he is to reign over? How could he have neglected to think things through when they ultimately are so obvious? His mind feels paralyzed under the weight of these kinds of thoughts, and his arms grow limp all of a sudden.

"I also have a confession to make," he admits. "My father has been pressuring me to become what he terms a more responsible young mer-prince who shows more interest in the political affairs of the Underwater Kingdom and thinks about settling down with a mermaid princess from one of the neighboring kingdoms. Tomorrow, actually, my father wants to throw a ball in my honor, inviting all kinds of prospective princesses from the surrounding kingdoms and hoping severely that I will find this special someone that he himself has had the fortune to have found when he was my age." Loriolan confesses that his father's pressures have reached a certain degree of discomfort where a choice on his part has to be made if he does not want to anger his parents beyond irreparable damage.

Indirali is hit by this news as well. But something in her does not want to give in to these separating forces and the overwhelming pressures they constitute; instead, she feels her fighting spirit welling up and overtaking her being in an attempt to save the one and only source of hope and ultimate wellbeing she has had the fortune to encounter in her life: Loriolan! She notices his inner turmoil and distance and tries to get his attention again. She unwinds from his arms and stands right in front of him. She lifts his head gently and gazes deep into his eyes: "We are not giving up, my love. I never will! Our life and love belong to us, and no one can take it away from us, ever!"

Loriolan looks at her with a spark of hope returning to his eyes. If she feels that way, then he certainly does as well. "Together we are unbeatable," he reiterates, "and we shall certainly be victorious against all odds and over all circumstances!"

She smiles at him and nods her head with full conviction. Life is coming back to his limbs, and Loriolan feels his old, optimistic self again. For as long as Indirali loves him, he feels he can achieve the impossible for their common benefit and promising future. He pulls her gently to a smooth rock where he invites her to take a seat while he tries to think things through with her and come up with a solution. Then he begins to pace back and forth in the water, intently reflecting on possible solutions.

"How long do we have until Hecto comes for his betrothal ceremony?"

"Our palace expects him this week, in only three days!" Indirali gives him the shocking news. Loriolan winces but tries to stay calm.

"That doesn't leave us much time at all, does it?" The pain is written in his face. "We'll have to be very vigilant in coming up with a workable plan and executing it," he emphasizes. Indirali nods strongly. She is completely with him. Loriolan continues to pace for another few minutes when, all of a sudden, he stands still and looks up with an air of illumination in his eyes. "This is it!" Indirali is all ears, excited at the potential turnaround of their situation. "It's not much, but maybe we can make it work if we give it our best effort," Loriolan explains and then moves close to fill her in.

"My nanny used to read fairytales to me when I was young, all of which seem to have some reminiscent core of truth to them, some faint origin in a life story that happened in the distant past, long, long ago. Sometimes Harla would tell me that she remembers certain mer-beings talking about their ancestors and the adventures they went through. I found a lot of facts in the fairytales that matched with accounts from those narrators, convincing me of the truth that those fairytales are based on real facts."

"Yes!" Indirali is trying to follow his line of reasoning.

"If we want to overcome the impossible odds and not only vanquish our adversities but also unite as a couple that is able to live together always and maybe have children one day and enjoy everything else that deeply united couples do in any and all of life's circumstances, then we must seek the advice of the wisest beings on Earth and in the Water. We must go to any length to find them and question them deeply as to the extent of their knowledge in regard to our situation and the answers that lie deep within our psyche and soul."

"Yes, you are right!" Indirali agrees, getting more and more excited all the time.

"One of the beautiful tales Harla used to tell me, which impressed me very much at the time, and which for some reason got stuck in my memory," Loriolan continues, "is the story of a human girl and a merman who, like us, fell in love one day and went through extreme lengths to be together in an ultimate way. They both had to separately overcome the dualism reigning on Earth, each in their own unique way. I think he had to prove himself in regard to fighting some deep-sea monster, and she had to prove her impeccable purity and devotion by serving the Goddess of Love. In the end, however, they were miraculously united, able to live and be together in mind and body for the rest of their lives."

Indirali smiles. "Sounds like a wonderful story, like ours should end!"

"Exactly!" Loriolan confirms. "We just have to get the right advice before we go our separate ways and try to find the solution each on our own. And once we have found this advice, we need to implement it immediately since our time is so short in which we can still be single and available for each other."

"We need to be able to communicate our findings with each other, don't you think?" she wants to know.

"Of course, my darling. We should always act in one accord!" he agrees and gently places a kiss on her forehead. Indirali feels this irresistible attraction to him and would like nothing more than to succumb to it this very moment. But it is clear to both of them that matters need to be dealt with first before such elevated feelings can find their lasting fulfillment.

"Indirali, this path sounds very vague and difficult right now. We won't be able to see each other for quite some time until our obstacles are cleared away.

If I could see another solution, I would certainly opt for that, but unfortunately I can't …" His view begins to darken as he imagines this bleak and harrowing time ahead of them. How will he be able to not see her every day like he has grown used to and fond of? He will miss her more than he can express; his soul will feel strangely torn apart, like a body that has split in half.

Indirali picks up on his sentiments, which she shares fully. Still, she tries to lift him out of this threatening despair by encouragingly smiling at him and continuously assuring him that they will be successful, because there is nothing else left for them in this world except for the love they share for each other. "Nothing else is as true and real, Loriolan," she implores. "Nothing comes even close to it!"

A smile of regained confidence shows on her face; she knows there is only a 'forward', no matter how hard, lonely, and challenging this path might become, because the 'here and now' is solely taken up by tragedy and misfortune.

"I will send Hedna if I can't come to see you for any reason," she assures. "She will be my trusted and loyal messenger. — I hope, though, that the time of our separation is short, and our lives together long and everlasting!" She spins around, as if to convey a feeling of lightness and confidence.

Loriolan smiles. Oh, how he loves her and wants to be with her always. He hopes so much that their desperate plan will work and that they will find effective and powerful help along the way. Then he hands her a nicely shaped pearly shell, which he shows her how to blow and summon him with in the event that she wants to meet him and he isn't here. He says that unless he is caught up in fighting the monsters and overcoming any challenges in his way that separate them, he would be here in an instant. "I hope you don't have to go through with the betrothal, let alone the wedding!" he asserts. "This would be more than I can bear, I think."

"Loriolan, please don't go there. Nothing of the kind will happen. I would rather die and see you in Heaven than become someone else's wife. — But of course this won't be necessary," she quickly adds upon seeing the startled look in his eyes. "As we said before, all will be well, because we just won't give up."

"Yes, my love, for you I will go to the end of the world and to the deepest depths of the sea if necessary. Nothing will stop me if our good fortune awaits at the end of the dark tunnel!"

She feels the same way, and together they sit quietly for many hours this night, tightly embraced as if neither of them dares to let go of the other. Hedna and the two mermen brothers patiently wait in a nearby cave. They know not to disturb the two lovers and are more than happy to give them the space and this last night alone together.

The full moon is shining down on the two melancholic lovers as they sadly say good-bye to each other, their hands and fingers slowly slipping apart, as if a beautiful dream has just come to an unfortunate turn.

"Until we see each other again," they both whisper softly, then turn to tackle the task of their challenging unification process.

Chapter 7

Hadores, proud and accomplished ruler of the Underwater World Kingdom of Azuris, has certainly shown tremendous tolerance and patience with his freedom-loving son Loriolan. Throughout the prince's upbringing, the royal parents have pampered him and his sister, Arilene, with any privileges and affections children of their position could ever expect and want. They certainly didn't lack any love and attention, and they certainly didn't lack any material goods they put their mind on having and enjoying. There always has been much laughter and joy in the palace, as the family enjoyed each other's company in an atmosphere of unconditional love and abundance of every good thing. Often, as children, Loriolan and his sister would chase each other around the palace, and even as young adults they continued on, playfully and irreverently interfering with their father's official obligations and tasks. Sometimes even his balanced temper had enough of it, and then he would put them in their place, asking for more rules and restrictions to be observed in regard to their frisky and rumbustious behavior. But his children always knew that they could ultimately count on his love for them, and even though they began adjusting and accepting more adult-like behaviors over time, there still remained an air of wild and untamed playfulness in them, a love for all things free and all things uplifting. And deep down, their parents love their children for it, glad they have held on to their innocence and to their infinite capacity for unconditional love and compassion, which the parents unfortunately see getting lost in many young adults around them who either try or are forced to grow up way too fast and adjust to the responsibilities of adulthood before they are truly ready for them. This was also the reason he and his wife have been consenting to Loriolan's wish to forego an invitation to Poseidon's palace and not be sent off quite yet to undergo higher political and spiritual training befitting the heir to the throne. They have, instead, allowed him to continue spending his last quality time as a youth with his best buddies, a decision King Hadores has lately begun to question, as his son seems to take blatant advantage of his granted liberties. But the time has come where King Hadores wishes to think about retirement and of handing the crown to his son, as well as seeing his daughter married off to one of the select, well-off royal suitors from one of the neighboring kingdoms. The time has come for Loriolan to take the scepter into his hand and relieve his father of his many burdensome duties. And for that transfer of office to take effect properly, Loriolan is expected to find himself a suitable companion and wife, and Arilene is expected to finally, after rejecting many decent, well-off, and even handsome suitors, accept the hand of a stately prince. But unfortunately, both of his children have been very slow in pursuing their planned out futures; in fact, their spirits seem to roam around in any realm but the ones their parents and ancestors have laid out and predestined for them. Lately, King Hadores has become increasingly irritated with his son's behavior, as he doesn't seem to give in at all and finally make his father proud and happy. In fact, the more Hadores and Queen Lilliane implore their son to heed their requests, the more elusive he seems to become. He hasn't been seen much around the palace lately, and a great concern has overtaken the royal parents' hearts. Desperate to get through to him, King Hadores has been resorting to all sorts of devious tactics to get his son's attention, including denying him certain privileges he enjoyed for most of his life. The atmosphere around the family household has become strained, to say the least, and a great change of attitude and behavior from both their children, especially from the heir to the throne, is now expected in order to avoid a nasty confrontation and battle of wills between the generations.

As a way to force the issue, Hadores and Lilliane have organized a royal ball in their son's honor. Many beautiful princesses from faraway kingdoms are expected to arrive with their entourages, and much elaborate preparation has been put into action to guarantee the grandness and splendor of this auspicious event. For many weeks now, the palace has become the magnetizing point for all things superlative, expensive, and precious. King Hadores and his wife spare no costs and efforts to turn this ball into one of the most memorable events of their lifetimes. So grand are their hopes that their beloved son will come to his senses once and for all when he hopefully meets and finds this special someone, who surely must have been waiting for him all her life in the same way as he, deep in his heart, must also have been waiting for her, probably without realizing it in his youthful preoccupations. But the parents' patience has reached its limits, and any and all efforts and precautions are about to be implemented to guarantee the Prince will show up to his own bride-choosing ball. King Hadores has asked the servants to immediately bring Loriolan before him as soon as he shows up at the palace. He intends to have one last conversation with his son where he will put all the issues at risk on the plate for him to decide whether he wants to lose his privileges completely and become a stranger to his family or whether he finally treats his parents with the respect they deserve and shows up at the ball, with dignity and respect for all the distinguished lady mermaids that will have come from many faraway kingdoms to offer themselves to his choice and companionship. King Hadores strongly counts on his son's decency and maturity and on the fact that he is ultimately interested in falling in love and founding his own family, as well as in starting his official training and soon stepping into the office of King over Azuris, able to handle the political challenges and the social care for his people with all the poise and equanimity he and his wife have tried to equip Loriolan with throughout his privileged upbringing.

But all this hustle and bustle could not have come at a more inappropriate time for Loriolan. At any other time, he would have considered making at least the concession of attending this undesirable event held in his honor, but with Indirali getting betrothed in three days, attending this ball just seems like an incredible waste of time, an irritating distraction from all the things that matter most to his heart. He has not confided to his parents that he is in love with an earth human, and that he intends to fight for her even unto his death if necessary, if that would allow him to spend even just a mere moment with his eternal beloved. He hopes his parents will understand and support him since his path and challenges seem overwhelming enough without him having to also stand up against his father and fight him on his insisting expectations and views.

But Loriolan is not in great luck. His father has made up his mind, and when

Loriolan finally breaks the news to him that Indirali has conquered his heart and that there is no room for anyone else, his father explodes into an irrational anger that threatens to destroy the relationship with his son to a considerable extent. He reminds Loriolan about Poseidon's curse on the human world, one that is based on the fact that the human race has lost itself in arrogance, ignorance, and violence, and that it is only wise to stay out of Poseidon's way if peace for Azuris is of any importance to the King's son. He is so frustrated and disappointed with Loriolan's irresponsibility and foolish distractions that he authoritatively puts him into his stately place, namely, locks him into his chambers until the hour of his appearance at court in front of the princesses. In his kingly mind, his son needs to finally grow up and forget about all things impossible. Loriolan had brought up the fairytale of the cross-world lovers who succeed in their quest for unification, but King Hadores only had a dismissive remark about it, hoping that his son has not given in to some irrational hope and dream about becoming someone he is not. Loriolan belongs to his mermen people, a ruler of distinguishing traits and abilities, fair and just and immensely capable of meeting any challenges with the calmness and power of a true Underwater Ruler. Hadores just has to help his son to discern right from wrong, and all will be well with the kingdom. Or so he thinks.

CHAPTER 8

*H*is mind is racing, his heart pounding. Loriolan cannot afford to stay put at this most urgent of times. Angry with his father for trying to break his free will, Loriolan lets the steam off by throwing things against the wall. He wants to punch a hole into the wall, if necessary. He needs to escape. He needs to talk to someone who will understand and help him. His nanny comes to mind. Loudly he calls for the guard to listen to his request. He wants to talk to his nanny. He says he needs comforting so he is able to let go and come around to fulfill his father's wishes. The guards send the message to the king, who fortunately sees a good sign of reconciliation in this request. And so Harla is allowed to enter the Prince's chamber, happy to be of help and happy to see him coming around.

After a moment of enjoying her nourishing presence and words, Loriolan presents his dilemma to her. If anyone will understand, it must be his dearest nanny, the mer-woman who helped raise him and who always showered her love abundantly on him. He reminds her of this particular and special tale she narrated to him when he was a child and which has become so relevant to him in his present situation. He continues to disclose to her how he met Indirali and how their love for each other goes beyond the two worlds that seem to keep them apart. He conveys to Harla how deeply and for all of eternity he loves his Indirali, and that if Harla ever deeply cared for him, he would like to be able to count on her help now, because his soul is about to be sold off to the most competitive, accomplished young mermaid princess his father has invited, and he is not ready to let this happen. So if she could please help him escape and also advise him on where to turn in order to get reliable advice from the wisest person she knows and who would be able to point him in the right direction, and help him on how to begin his arduous path of love's redemption.

Harla is taken aback at first. But her initial shock quickly yields to her inherent good nature with which she was always able to conquer little Loriolan's heart anytime there was some lesson to be learned or rule to be followed. She attentively listens to his heart's plight, and the more she listens to his heartfelt words, the more she sympathizes with his unfortunate situation.

"If you have found her, your eternal beloved that is," she assents to his pleas, "then you would be foolish not to do everything in your power to win her into your life. I know how empty a life can be if that special someone never shows up because you are either preoccupied with other things or you are not ready for this most exquisite, ecstatic love that only few are able to savor to the fullest extent. As much as I love you and your family — you all have been so good to me always — I have to admit that I sometimes wonder what would have been if I had stayed available on the dating scene for just a little while longer. But then this opportunity came along, and I have not really regretted my decision to serve you and your loving family ever since."

Then Harla tries to bridge the gap between father and son, trying to make Loriolan see just how much his father loves and adores him and that she wishes they will reconcile again as soon as possible. Loriolan tells her that this will only be possible once his father accepts Indirali as his daughter-in-law, and for this to happen, he must leave now or be branded with failure for the rest of his life. Harla understands, but can't help to emphasize to him how important in the overall scheme of things it would be to leave on such a life-risking mission with his parents' blessings, and that it would be awesomely nice and respectful of him to attend the lavish ball being held tomorrow night for his benefit, so generously organized by his loving parents. If, after looking at several princess beauties, his heart is still with Indirali, then in her opinion, he has met them halfway and absolved himself a great deal towards his duty as a son — considering the great love and hopes his parents have invested into his upbringing and education — and can then with good right and conscience pursue his heart's quest, even if it means risking his life in the course of it. She imploringly looks into his eyes, waiting for a concession. Loriolan lowers his eyes. He knows she is right on one level, but she and his parents cannot possibly know the extent of his heart pain, caused by the fact that forces beyond their control are trying to tear Indirali and him apart. A deep despondency overcomes him.

"Harla, if I cannot do something right now to ease the pain of separation from Indirali, if I have to wait until after tomorrow to prepare and start on my journey to find the solution that allows us to unite for all eternity, then I shall just be an empty shell at tomorrow's event, an emotional wreck, good for nothing, and probably even an embarrassment to my parents. So please help me to get started tonight. Tell me whether there is someone wise enough to not only make sense out of my situation, but also able to point me in the right direction and give me sound, helpful advice that I will be able to use along the way. I promise, I will be back in time for tomorrow's festivities! I won't let you or my parents down. But I have to go now, I just have to!" He looks pleadingly into her eyes, and she cannot resist his heart's cry for her help. This viewpoint on the situation puts Harla right back into the position of wanting to help him, and she suggests he go to Rachtan, the King's spiritual advisor, who lives outside the court in a relatively humble cave in which he practices the spiritual rituals so helpful for his father's kingly duties.

Loriolan thanks her with a big hug, and they agree that she will wait for him at the sea horse stables so she can accompany him back to his chambers, as if he never left. She says she will take care of the guards somehow and hopes all will go well for him.

Then she pokes her head out the door and sends the guard off to the kitchen to fetch a glass of seaweed lemonade. The guard willingly hurries off.

Loriolan looks at her, relieved. "I won't ever forget this, Harla! You always have been my biggest support!" Harla responds with a big smile, then lovingly pushes him out the door, telling him that she has it covered and for him to rush off now.

Loriolan smiles faintly and then escapes into the dark of the night.

CHAPTER 9

Rachtan is a stately merman with numerous awards and recognitions for his invaluable service to the palace and the spiritual elite of Azuris. He has served several generations of kings and is older and wiser than most mer-beings of Azuris combined. The ability to not age stands in direct connection to the degree of spiritual realization a mer-person has achieved and demonstrates spiritual competence of a very high degree. Many precarious situations have been successfully avoided or resolved thanks to the clear perceptions and uncanny magical and healing abilities of Rachtan, as this evolved Master has served his kings with lifelong loyalty and devotion and has always come out the prophet and hero of any political and personal challenge. King Hadores, like his predecessors, has come to heavily rely on Rachtan, and not a single crucial state decision has been made without him first consulting with his much-appreciated spiritual advisor. Despite King Hadores offering Rachtan great amounts of his wealth for solving many of Azuris' most difficult crisis situations, Rachtan has stayed humble and light-oriented, declining excessive material compensation and adhering to his simple and self-sufficient lifestyle and abode.

It felt quite awkward to Loriolan to approach Rachtan for his guidance and wisdom, for he, out of all mermen, would be the most devoted to his King, and most likely will not want to have to wonder about his allegiance when asked to support Loriolan in his heart's quest against the King's will. But his situation doesn't leave Loriolan much of a choice, and so he humbly waits by the cave's entrance for Rachtan to invite him in.

Rachtan's young apprentice, a gentle, good-looking young man, greets him by the entrance, indicating for him to follow. The cave has a long hallway leading into a mysteriously lit, spacious inner hall that resembles, quite remarkably, the outer universe, with fluorescent dots decorating the ceiling like the stars sparkling across the night skies. There are planet-like balls circling a sun-like inner core at the center of the hall, just as if the solar system and our galaxy have been recreated in miniature form to please the onlooker with all the intricate movements and cycles that constitute the astrological and astronomical secrets and revelations influencing and determining the life cycles and conditions of all species inhabiting the cosmos on various planes and worlds known to life. Loriolan feels his breath taken away as he is overcome by the elevating warmth and elusive mystery of the atmosphere. A deep, comforting humming sound reverberates throughout the hall, soothing Loriolan's nerves and easing his subtle tensions away, making him immediately feel deeply welcomed by his so far elusive host. Loriolan has never been to this cave of Rachtan's, for it is always the Master himself who comes to the palace whenever he is needed. In fact, Loriolan hasn't had much contact with Rachtan so far at all, so little did he think and care about the state affairs his father has to deal with on a constant basis. But his request, nonetheless, comes from a deep heart place and should deserve the Master's attention, he reasons. But where is Rachtan? He looks around, turning his body and noticing how everything in this water-filled hall seems to happen in slow motion, as if time stands still. The apprentice seems to have vanished into thin air, and the ominous and mysterious keep beckoning Loriolan at every turn.

And all of a sudden, Rachtan addresses him. Loriolan continues to turn, confused as to where Rachtan's voice just came from. He detects, next to the entrance hallway, another three hallways, with each of those four leading into one of the four cardinal directions. Rachtan seems to have stepped out of the eastern hallway, looking all impressive and wise. His long, white hair floating in the soft, undulating waves, his flowing purple robe leisurely thrown over his shoulder, he stands tall and sparkles at Loriolan with eyes that express the expanse of his inner worlds.

"Loriolan!" he greets with a crystal clear voice resounding from the humming-suffused environments like a melody riding on the waves of its orchestral ocean and worlds. "Nice of you to come! I have been expecting you. Here to figure out your destiny and vocation? Seems to be perfect timing!"

Loriolan feels a shudder running down his spine. Is there anything he can hide from him? When Rachtan looks at him, he feels strangely found out and pierced by the arrows of truth that seem to shoot from his all-knowing mind.

"Harla recommended I see you," he begins to introduce himself. "I have an issue of the heart that I need help and guidance with. She thought that you probably would be able to help me." He looks at the Master with a big question mark on his face.

Rachtan bursts into a laugh. "You have come to the right place, my son. In fact, all your forefathers once stood there in the same spot as yours with the same heart issues, wondering about pretty much the same things and wanting help in getting to where they wanted to get. I am used to lending this kind of help; in fact, I see it as my great honor and pleasure to lead you onto the right path, the one that allows you to unfold your full potential and helps you to become your most original self, the immortal, powerful, and enlightened self you already are — and always have been — in the deepest depth of your soul and being."

He moves towards the light-emitting center globe. "And this is who you are, Loriolan! The sun-like center of your own being and world, able to illuminate all your problems and drown them out with the power of your inner bliss radiance! The answers all lie here!" He points towards the sun, and then to his heart and third eye chakra between the eyebrows. "You just have to remember, and for that to happen, you must first vanquish your fears and self-doubts; you must overcome the monsters of your own vain imaginings, those devious creatures of the dark that feed off the fears and anger of those who are caught within their own swamps of ignorance and arrogance."

Loriolan would like to sit. He takes a few steps back, trying to keep his composure. So, that's how easy everything seems to be?

Rachtan opens his hand and several rune tablets fall to the ground. Loriolan stares after them, and the most amazing sensation overcomes him. It feels as if the planetary revolutions within our cosmos just revealed themselves to him, enlivening the knowledge of their influences on his life, and making him feel like this moment is in alignment with a new and meaningful beginning.

Rachtan holds his hand stretched out for Loriolan to catch another set of rune tablets. Intuitively, Loriolan opens his hand, holds the tablets for a moment, then follows Rachtan's lead, indicated by his face, and lets the tablets fall on the ground as they may. And again, a certain magic begins to unravel, telling Loriolan everything he needs to know about his situation in the most subtle, intuitive ways, pointing out his weaknesses and strengths so he may steer clear of certain temptations, distractions, and pitfalls, and also showing how he will be able to use his skills, abilities, and powers for the accomplishment of his mission and the realization of his Higher Self qualities and fulfillments. Loriolan sees his deep interconnections with the stars and planets, lifetimes he spent in various fields of existence, and the karmic entanglements he created within those fields that now constitute his past in regard to these places and times. He understands that, according to the karma he created, he has negative and positive connections that bind him to certain star and planetary systems, causing these celestial bodies to either support or challenge him at certain times of their revolutionary phases around the center star of their own cosmic cycles, throwing the lassos of their karmic resonance fields at him as if trying to pull him back to the cosmic locales from where the seeds for his present lifetime and worldly existence originated. The runes fell to the ground in the blink of an eye, but the story they tell seems to have lasted an eternity. The fall of the runes enlivened his own past history within the cosmos, and as they hit the ground, they show his present spiritual makeup and destiny that connects him with and is influenced by the celestial mysteries and worlds. Loriolan's eyes gaze into these realities, trying to fathom the deeper meaning of the unraveled mysteries of his expanded, immortal being when, all of a sudden, Rachtan snaps his fingers to catch his attention.

Mesmerized, Loriolan follows Rachtan's eyes as they lead him to take a good look at the center sun, stationed within his universe-feeling hall. Gently, Rachtan places his hand on Loriolan's back between the shoulder blades to support him even further in his self-introspection with the light and protection streaming from his palm. Loriolan begins to feel like melting ice, his physical existence dissolving and his inner essence shining forth; a sea of consciousness begins to take him over, allowing him to feel at One with All of Existence. The sun's light begins to turn brighter the longer he looks at it, absorbing his whole attention and causing him to identify with its radiant brilliance and power. And then the blinding light gives way, and exposes a transcendental realm of existence only privy to the pure and enlightened ones; beautiful, angelic beings float in the light-filled spaces, their refined, sublime, delicate, alluring, and breathtaking scents aromatizing the atmospheres of bliss, and celestial choirs and music intoxicating the senses with their stunning, divinely inspirational beauty, expressed in cadences of elaborate, sacred rhythms and melodies. Their shapes and forms adjust with every thought and feeling of highest joy and freedom, ranging in color and brilliance from the deepest, most saturated scarlet reds to the most lovely pastels of the violet and lavender tonalities, with every color being represented in endless possibilities of its shades and hues. And in the midst of all this splendor and exalted living, Loriolan detects the nature of these Divine Beings as being beyond any dualities of the mortal worlds. Androgynous beings roam around the celestial spheres next to beings identified with either their male or female sides. He also notices that devas of all kinds and races peacefully and joyfully coexist and occasionally merge with enlightened members of the human race, and with higher-dimensional races he has never seen before. An inner light of recognition and remembrance lights in his mind as Loriolan experiences the vast scope of possibilities of harmonious coexistence and cross-race identifications, and a deep inner conviction spreads in him that Indirali and he can absolutely unite with one another in the same way as these beautiful transcendental beings do. The Source of all beings seems to be strong on this wondrous plane of angelic existence, spreading the umbrella of Its protecting and nourishing influence over all the sentient beings of the Heavens. Loriolan begins to feel dizzy from all this elevation and highest triumph over life and death, and he would have liked to dwell in this place of mind-blowing peace and ecstasy forever if Rachtan would not have removed his hand from his back, causing him to plunge right back from whence he came.

"Now you have seen your goal, my son!" he exclaims. "The rest is just removing the debris along the way so you can live and be at one with your goal at all times. And of course there are innumerable goals beyond the one you just perceived, always beckoning your adventuresome spirit to grow beyond the confines of your mortal self so you may, at one moment in the blink of the eternal eye, realize the full potential of your Highest, Divine Existence and Calling. That, my son, is true statesmanship and honor!"

Rachtan claps his hands, and the apprentice reenters the hall. He balances a golden plate with silver goblets on it.

Loriolan comes slowly back to his physical senses, and gratefully accepts the offered drink.

"Let's drink the wave-surging nectar of the Gods to the accomplishment of your mission, my son!" he invites, gracefully holding the goblet up for a toast.

Still in some haze, Loriolan concurs with the offered gesture, and raises his goblet as well.

"May the Gods be with you, and guide you along your way always!" He takes a big sip and smiles broadly.

Loriolan hesitates. "I certainly got a glimpse of the truth I seek, vast enough to encompass the worlds and lives of my beloved and me," he admits, "but I still seek your wisdom and guidance in regard to exactly where to go from here, what to expect, and what to do!" He looks at Rachtan with humble eyes expressing his request.

"You are right, my son! The first step is always the most important, as it gives the direction and lays the foundation for the whole mission. Like the saying goes: Well begun is half done!" He points at a soft coral seating area, warmly lit by phosphor-light emitting plants, decoratively arranged around the lounge area, and indicates to Loriolan to make himself comfortable. A nice, soothing, ambient music begins to play from out of nowhere as Loriolan and Rachtan begin an intimate conversation geared to help Loriolan in his quest. Throughout it all, Loriolan experiences again and again that Rachtan seems to know him inside and out; somehow he foresaw that Indirali would enter Loriolan's life and take his breath away. With cogent words, Rachtan lays out what he sees to be the most direct path to a deeply longed-for unification between their two aching souls.

"What separates you both is the angle you took when you incarnated into these lifetimes of yours," he explains. "Your infinite love for each other sought the greatest of challenges, namely, to undertake the overcoming of the full scope of dualism reigning on Earth, from the deepest depth of the earthly subconscious regions to the highest peaks of the superconscious realms of this riddle of a planet." He looks at Loriolan as if to convey both his puzzlement and his admiration for such a courageous act. "Once solved, however, this enormous challenge certainly bears the potential for accelerated growth along the evolutionary line of supernatural unfoldment! You have chosen the superhighway to highest existence and learning!" He makes a gesture as if he were to tip his hat to Loriolan.

"Couldn't you just teach me, Rachtan? You already gave me a glimpse of what inner realization I'm looking for. Why can't I just stay here with you?"

"Wouldn't that be nice!" Rachtan agrees. "However, your Higher Self tells me that you are not interested in yearlong studies of the human soul landscape and in the disciplines and routines of a lifetime that lead to higher-self realization. On the contrary, your soul feels very much under the pressures of time, and the longing to be with your beloved rather sooner than later will always shortcut your meditative attempts for self-liberation." He smiles at Loriolan. "No, you need the instant-gratification way, the how-to challenge that keeps your soul going under extreme stress and adrenalin pumping, the overcoming of obstacles so severe, they conjure your deepest inner resources in a jiff, allowing you to perform supernatural acts of overcoming the most difficult of hindrances, and thus marking you as the hero you are and will be unto your people." He takes a moment to let his words sink in. Upon seeing Loriolan's reflective face, he continues to add: "Yours is the life of a king! You have enormous powers latent within you that just need a short rekindling, and you will lead the most fulfilling life beside your immortal beloved that any merman can dream up for himself."

Loriolan has to admit that Rachtan's words express his truth. Until he met Indirali, he wasn't even interested in any spiritual matters at all. Why would he make a lifelong sport out of it now? "But I can count on your services always?" he asks Rachtan, needing to make sure he will always have the same high quality assistance from this spiritual Master that his father has the fortune to count on for all of his affairs.

Rachtan smiles this mystical smile of all times, gently nodding and confirming his everlasting loyalty and accountability to the Royal Family, to his father and him. He also tells Loriolan that he is a multidimensional being who exists on several planes of existence and that this lifetime of a spiritual advisor to the mer-kingdom is a dedication he will keep for as long as Poseidon wishes to keep peace and prosperity among the mer-folks.

Loriolan's mind feels stretched, but his heart and soul are comforted. "Where do I go from here, Rachtan?"

"You visit Velvetia, the atmospheric Ring Guardian of all the known mer-kingdoms of this planet. She dwells in the twilight zone between the mer-worlds and the fiery, high-pressure underworlds of the life-threatening Earth magnetic ring zones and realities."

Loriolan is caught by surprise. He has never heard of such a being. "Who is she?" he wonders out loud.

"She is the aim of the spiritual merman seeker, when he is ready to confront his roughest survival issues, and, with that, his most frightening fears and doubts. She is the guardian that keeps the immature soul from entering the death zone of Earth, the core chakra of the planet that symbolizes the gateway to an either higher or lower dimension — depending on the predominantly good or evil nature of the journeying soul — ultimately presenting the seeker with the rewards of his actions and works. The Earth's core chakra is only a gateway to higher dimensions for those who are strong, courageous, and evolved enough to defy the life-threatening influences of the absolute gravity, dark hole vortex-like source at the bottom of the combined subconscious mind of Earth's population, underwater and on land. In the same way as fire burns the hand of the ignorant person, the burning-hot atmospheres of the magnetic ring realm of the planet destroy whoever approaches it before their time, their impurities, fears, and arrogance causing them to fall prey to the purgatory hell rather than being redeemed by it through trials and tribulations that would otherwise lead to enough inner purity that no fire could harm such an elevated being anymore."

Loriolan thinks he understands the scope of what was just said. Nevertheless, a shudder runs down his spine. Is he to risk his life trying to traverse this hellish sphere?

"But in the hands of the pure, fire can become a complete ally, a means for great good and societal advancement," Rachtan reminds him. "And he who makes it through the valley of death, pure and persistent enough to be able to withstand any onslaught of death with the transcendent mindset of a gentle seeker of the truth and the adamantine braveness of a true warrior heart, will win not only his soulmate, in your case the princess of your heart, but also the eternity of his soul, the vastness of a life in ever-flowing abundance!" Rachtan pauses.

Loriolan needs a few minutes to reflect on this mission. He already feels fear and resistance creeping up on him. But the thought of Indirali gives him the much required impulse and motivation to tackle this impossible seeming task for both their sakes, for a life of sweet unison of their souls, and hopefully a common kingdom to reign over, in peace and harmony between the two worlds, underwater and on land.

"And Indirali needs to climb the highest mountain top in order to find the gateway to Heaven?" he asks, wondering a little bit about the difference of their directions. He loves her so deeply, and his gentleman's heart completely wants her to be as safe as possible and to succeed in her mission as well, so they definitely will unite on a higher plane and be happy for all eternity.

"Hers is the task of sacrificial devotion to a higher source and cause!" Rachtan confirms. "She is your guiding light, and together you shall overcome and transcend the positive and negative attractions this planet lures you with into its karmic influence sphere and electro-magnetic pull. Your combined soul essence is to outgrow the death-like limitations and energetic blockages that bind you to this planet so you can restore within yourselves, along your united chakras or bodily life force centers, the flow of the cosmic nervous system that runs through the planet like a string runs through a pearl in a whole network of pearls or other stars and planets."

Loriolan looks at him in bewilderment. "Really?" He kind of has to get used to this grand idea. Everything in his life so far was about play and learning to be a man. Now all of a sudden, he has to confront what even the most daring of soldiers and generals on the battlefields don't often get to do: face your most certain death, and live to speak about it! Loriolan reels with discomfort but wants to get on with things as quickly as possible. At least there is a way, and soon he will be with his beloved for all times!

With tears forming in his eyes, Loriolan thanks Rachtan for his guidance and wisdom. They still sit for a while, and Rachtan continues to illuminate Loriolan's mind to all the possible dangers and challenges along the way, describing how he got to know Velvetia quite well, learning many surpassing mysteries from her wisdom-pouring mouth, admitting that he feels quite humble in her all-knowing presence, and that she performs an invaluable service to both mer-beings and humans, as her powerfully anchored presence in Source allows her to be an immense magnetic shield that protects and safeguards the mer-kingdoms from being drawn in and collapsing into the immensely dense magnetic ring of the Earth — the source-level of Earth's gravity pull — thus helping to maintain the delicate balance between all underwater-worlds that allows them to continue to survive and thrive in their own respective atmospheres.

Loriolan acknowledges that the world is lucky to have such a powerful guardian and looks forward to meeting her soon.

"Such a journey has not been undertaken for thousands of years," Rachtan remarks. "It takes a special, highly evolved being, a hero and heroine, to even think of tackling such a larger-than-life task. If you do this, my son, Azuris and Lucania, and the Earth as a whole, for that matter, will be thankful to you and Indirali until the end of measured time, and Poseidon will see no reason anymore to hold a mirror up to the faces of those who like to destroy everything that makes life worth living!" he promises with a mischievous look. Because for quite a while now, Rachtan has quietly been longing for the day Poseidon will be pleased enough with mankind so as to not have to punish them anymore for their own wrongdoings with his vanquishing oceanic powers.

In the end, Rachtan lifts his glass for another toast, which Loriolan joins, and with his warm, resounding voice, Rachtan assures Loriolan that he will be successful and that he will be united with his beloved Indirali for all times to come, reigning over the most magnificent queen — and kingdom this Earth has ever seen.

CHAPTER 10

$\mathcal{L}$oriolan sleeps late into the day, like a turtle, all curled up in his maiden's hair plant bed. It has been a long night, and he didn't get much sleep. He also is not particularly interested in today's festivities and challenges and would like to actually skip the whole day if he could. And so he prefers to stay in his dream world, resisting the moment he has to face the unavoidable confrontation with his father, which he has to have in order to make him understand and get his blessings for his soul journey.

Arilene quietly sneaks into his chamber, slowly pulling the maiden's hair cover from his coiled-up body. Loriolan begins to move and stretch.

"Hey, sleepyhead," she cheerfully calls to him, "you are the guest of honor today, and here you are fast asleep!" She laughs, and then kneels in front of him to have a better look at his face. Her little Blue Tang pet fish 'Shmootch' is right beside her, looking all curious at Loriolan and trying to help her wake him up by nudging his nose a bit. "You really astonish me! Come on, Loriolan, you won't miss your own wedding ball, will you?"

Loriolan sneezes, then gives off a heavy sigh and pulls the cover back over his face.

Arilene waves her two maidservants in who have been waiting by the door. Together they tease Loriolan about his sleepiness and resistance, trying to jumpstart him into the day. They talk about the delicious food lined up on the endlessly long buffet tables, and about the excellent, cool musicians the royal parents have invited to perform on this grand occasion. They also mention that the halls are festively decorated, looking amazingly beautiful, with loads of sea flowers hanging from the walls and ceilings as well as entwining around the marble pillars to delicately perfume the atmosphere with their lovely scents. Everything is so beautiful and festive, and they cannot understand why Loriolan is taking his time.

"Are you not in the least curious about the princess mermaids that are coming?" Arilene asks.

"No, not really," Loriolan dumbfounds his sister. "I wish it could just all go away, right now!"

"What?" The girls are puzzled. But then one of them has espied through the window the highly anticipated royal carriage from the neighboring kingdom of Aquamaralis, with the Princess, the secret champion of most of Azuris' mer-citizens, descending from it onto the palace grounds — Charmeline, the most beautiful young mermaid many have ever laid their eyes on. Her golden, long hair is undulating like the sun itself, radiating from her graceful figure as if to outshine everything around her. If this bombshell beauty will not arouse Arilene's brother's interest, then nothing will. The girls giggle and whisper excitedly about all the interesting developments and exciting new guests arriving at their palace.

Then Arilene sends her maids out to have a private word with her brother. With a questioning face, she stands right in front of him, prompting him to explain himself.

"What?" Loriolan plays dumb, ready to roll over to the other side. But Arilene won't have any of this anymore.

"Loriolan, please, what's wrong with you? Here the most beautiful mermaid princesses come to woo you, and you act like you couldn't care less!"

"That's because I don't!" Loriolan just isn't in the mood. If it were up to him, he would sleep through the day or leave right now to begin his long journey. But instead, he needs to satisfy his parents' wishes and endure the charade, and a charade it is since he cannot live up to their expectations and pretend to be seriously interested in another woman. It would be tolerable if this were just any party, but this ball is specifically meant to hook him up with any stranger he just might happen to stumble across within the crowd of vying girls. The truth is that his heart is taken, and nothing will change that!

With a grouchy face, Loriolan finally sits up and looks Arilene straight into her caring eyes: "I'm already in love with someone else, Arilene!"

Arilene takes a step backwards, startled. But then she continues to look at him with her warm and openhearted eyes, revealing a spark of interest.

"I met her several days ago at the crescent bay pool where we used to play hide and go seek when we were little!" he discloses. "She is the most amazingly beautiful girl I have ever laid my eyes on. She completely stuns and turns me on, on all kinds of levels," he admits.

"Uhum!" Arilene clears her throat with an air of played offence taken.

"Of course you are as beautiful, in your own way," he grants her smilingly. "You know what I mean!"

"Yes, I do! You want someone to love romantically, as I'm getting ready to do as well," she reflects. "I guess we have truly grown up. We don't get to play around much together anymore," she complains a bit. "I noticed you were gone a lot lately, and I get to hang out with my female buddies!"

"Are you okay?" he wants to know. "I just noticed that our interests have shifted away from each other's as of late, and you don't want to hang out with us boring mer-lads much anymore anyway!"

"It's alright!" she concedes. "Who is this attractive mermaid that I have not heard of her before?"

"She is not a mermaid," he explains quietly. "She is a human, and she lives in a palace on land with her family and friends." He lowers his gaze, knowing that all this might make little sense to his sister, as it did not to his father. But to his surprise, Arilene is quite open to the idea.

"She must be quite a girl to have captured your heart to such an extent that you want to forego a ball where the most beautiful mermaid princesses of the Underwater Kingdoms are lining up for your selection, happy to get a dance with you or for you to even just look at them. You are such a fortunate guy, Loriolan!" Her voice falters, and she lowers her eyes now as well. Loriolan lifts her chin to see what's going on in her. "What's the matter, Arilene?"

She looks up: "Do you know why I insisted on continuing taking voice lessons at the Music Academy of the Sirenes, even after Mom and Dad offered to get me a private tutor instead?"

Loriolan is all ears.

"It's because I fell in love with a boy there, a harp player of the most accomplished and magnificent nature!" Her eyes begin to sparkle with the light of love. "When he accompanies my singing, I feel like we are in the Heavens, completely united in bliss and highest, purest love. I have never felt that way before, Loriolan!" She looks at him with these vulnerable, pleading eyes as if it is up to him to give her permission to love her love interest.

"Of course Mom and Dad want me to marry a prince from another kingdom. But I want him, Loriolan, a non-royal: he is not a prince, but he is the prince of my heart!"

"What's his name, Arilene?" he wants to know gently.

"His name is Shantiloh, and he is Rachtan's apprentice!" she reveals. "His wisdom is beyond his age, and that means more to me than material treasures or royal rank!" All of a sudden, she is close to tears.

Loriolan comforts her, taking her hand into his. After a moment, she pulls it away and stands up, walking to the window to take a peek out. "Enough about me. It's your day today! What are you going to wear?"

Loriolan doesn't want to get distracted from matters of the heart. He doesn't care to live a life of pretense and denial. "I met Shantiloh yesterday, at Rachtan's!" he reveals. And upon receiving an incredulous glance from her, he continues: "I sought Rachtan's advice because I want to marry Indirali and live happily ever after with her!"

Arilene sits down, her eyes big with anticipation.

"He said I have to traverse the underworld and not only get to the very bottom of our oceanic world, but encounter and master my deepest fears and weaknesses as well, so the gateway of hell will let me pass through to the other side, and then — miraculously — I will be in Heaven, I hope!"

"Wow!" Arilene gives off a deep sigh.

"Yes!" he concurs. "That's why it is important that I get on my journey as soon as possible. Because on top of that, Indirali is to be betrothed to some war hero she doesn't like, in just a couple of days."

"Not much time then!" she realizes.

"I just need to get Mom's and Dad's approval for my trip, and then I'm outta here!" he wishes.

"Good luck with that!" she laughs. "Will I see you again?" She looks at him with a hint of fear in her eyes.

"I strongly anticipate 'yes!'. I want to succeed and have it all: Indirali, ruling over Azuris, and you and Mom and Dad close by, of course. Just everything that makes us all happy! I want it all, is that too much asked?"

"I guess not," she admits with a reflective face.

"And you should have your Shantiloh as well, if he makes you happy!" He looks at her encouragingly. "Does he share your feelings?"

She blushes. "We haven't really admitted our love to one another yet. But it suffuses the whole atmosphere when we are together. I think everyone can see that we are in love; it's as if we're radiating bliss to all corners of the universe, enveloping and inspiring everyone around us to share in our infinite happiness and ecstasy." Her eyes begin to glow again.

"Then you should definitely be together!" he reassures.

"You think so?"

"Definitely! He seems as much into you as you are into him. I just hope Rachtan will let him be with you." Arilene winces under what he just said. "Which I'm sure he will," he quickly adds to encourage her, "if it is meant to be." She looks at him, vulnerable. "And it is meant to be if you love him the way you do!" He smiles at her. "You just make it happen!"

"How?"

"Envision yourselves together — it all starts in the mind anyway — and talk to him about your feelings!"

"I feel shy about that, Loriolan. I wish he would take the first step."

"He might think that you are unreachable because you are the daughter of the King of Azuris, and he knows that you are supposed to marry another royal prince."

"Which I don't want to do now that I know Shantiloh exists!" she reacts.

"Exactly! Let him know that! You might be surprised at his reaction. Maybe he is just waiting for you to tell him!"

"I think I will!" she decides. "I guess I have nothing much to lose."

"And, if after I come back, the two of you are still not together, then I will ask Rachtan first and personally offer Shantiloh your hand in marriage!"

Arilene lets out a shriek of joy. "You would do that for me?" She cannot believe her fortune. She always is able to count on her brother for such brave actions. He always looks out for her wellbeing, and she will miss him terribly once he is gone. The thought that he will traverse the spheres of darkness frightens her some, but if it is all for love and a good cause, then she will have to be okay with it and wish him well on his journey.

The two of them still sit for a while, chatting about their beloveds, when Queen Lilliane knocks and enters Loriolan's chambers, spreading her good mood and happiness around, then hurries the both of them on to get ready and come join the festivities that are to begin any moment now. Arilene helps Loriolan pick a nice, golden-purplish, beautifully decorated attire, places his princely crown onto his combed hair, and then smiles at him as if to confirm that he will be the handsomest of all mermen in the whole palace.

On his way to the celebration hall, Loriolan is joined by his two buddies Torilander and Chekilian. Quietly, Loriolan whispers a message into Torilander's ear. He is to go meet Indirali, or Hedna, if Indirali cannot come, and inform her that Loriolan is going to leave in the morning to vanquish the dark and meet her in the Heavens, and that he hopes she found a way as well, to meet him in the celestial spheres as soon as possible, because his love for her is infinite and eternal and he misses her already more than is bearable and hopes that she will not go through with that doomed wedding to Hecto, because that would be the end of him.

Torilander nods, then hurries out of the palace to accomplish his mission.

CHAPTER 11

The fanfares begin their majestic entrance hymn as Loriolan, accompanied by his mother, enters the foyer of the great festivity hall, proudly announced to all the anticipating guests by the Royal Ambassador of Azuris. Loriolan feels blinded by all the glittering lights and glamorous pomp, as well as overwhelmed by all the expecting faces he hates to have to please and justify himself to. Followed by the King and Arilene, the Royal Family slowly and majestically walks down the ruby-carpet, with courtiers and guests bowing before them in reverence, then take their elevated throne seats at the end of the hall to commence the festivities held in the Prince's honor.

One by one, the princesses and their accompanying entourage are introduced to the royal hosts, each making their curtsy, most of them painfully aware of the importance of a good first impression and therefore aware of how they look and come across, just so they can take their place afterwards on the dance floor with their adjoining male partners.

When the introduction ceremony is over, the King gestures with his hand to begin the event, and the Master of Ceremony bangs his staff three times on the ground, prompting the musicians to begin the orchestral entertainment with minuets of Azuris' most accomplished composers. Rows of mer-gentlemen begin to approach and bow to a mer-lady of their choice and company, and a baroque-like group dance begins to sweep the hall. Couples exchange partners and in rows dance by the Royal Family to offer especially Loriolan a closer look at the mer-princesses each mer-gentleman would be happy to give up and let the Prince dance with. Loriolan feels increasingly awkward. Face after beautiful face dances past him, each smiling at him with alluring eyes and pouting mouths. Even with his best efforts, he has a hard time discerning any particular mer-princess from all the others, simply because his heart is with Indirali and not in this tumultuous place at all. He feels strangely floating within a bubble that only his beloved Indirali and he share, with the world existing outside of it, unable to penetrate through to him at this very moment. And so he settles into an inner peace, knowing his heart is true to Indirali, and all the smiling, tempting faces soon become one big blur to him.

His parents, on the other hand, have a great time pointing certain princesses out to him who strike their fancy. Sometimes it's her beauty, sometimes the way she moves, and another time she seems to look wise and of good character. Only Arilene sits quietly, observing the spectacle with equanimity, occasionally indicating to Loriolan with her face that she is with him and to not let the flesh market get to him or dissuade him from his certain mission. Soon, however, a royal gentleman approaches the throne area and, with a bow of courtesy, asks for a dance with Arilene. Arilene looks at her father, and he agrees. Hesitantly she joins the dancing couples and — looking extremely graceful and pretty in her lovely, azure-blue gown and long, wavy, light-blue hair — begins to weave her own beautiful magic on the dance floor that quickly seems to overtake and intoxicate the senses of a crowd of royal mermen, much to the delight of the King and Queen. And so the music and dancing continue, piece after piece, until at some point Loriolan's father thinks his son has watched enough and now it is time for action, to throw himself into the sea of possibilities any healthy merman would fight to have.

But Loriolan doesn't feel ready, the truth is he never will! The thought to pick a certain lady just rubs him the wrong way. If he obliges, then only to get his parents off his back! And so, under their continued urges and pushes, Loriolan steps onto the dance floor. The music immediately stops, and everyone looks at him with eyes as if fortune could strike at any moment. Loriolan turns around, trying to find a face that doesn't besiege him with highest anticipation and futile hope. He wants to find someone not interested in him romantically, someone who will leave him to his freedom and not bother him with her romantic or ambitious desires. He glances into the round like lightning trying to find a rod to unstress on, starting to sweat as he feels the attention mounting and the hall growing increasingly impatient, and finally two invisible mer-people seem to push him together with Charmeline, the blond bombshell of Aquamaralis. On one hand,

Loriolan feels relieved to have finally found someone to dance with and thus fulfill his obligation, but on the other hand he feels strangely trepidatious about what move Charmeline might make on him, now that he is in her clutches.

But to his relief, Charmeline doesn't exude this intense interest in him that he feels coming from all angles and corners of the palace. Instead, he feels her almost aloof and disinterested in his deeper feelings and being. She dances gently with him, following all the programmed dance moves to the letter. They make a splendid looking couple, the palace crowd agrees, and Loriolan's parents couldn't have looked any happier than at this seemingly very auspicious moment. What no one, however, seems to pick up on is the fact that Charmeline feels the same way about her being here at the ball as Loriolan does. When the two of them begin to exchange words, she quickly confides in him that she is in love with someone else, but that she has to fulfill her parents' request and show up at his bride-choosing ball. Loriolan laughs a laugh of relief and confides in her that he has the same problems as her. That causes Charmeline to open up more, and from then on, they both seem to chatter vividly with each other as if they are forgetting the world, causing the King and Queen, and any interested parties among the crowd, to cross their fingers and hope for the best, namely, a wedding in the near future.

What holds Loriolan and Charmeline in this misinterpreted bond, however, is the fact that they are both in love with someone else and that, for now at least, they don't have to pretend otherwise but can instead encourage each other to follow their hearts and hopefully end up with their true lovers. Charmeline agrees to go along with the charade and keeps dancing with him until the party begins to slow down, because everyone feels the Prince has made his choice. The royal parents look very satisfied when Loriolan finally ascends the stairs to their thrones, Charmeline right behind him.

"I have made up my mind!" he announces to his parents.

"We see!" they smilingly acknowledge his decision.

"Can we go now?" Loriolan pressures.

The King laughs. "You are not a man of many words, are you?"

"Well, like his father, he seems to know what he wants!" the Queen concedes, happy with her son's choice. "I guess this celebration has served its purpose and come out a success!"

"If you say so," the King obliges. "Let's thank our guests for coming, though, before you rush off to savor your newfound feelings for this young, beautiful lady here!" he smilingly recommends.

At this moment, Loriolan notices Torilander waiting by the entrance. His heart skips a beat. His lifeline to Indirali has returned. He aches to hear the news from his mouth. And all of a sudden, he has a hard time keeping up appearances.

"Father, I have to go. Please thank everyone for me for coming!" he apologizes before taking Charmeline's hand and placing her back into her company's care, then retreats towards the entrance. The King is speechless at his son's odd and bold behavior and is about to call him back, when the Queen lays her hand on his to calm him down, indicating to let Loriolan go for now.

The festivities end with the King holding his thank-you speech and the musicians performing the finale crescendo that leaves everyone whirling across the dance floor one last time. Then the guests are invited to continue enjoying the gourmet food at the lavish buffet, which had been deliciously arranged for the enjoyment of their visionary senses as well as their taste buds. And with a sense of fulfillment hanging in the atmosphere, the celebration slowly fades into the departures, with guests saying good-bye to friends they hadn't seen in a long time, and then driving off in their sea horse carriages to the tune of the full moon lighting the water in the early evening hours of this glamorous, eventful day.

CHAPTER 12

Indirali had sent her maid, Hedna, to convey a message to Loriolan as well. She wants Loriolan to know that she will endure the betrothal ceremony because she doesn't see any way to avoid it at this late hour, but that she will leave the palace immediately thereafter to search for an old, wise Oracle that the father of one of her maidservants still remembers from his past. This Oracle is known for her healing and magical abilities, which she applies very much to the benefit of all who seek her help and guidance. Indirali is hopeful that she will find what she is looking for, namely, a way that will ultimately unite her with Loriolan, the love of her life.

Loriolan can't help but feel tears forming in his eyes. How long do they have to be separated? How he longs to behold her beauty and to touch her glowing, velvety skin!

Torilander adds that Hedna confided Indirali spends many hours crying silently, wishing the betrothal ceremony would be canceled or at least be over already.

Loriolan stares into the dark, hazy-eyed, mulling over their unfortunate, separated destinies. Torilander lays his hand on his shoulder, demonstrating his heart is with him, when suddenly, Loriolan inquires: "Do you love Hedna?" Torilander backs off with an abrupt laugh, as if a nerve was hit and he is afraid to be found out. But when Loriolan holds his questioning gaze, he begins to admit he has feelings for Hedna, explaining that she had decided to not reciprocate them at this time.

"Why?" Loriolan wonders.

"Because her first loyalty lies with Indirali, her Mistress!"

Loriolan nods, "Very good of her. Indirali will need such a good-hearted, loyal maidservant and friend like her if she is to go on her arduous, challenging journey. Hedna is going with her, is she not?"

Torilander nods, and now it is he who looks melancholic.

Loriolan begins to fill Torilander in on his visit to Rachtan and on the necessity of his soul's journey through the gateway of the most dark, describing his expectations of what he thinks will happen along the way according to Rachtan's knowledge and cautions. Torilander feels he cannot let his friend go alone on this dangerous, life-risking quest and insists he be allowed to join him. After a few feeble attempts to thwart him, Loriolan finally agrees to have his best friend accompany him. He tells Torilander to get his parents' approval first, and if they consent, he should be ready in the early morning. Torilander nods, greatly excited!

At that moment, there is a loud knock at the door, and a guard insists Loriolan accompany him right away to the King's office. He wishes to speak to his son on important matters.

Loriolan throws a somewhat trepidatious look at Torilander, then leaves with the guard.

King Hadores has a broad, happy smile on his lips. Today his son has truly made him proud and hopeful for the future. He wants to convey his congratulations and get a feeling about how serious Loriolan is in regard to Charmeline, and just how fast he wants to proceed with dating and getting to know her better. He knows her father, the King of Aquamaralis, very well and is absolutely excited about this ideal match that will also benefit the two neighboring kingdoms very nicely.

"I love Indirali! Always have, always will!" Loriolan blurts out, seeing no other option but to confront his father straight on rather than hide the hurtful truth from him.

King Hadores stops in his tracks. What did his son just throw at him? The color fades from his face as he tries to understand what just happened.

"What did you just say?" he wonders out loud, thinking there must be a mistake in the choice of his son's words since the experience of today conveyed a completely different picture.

"And Rachtan knows about it and encourages me to go for it!" Loriolan informs his father. "He thinks I should follow my heart and not compromise on something so important as true love. He even showed me my destiny and gave me information about the path I have to undertake to finally unite with my true love. Nothing is impossible, Father! I will and can be with a human girl! Our ancestors knew how to overcome any obstacles in their way to be able to love and be with a human! The tales of old speak about it!"

King Hadores takes a seat. What nonsense has his son been bothering with? "Rachtan? Ancestors?" he tries to catch on. While he was entertaining in his mind his son's wedding to this gorgeous Princess of Aquamaralis, his son has been scheming his own plans of getting married to an Earth human woman. His stomach begins to turn and his anger to rise. How dare his son oppose him on such important matters?

"I thought we were over this!" he roars. "Didn't we agree that this fairy tale doesn't apply to today's realities anymore?"

"I think most fairy tales are actually legends of old that are based on true events, events we can hardly remember anymore, but which are real nonetheless! I believe in them and so does Rachtan!" Loriolan knows to bring the revered name of the King's advisor up in this conversation as much as possible, kind of like a protective shield against the wrath of his father. And it seems to work. King Hadores' look changes; puzzled, he stares in front of him as if to reconcile these two opposing viewpoints.

"What exactly did Rachtan have to say about this topic?" he finally yields.

And so Loriolan describes his visit to Rachtan and tries to convey the gist of his teachings and guidance to his father, who suddenly is all ears. After Loriolan finishes his report, the King tears his hair, looking all disheveled and confused.

"I guess I have to get used to the idea of having my own flesh and blood cross-merging with a human!" he admits. "What did Rachtan have to say about Poseidon's curse on the humans though? How does this factor into your future plans?"

Loriolan tries to placate his father, telling him that Rachtan expects many circumstances will change for the better once Loriolan succeeds in his mission, and that Poseidon most likely will be pleased with the idea of having peace between the oceanic kingdoms and the ones on land, very likely prompting him to release his stronghold on the humans when beholding the immense love he and Indirali will share as rulers over the kingdoms.

The King can't help but all of a sudden feel pride welling up in his fatherly chest. His son certainly has high and lofty goals and ambitions. Who would he be to stand in his way and go against his own spiritual advisor's wisdom? Sure, it irks him that his son went behind his back and sought guidance from Rachtan rather than from him, but he realizes that he hasn't been a good father to the inner, pressing needs of his lovelorn son. And so he gives him a big, long hug now, conveying his fatherly consent to this ambitious journey even though he wishes his son would still change his mind.

Grateful for his blessing, Loriolan responds heartily to this hug, and a big sigh of relief escapes his lips.

His father tells him to leave it up to him to break the news to his mother and that he will make sure she will understand and support his decision and love for that human girl as well. Then he wonders when he might meet the girl who captured his son's heart, whereby Loriolan responds by telling him about her plight, as well, of how she needs to dodge an arranged marriage like he had to, and that she also must go on a soul journey that will help them both to unite in a higher, transcendental sphere from which they intend to return as a couple united by God.

Father and son look into each other's eyes, with Hadores trying to fathom the courage and determination of his son with which he intends to overcome impossible odds, and with Loriolan succumbing under this probing gaze with a faint smile, as if to retreat to his inner resources that he still needs to draw upon to such an extent that he can withstand any questioning of his integrity and deep resolution in regard to going on such a life-endangering mission, which surely must be the biggest nightmare any parent can face in their life.

Loriolan leaves his father's office wondering whether his father stands really, fully behind him or if he is just still trying to get there. Anyway, a big breakthrough just occurred, and Loriolan would be deceiving himself if he wouldn't admit how relieved and happy this meeting ultimately made him.

He decides to swim up and take a look at the night sky. He wants to be as close to Indirali as possible. He wants to convey his love to her, every minute of the day, for all eternity. She is the Goddess of his heart, the center of his universe! She makes him tick, she makes him smile, she makes him feel alive as he has never felt before. And so he glides up to the surface, surrendering to the drift he caught, and begins to float on the ocean's surface, face up, losing himself in the mysterious dark of the sky. The moon shines brightly, and the stars sparkle like an infinite ocean reflecting the sun's light rays, enlivening his mind and heart with the beauty of their endearing constellations and elusive distances. Loriolan basks in the cosmic rays and energies, envisioning a life with Indirali, wishing she could be here with him, sharing his dreams, and helping them to come true. Where is she right now, and how does she feel? Does she think about him right at this very moment as well? Such are his love-suffused thoughts and feelings while the night begins to slowly envelop him in the dark of a setting moon, leaving him wanting and hurting for his one true love of all time!

CHAPTER 13

And Loriolan's love is responding in like manner! Indirali sits on the rim of the fountain within her private garden, gently splashing with the water as if caressing her lover. Overwhelmed with the happenings inside the palace and afraid of what tomorrow will bring, she is bent on losing herself in thoughts about Loriolan. She misses him terribly and resents the fact that she can't win her parents over to her cause. Instead, she is forced to go along with their scheming wedding plans with a man she would give anything to never have to meet in her life. Her heart has chosen her lover, and as strange and impossible as it might seem to the outsider to consider a union between the two different worlds, for her it feels almost the more natural choice at this point simply because her feelings for Loriolan border on the sheer magical and Divine in nature, and it would break her heart if she would have to betray this most sacred of unions she could ever imagine and feel.

Tears run down her cheeks and mingle with the water she reflectively plays with. How she wishes Loriolan could be by her side right now, comforting her soul and easing her pain! Does he think about her this instant as well? Does he ache as much as she does to finally unite in heart and soul and body? Longingly, she looks up to the bright shining moon, asking for its help in bringing her and Loriolan together in an ultimate and final fashion. The moon smiles down on her, taking pity and promising her that all will be well if only she continues to follow her heart. In all her radiating wisdom and essence, the Moon Goddess takes the two hurting and longing lovers into her protective embrace and vows to accompany them on their soul-uniting quest until true love for all eternity has been restored to them!

Indirali is found in the morning, asleep by the fountain, a faint smile on her lips and the water mist sprayed on her long, beautiful hair! So deep and mystical has her inner connection with Loriolan been throughout the night that it reached into her dream world, causing her to revel in the bliss they trigger in each other and which they share so intimately.

Today is the day that Hecto is expected to arrive and claim his bride-to-be as his! The palace is hustling and bustling with last minute preparations in order to impress the neighboring king's son with all the pomp and glamour King Eurylochos is able to conjure up and muster. And tomorrow's betrothal event is to outshine everything! The King has put in an extra effort and financial expenditure in order to make sure Hecto understands that his bride is of royal and prosperous descent! A considerable amount of precious dowry gifts have been lined up to ensure Hecto's good will and marital commitment. Nothing has been left undone to win this stallion of a man over to the much-needed union between the two kingdoms, and if it means to sacrifice Indirali's heart on the altar of political strategies, then King Eurylochos has decided that it be so!

But deep down in his heart and soul, the King is hurting for his daughter and for his kingdom as a whole. Because just this morning the news has been brought to his attention that yet another fleet of his trade ships has been destroyed by the angry waves of Poseidon, a fleet of greatest, most desperate hope to bring much-needed resources and products from the southern provinces to Lucania, meant to fill the empty storage facilities and refill the empty treasure chests with the exchanged gold for Lucania's grains and other agricultural goods. Without the ability to undertake trade exchanges with the southern provinces, which, incidentally, enjoy a warmer climate that allows growing a different variety of foods and spices, commercial life seems to take great losses, and profits and prosperity have dwindled to an all time low, leaving farmers and salespeople destitute and despondent. Yes, King Eurylochos feels his hands are tied when it comes to the wellbeing of his daughter. She seems to be a precious bargaining chip he can't afford to not make the most of. Her marriage to the successor of the King of Neapolis is a strategic move that King Eurylochos hopes will ease his kingdom's hardships. It is well known that Neapolis's fertile volcanic soil yields more produce and grain than other kingdoms on the Italiot Peninsula, promoting Neapolis to a more privileged status and political esteem among all other kingdoms. To align himself with a kingdom that seems to have an advantage in almost all areas of its political and commercial interests is just wise statesmanship, the King reasons. As much as he loves her, he has to see her off to this ambitious war hero lest his kingdom's fate be sealed and its demise become inevitable. With a heavy heart, he awaits the arrival of Hecto's delegation, ready to sign the marital contract and thus give his beloved daughter away to someone he doesn't even trust at the very bottom of his fatherly heart.

The tension mounts towards the late morning, the time of day Hecto announced he would arrive. The King and Queen grow increasingly nervous, wanting to make sure that everything will be to his liking and much-coveted approval. If there wouldn't be so much at stake, King Eurylochos would not have bothered with all the extra luxuries nor would he have rounded up the great number of artistic performers from within his kingdom to ensure this crucial guest won't lack in entertainment. No, if it were truly up to the King's heart desires, he would have liked to keep it all to a basic minimum. But life has its quirks, unforeseen surprises, and challenges, and he better not leave anything about his daughter's marriage up to chance. And so the palace awaits the betrothal delegation as if the destiny of all of Lucania depends on it, nervous to convey an advantageous impression and eager to catch the prey in their cleverly laid out net of offered hilarious entertainment and carnal pleasures.

Indirali sits by the window of her chamber gazing at the sky as if wanting to fly away. Hedna silently sits by her side, gently combing Indirali's long, shiny hair, sometimes quietly humming a melancholic tune as if to appease Indirali's aching heart. The clouds slowly blur as Indirali's eyes begin to tear. But deep within, she knows all will be well! This is just a charade she needs to endure so she can ultimately be with her true love! Her heart begins to ache the closer the hour of Hecto's announced arrival approaches. It's as if she picks up on everyone's expectations and nervousness in the palace, most of all that of her father's, who just recently implored her again to understand the urgency of his state business and affairs, making it very clear to her that her wedding is nonnegotiable and absolutely the last chance of survival for his people, because peace and cooperation between Lucania and Neapolis are the only hope for his weakened kingdom that he can see at this late hour, and as much as he regrets the whole arranged marriage, he also must insist on it as well.

The hour of Hecto's anticipated arrival comes and passes without the Prince showing his face. Still, the expectant crowd is in a good mood; it is not every day that the Princess gets betrothed, and it is very seldom that the Lucanians can find a reason in their lives to celebrate anymore. Life has become barren and empty for most citizens, with growing poverty and misery encroaching upon society's life, unstoppably escalating and threatening to overtake even the royal palace until there is not one man left standing in his original honor and dignity and no woman to celebrate the beauty and goodness of life anymore. No, this sad fate must be avoided at all costs! King Eurylochos does not want to bring war upon his people as an answer to the pressing needs of his kingdom nor is he interested in turning his neighboring kingdoms into enemies and aggressors. His father has taught him well, recounting endless stories of the long Greek wars of previous generations, talking about the uncountable deaths that occurred at the hands of other Greek kings and war heroes only because pride and ignorance prevailed in those days, turning city against city and brother against brother. Eurylochos had shuddered upon hearing about the senseless bloodshed and the demise of many brave and heroic men, who unfortunately threw their valuable lives away in the misguided pursuits of false glory and victory. In King Eurylochos' opinion, life is more valuable than death, and the wellbeing and prosperity of his people mean more to him than the awards and useless medals the war can give to those who err on the path of murderous killings. He swore early on in his office as king to put his life-affirming values first, to try avoiding war at all costs, and to always hold precious the lives of all those he reigns over.

But how unnerving becomes the atmosphere in the palace as not only the lunch hour passes, but also the early afternoon goes by without the much-anticipated guests showing up. The tension begins to subside into a feeling of subtle irritation and despair. The food is cold, the hosts are hungry, and Princess Indirali is ground through waiting hell as her forced-upon suitor continues to not show up. The collective morale at the palace is sinking rapidly, with King Eurylochos hiding in his office to avoid the questioning eyes of his ministers, courtiers, and staff. Frustration grips him that seems to trigger his anger with the whole situation. Here he is willing to sacrifice his daughter to this vain prince, and he does not even have the courtesy to show up in time for his splashy reception! The understanding was that Hecto and his entourage would overnight in a nearby village especially prepared for their repose from the long trip, and that they would show up at the palace early in the day to be greeted by the euphoric crowd and anticipating Royal Family. Eurylochos begins to feel his anger growing at an alarming rate. He condemns the situation he is in. He would prefer nothing more than to send this arrogant twit right back if he still chooses to show up, now after most of the day has already gone by and much of today's entertainment and food has been wasted. He feels rendered a fool, and he does not like it one bit! How deep does he have to sink in order to win back the mercy and benevolence of the Gods in order to save his kingdom, not to mention his darling daughter's love life! His heart cries out in anguish, when all of a sudden, the guards knock at his door, informing him of Hecto's arrival. King Eurylochos tries to regain his composure, then walks out and joins his wife to regally stride with her onto the grand balcony. With a forced smile and gracious wave of his hand he greets his future son-in-law, causing the enthusiastic crowd to burst into a jubilant cheer.

With the smile of a victor, Hecto rides his horse ahead of his brigade, proudly waving his city-state's flag, enjoying every moment of his pompous reception. The palace crowd, quietly sighing with relief, joyfully applauds as he rides along the flower-strewn path; the Prince, after all, has not reneged but rather seems to have been delayed through circumstances along the road. And Hecto brims with confidence. He looks forward to refreshing himself with all the delicious food and luxurious accommodations he expects, and is very much looking forward to meeting his future in-laws to exchange vows and precious gifts.

Indirali is finally summoned as well. She is to join her parents in the assembly hall to permit her suitor a glance at her for the first time. With a feeling of extreme awkwardness and resentment, she enters the dais on which her parents occupy their thrones, her long, flowing dress caressing her figure as if to buffer her from the harshness of the situation. As previously advised, she takes a standing position near her mother's throne to allow Hecto his much-awaited first look at her. She doesn't want to meet his eyes; she'd rather leave or crawl into a hole to hide away than to get entangled with him on any soul level and in any other way. What ultimate degradation and humiliation! Indirali endures the welcoming ceremony with an air of indifference and aloofness, making it an art to seem present but inwardly be as far away from the event as possible. She thinks about Loriolan, and a smile begins to spread faintly on her face.

Hecto is pleased with what he sees. In his opinion, the betrothal ceremony tomorrow can proceed as planned. With mutual words of flattery and kind approval of their exchanged gifts, the two parties separate at the end of the day to rest for the upcoming festivities. All seems well in the palace household: all members seem to feel a spark of hope reignited, and all wish the Princess well on her new and upcoming journey to eventually become the queen of the neighboring kingdom of Neapolis. Peace has been secured, and tonight the palace inhabitants go to bed with a feeling of lightness and relief.

Only Indirali couldn't be farther away from her happiness. Even though she knows she will leave to go on her soul journey the morning after her betrothal, she can't shake this irrational fear that somehow she might get caught in the net of deception and sacrifice her parents have put her in and that for some inexplicable reason, she will never be united with Loriolan but must suffer till the end of her days on this planet until she might see him again in Heaven. So deep is her despair in regard to the upcoming betrothal that she can hardly sleep, restlessly tossing and turning and hating every minute that brings her closer to the moment where she has to agree to his hand in marriage. She hopes with all her might that this engagement won't really matter in the eyes of the Divine and that the real truth about her loving feelings for Loriolan will outshine everything in the end. This thought is all she has right now, the only lifeline that keeps her alive at this very moment, alive and hoping for the best possible outcome! For that she is willing to risk her life and go against her father's decision! For her true love she is willing to leave her life as a princess behind and step into the absolute unknown, willing to overcome any obstacles in her way, and willing to sacrifice everything in order to transcend into the Heavens where alone she hopes she can unite with Loriolan forever!

CHAPTER 14

As much as Indirali tries to fall asleep this night, she just isn't able to. Over and over, she sees playing in her mind the victorious grin of Hecto with which he approached her parents and her this evening. In his opinion, she already is his, no matter how she feels and no matter that she is in love with someone else. Her feelings are just not important to anyone here in the palace, it seems, except for her loyal maidservant, Hedna, who herself is not able to change anything about this fixed matter. A deep desperation grips Indirali, and if she could, she would escape right now from this unfortunate place and event, leaving everyone to their illusory expectations in regard to the real truth of her life and love. If only she wouldn't love her parents so much. They raised her with much love and care, but lately, all this seems to have gone up in smoke as they try to match her up with this arrogant behaving man, as an attempt to patch up the kingdom's underlying problems. As much as she would like to help, she can't make herself believe that it is her duty to be miserable for the rest of her life so everyone else in her father's kingdom can be happy. She wouldn't be at all surprised if the expectation of her marriage to transform Lucania's fate for the better would actually be a futile one and her misfortune would rather beget more misfortune for her father's kingdom. How can anything good ever sprout from anyone else's misfortune? Certain cruel Gods of old used to demand the sacrifice of a virgin's life just to satisfy their blood thirst, but thankfully, today's societies have assumed a more enlightened stance in the matter and have given up the physical life sacrifice. But, in a way, this sacrifice continues to exist when girls like her are sacrificed on the altar of an undesired marriage, a bond meant to foster a political or societal alliance rather than individual happiness and freedom, the very foundational blocks of a healthy, prospering society and of collective wellbeing! In like way, her life is readily given over to a man who doesn't deserve her because he believes in killing and death, and she believes in peace and eternal life! They couldn't be any more different than they already are, and life alongside such a killing machine would be her certain death, first on the inside, spiritually and emotionally, and very soon on the outside, physically. Indirali is certain that she needs to act promptly in order to avoid this agonizing, prolonged death experience. Nothing could be more painful than to stay and become this man's wife, she decides, nothing! Not even being incarcerated or hung for her disobedience! At least then her mind and spirit could still be free and with Loriolan, the true love of her life!

Such are her desperate thoughts and feelings that keep her awake and restless until the morning dawn. Soon she is jolted out of bed by the bell ringing, informing her to get ready for the common breakfast with Hecto and his entourage at the breakfast pavilion in the East Wing of the palace. Indirali feels nauseous. Her stomach is upset, and she doesn't want to join the breakfast to make another fool of herself. And so she stays put, lying back down on the bed with the comforter pulled over her face. She wants to forget everything about today; she wants this Hecto to just go away and leave her alone!

After breakfast, however, King Eurylochos comes to her chamber to check up on her and to make sure everything is still on track. He absolutely cannot have any missteps happen, not with this Hecto being right under his nose and looking already pretty puzzled in regard to why Indirali wasn't able to attend the breakfast with him and everyone else. Because this is the reason he came here for: to get a good look at the princess he is to marry!

Indirali doesn't look out from under her comforter; she just doesn't want to have any part in all this. Eurylochos implores her to explain her strange behavior, but when she does, he gets angry with her. He can't believe that she still thinks about this cursed merman, a member of the water race, who in some way must surely have his part in the whole Poseidon curse that hangs over all the innocent men who lost their lives on the ocean in the recent years and all the many loaded ships that went under, creating untold losses and bringing not only Lucania to the brink of annihilation but all its neighboring kingdoms as well. How can she possibly still entertain having anything to do with the water creatures, let alone be in love with one of them, ready to throw her life away for some impossible union between the races? King Eurylochos can't believe this nonsense that his daughter confronts him with and is getting quite angry with her now for being so stubborn and uninsightful. Does she not have any compassion with the sailors who lost their lives, and what about their families who are now left without a father and provider? And what about the kingdom's failing economy? Such are the accusatory questions he lays on her, trying to burden her and make her feel responsible for circumstances beyond anyone's control.

Indirali pokes her head out from under the comforter and looks at him with glowing eyes: "Why do you think anything will change only because I might marry this Hecto?" she wants to know.

"Because!" Eurylochos retorts. "It's at least a step in the right direction! To have peace between our kingdoms will help tremendously!" he triumphs with his reasoning.

"Did they declare war on you, or why is it so important that we have this union with them?" she wonders.

"No, they haven't yet. But that doesn't mean they might not declare it at any moment. Neapolis might not lack in grain and certain other commodities, but like us they are impoverished in many other areas of their economy, reeling just as much from Poseidon's relentless and unjust curse and jeopardy of all of our commercial efforts. Poverty can turn even the most reasonable ally into your worst enemy if it means having priority access to our dwindling resources! And with your marriage, we would have preempted that strike: we would have prevented the war from happening!" he asserts as if completely in the right. "Plus, this alliance could give us the necessary advantage over any possible alliance of several other kingdoms presently threatening our borders," he argues.

"So you marry me off because you engage in thoughts about war with whoever might attack you in the future? Don't you think that this kind of focus and attention might actually attract what you are afraid of most and will start the war you deeply dread and want to avoid?" Indirali feels almost offended at this thought.

"That might be the case, yes!" he admits with a slight tremble in his voice.

"You would use your own daughter for such a gamble?" she asks. "I thought that the real problem is Poseidon's curse! Without it, there would not be any destruction on the seas, no loss of lives and riches. Our kingdoms could prosper again, and any thought about war could be abandoned! Where there is abundance of every good thing, there is no need to fight over resources and unload any pent-up stress on another kingdom and people, because people who don't lack the necessities of life don't look for any scapegoats to blame for their lives anymore; they are way too busy leading their happy and fulfilled lives. It's when they are being deprived of the necessities of life through the irresponsible and selfish traits of their leaders and enforcing armies that the simple people get oppressed and angry, willing to be misled and let their anger out on anyone when they are ordered and forced to do so. And that leads to these unfortunate, detestable wars, Father!" Indirali is close to tears as she tries to get through to him. "So why don't you focus in the direction of restoring the wellbeing of our people through love and try to fix the real issue here, instead of trying to appease a quarrelsome neighbor who seems to threaten your borders because they are suffering from Poseidon's curse as much as we do, and as much as the other kingdoms all around us do. Why not find a way to create peace with Poseidon and try to win him over to the human cause? Why not find a solution that could even allow us to approach Poseidon with a reason for him to forgive the war-lusting humanity their sinful ways and trespasses?" Indirali looks at her father, and her father stares back at her. After a long moment, he gulps. There seems to be a kernel of truth in what she just suggested; he can't deny that.

"But how can such an impossible task ever be approached?" he wonders out loud. "How can Poseidon be made to back off and begin to support humanity in their trade efforts again?" As soon as he utters these words, however, he already sees the answer written all over Indirali's face. The merman! This Loriolan she keeps talking about! King Eurylochos' throat tightens, and he feels left without air for a moment. All this is way too fast and way too dangerous, he decides. He cannot, and does not, want to look in that direction. Not at this moment, at least.

But Indirali doesn't let him get away without rubbing the total sense that all this makes in his face. "Don't you see it, Father? A union between Loriolan and me could appease the God of the ocean and sea. He could be taught a lesson that love between a human and a water man is not only possible but also very inspiring, because by that time we will have conquered hell and the Heavens and proven that no obstacles are big and fear-inducing enough to make us stop and give up on our eternal love for each other! Poseidon will have to yield his powers in front of such infinite, eternal, and unconditional love. He will have to acknowledge that there are good human beings who deserve a chance on life and happiness, and that he better not mess it up with the rest of the heavenly worlds unless he wants to incur the wrath of the other Gods, who will be on our side because of all the tests and tribulations we will have gone through and mastered by then." Indirali lowers her gaze, and her father can't help but feel in quite some awe of her. Nevertheless, he doesn't believe that such a feat can so easily be accomplished as she is describing here. Not everyone traverses the valley of death and comes out alright and still alive at the other end of it, and not everyone climbs the highest mountains to join the heavenly beings in their eternal dwelling places, and then still returns to their earthly home kingdom to uplift and help those they left behind. He is, at the least, utterly skeptical about the success and good outcome for not only her but also his and the neighboring kings' kingdoms. It would be a very selfless act and challenging soul journey that she and this Loriolan must undergo if any of the desired outcomes should be anticipated as realistic and accomplishable. The King's eyes begin to tear up as he deeply reflects about what was just said. On one hand, it would save him and his family from locking into a bond with the royal palace of Neapolis, a bond he secretly detests and even is unsure of in regard to its ultimate higher purpose and benefit since Neapolis doesn't seem to mind Rome's escalating dominion, but on the other hand, it also confronts him with the absolute uncertainty of Indirali's reasoning and possible success, because if she fails, then all hell would break loose between the kingdoms, and his momentary advantage would be lost for good! This thought makes the King shudder.

"Father, I can do it!" his daughter reassures him. "I can face and conquer whatever demons and other obstacles are on my way! I will bring peace and prosperity back to Lucania and to all the other kingdoms presently suffering from Poseidon's curse. I will not rest until I have accomplished this task and have convinced Poseidon with my infinite love for Loriolan to give all of humanity another chance, because — as we both know — not all humans are evil in nature, and not all are bent on letting war loose on many innocent people the way certain war-lusting individuals and leaders irresponsibly are." Indirali takes his hand into hers and pleadingly looks into his eyes.

Eurylochos feels a wall of ice beginning to melt around his heart. Until now, he has not noticed how stonewalled he has become towards his daughter's wellbeing. In fact, he hardly knows her anymore. She seems to have developed a life of her own, and she is now trying to desperately connect with him and let him into her world again. Another tear begins to form in his eye, and the King turns to the side, embarrassed. He has to choke back this tear before she sees him falling apart and witnesses him becoming all emotional! But Indirali is intent on reestablishing this inner connection with her father they used to share in those most precious, carefree of times of her childhood. Oh, how he used to make her laugh when she was little, and how he read all her wishes from her face before she had time to even express them to him. Indirali longs to find his heart in all the weariness of the present situation, the place that used to make her feel safe and protected when life seemed to threaten her in any small but hurtful way.

King Eurylochos feels the love and concern streaming from her heart, and a warmth begins to melt the remnants of his indifference towards her fate, slowly spreading throughout his entire being and lifting him to a level from where he could no longer imagine continuing to hurt her and sacrifice her for his lack of ability to steer the destiny of his kingdom in the direction of an earned fortune and its much-deserved prosperity. All of a sudden, he sees that, in his ignorance, he expected Indirali to fix the problems he couldn't fix himself. Instead of praying to the Gods and trying to enlist their help and wisdom, he has basically given up on his own sense of responsibility and has put his burdens on her shoulders and, for that matter, on those of his son, who at this very instant is risking his life in order to guarantee protection for Lucania. Eurylochos can't help but laugh out loud abruptly. The whole idiocy of the moment comes to mind all of a sudden: how he sends his children into the risk of death, inwardly and outwardly, just so his kingdom might be saved. What he has completely lost track of, however, is the fact that only life begets life, and death only begets death. Where would his kingdom be without his son to live and to rule over it some day, and his daughter to inspire the beauty and wisdom of cultural life in everyone's hearts, qualities of a refined and higher nature that contribute as much to the meaning of life and prosperity as successful commercial trade can do. A veil of ignorance falls off his eyes and heart, and King Eurylochos wipes his tear away with his brocade-laden robe sleeve as if wanting to hide his face in shame.

But then he looks at his daughter with all the love he feels for her. "We have to have a plan though! At this late hour it is impossible to not go through with the betrothal! This offense alone could start a war if we are not careful!" he warns, and then he reveals to her a way that could extricate them from their obligation in an honorable and mutually acceptable way. He tells her that Hecto just informed him that the wedding can only take place after a year has passed because, as the superior commander, he is expected to fight against intruding forces from the north, whose conquest will very likely take him many months to complete.

Indirali is happy to hear the good news. She smiles at her father. Because so far, all she heard was that Hecto wanted to marry her within the next three moon cycles!

Eurylochos shares her sentiment and continues to explain: In the meantime, however, Hecto expects Indirali to wear the engagement ring as a sign of her loyalty and commitment to him. Eurylochos decides to now speak to Hecto and explain to him that he doesn't want his daughter to wear the engagement ring on her finger until she can be certain that Hecto is out of danger and has not been killed in war, which otherwise would stamp her as a premature widow. She will, instead, wear the ring on a necklace around her neck and will put the ring on her finger only after Hecto gives his word that his life is not at risk anymore until he is married to her. Eurylochos says that he will make sure Hecto understands that this twist in protocol is a necessary requirement for Indirali to wait out the unexpected and extra-long engagement period until the wedding, since the original agreement was that Hecto would marry her within three moon cycles and that he would not go to war before his wedding, risking his life with the possibility of maybe not being able to show up at his own wedding. King Eurylochos thinks that Hecto must surely acknowledge the fact that Indirali can't be made to wait for one year without either knowing that his life is safe and he will definitely come to marry her or having the mark of a widow on her, in case he loses his life in war.

Indirali smiles. This is the smart and resourceful father she knows. Proud of him, she gives him a hug and plants a kiss on his cheek. "Thank you so much, Daddy! I knew you would come through for me in the end!"

King Eurylochos enjoys this display of affection; deep within, however, he is sweating to make this truly work for now, lest his daughter's life hang on a fine thread.

"I'm sorry I have to still make you go through with the betrothal ceremony, my child!" he apologizes. "But it would be insanity to send this quite arrogant and fight-spirited man back right away when he came expecting you to conform to his will and become his bride-to-be." He looks at her lovingly: "Just endure it with an air of stoicism, and in a few days, you can go on your journey to find your fortune with Loriolan!"

She gives off a gentle exclamation of her joy and gratitude. Not in a million years would she have anticipated her father to come around so completely and wonderfully! She looks up to convey her inner thanks to Aphrodite, her guardian Goddess. Miracles are possible, she realizes, and the biggest of all miracles — her marriage to Loriolan — now all of a sudden doesn't look so impossible to her anymore!

"I hope you will succeed in your mission, Indirali!" her father prompts her on. "And I hope for all our sakes, and for the sake of our people, you will come back victorious and with Poseidon's blessings for us all!" He looks vulnerable but hopeful.

Indirali squeezes his hand heartily, signaling her commitment to the common cause.

"So, you are absolutely sure your love for Loriolan will give you the supernatural powers that are needed to help our kingdoms get back into the good graces of Poseidon?" he asks gingerly, hoping there might be a workable solution, after all, to all this grinding poverty and misery many nations of Magna Graecia have been enduring.

Indirali looks him deep into his eyes and then nods very strongly. "Yes, absolutely!"

And all that King Eurylochos can detect in her eyes is the absolute sincerity and truth of her words, enabling him to believe in her with his full heart and soul.

CHAPTER 15

From then on, the day seems to pass more easily for Indirali; with the wind in her back again and the love and support of her father secured, it feels almost like a piece of cake. Even though she still resents the fact that she has to act like she cares for Hecto and the betrothal ceremony, she inwardly feels relieved and at peace in the face of these unavoidable happenings. On some level, she almost even feels compassion for him now because, in fact, he did show up for her, hoping to have found his companion for life! And so she tries to be nice to him, although emotionally far removed from any true feelings towards him. With a graceful curtsy that would have stunned any wooing young man, Indirali offers him her hospitality and distinguished, elegant company.

Midmorning, the ceremony is held in the main temple. Hundreds of Royals have shown up for the occasion, to witness the ceremony that would bind the descendants of the Palace of Lucania and the Palace of Neapolis together in the rituals of engagement. After inviting the Goddess of Love, Aphrodite, and calling on Zeus for his ultimate Divine blessing, the priest affirms their bond but, to everyone's surprise, then allows Indirali to hang the ring with a necklace around her neck, as per King Eurylochos' instructions. Hecto complies, as King Eurylochos had a convincing argument about it in a short conversation they had before the ceremony, and when Indirali hands him the ring, he just puts it into a pouch and fastens it to his richly decorated leather belt, as if adding to his trophies, which incidentally, among other valuable items, holds his impressive, shining sword as well. Indirali tries to ignore the fact that he is wearing his general's uniform and army attire, fully equipped as if ready to march into battle. She can't help but notice the huge difference in outfits of the man the world wants to see her marry and of her true lover; while Hecto hides behind an armor of his past accomplishments and future battles, Loriolan boasts complete naturalness, innocence, and playfulness in both his outfits and movements. Much of Loriolan's scintillatingly beautiful skin usually shows, often adorned with sea jewels of various kinds, with pastel-colored, silken scarves and veils waving from him like dreams holding on to the reality they are born from. And his interaction with his natural habitat, the water, seems deeply interwoven and intimate, leaving her often marveling about his devotional alignment and sacred union with Nature and the Ocean that is his home. Indirali feels this mysterious pulling in her soul every time she thinks about Loriolan. She can't wait to get on with things and set out on her journey that will bring her close together with him. She can't wait to finally stop pretending and holding her breath, and instead begin living and breathing freely!

The congregation is ready to leave the temple, and in a long procession follows the betrothed couple out the temple gateway. Slowly, and under much jubilation from the waiting crowd, Indirali and Hecto walk down the flower-strewn path towards the palace. Indirali smiles at the people who seem to be so happy for her. Little do they know what truly causes her to be happy and how much she is willing to give up in order to make this happiness last forever and share it with everyone around!

Hecto and his delegation are invited to a splendid luncheon, a feast not only to satisfy his taste buds but all his senses, since King Eurylochos has spared no expense and has put on an artistic production of gigantic proportions, an entertainment menu guaranteed to please any man's desires and fantasies, a show meant to convince Hecto that his betrothed is from noble and prosperous descent, a pearl in the sand, and a gem in his crown!

The guests take their seats, with King Eurylochos and Queen Penelope sitting at the very center of the long, U-shaped, festively decorated banquet table, with Indirali sitting next to her father, and Hecto next to Queen Penelope. Exotic music begins to intoxicate the atmosphere, and guests begin to each move different body parts according to the magnetic rhythms and beats. Large flower bouquets accentuate the lush atmosphere, either hanging from pillars or the ceiling, or strategically placed around fountains and other significant, decorative junctures of the spacious dining hall, beautifying the buffet tables, and adorning the many beautiful women who have come to join and enrich the lavish meal and exciting performance with their smiles and quirky remarks. A host of sleekly dressed servants bearing opulent plates of the most selective, delicious foods offer these to the guests for their infinite pleasure and satisfaction. The best wine flows in gallons as the guests keep washing down the good food, getting merrier as time goes by.

Acrobats and seductive dancers begin to whirl across the dance floor in front of the dining table. The guests eat and watch, having a great time all around. At some point, King Eurylochos gives the much-anticipated speech, wishing the couple a great future and lasting peace among their kingdoms. Hecto feels like adding to the speech. He stands up, slightly drunk already, and lifts the chalice to toast his future wife, wishing she will give birth to many children and make him thus a proud father. Indirali lowers her eyes upon hearing this toast, ashamed to look into his eyes and let him see the truth of her feelings.

The festivities continue with full force: jesters playing tricks on the amused guests, jugglers and other artists triggering surprised reactions, singers and musicians accompanying beautiful, mysterious dancers to the tunes of ancient melodies and ballads — the whole hall echoes with the sound of laughter and joy. But soon the atmosphere begins to turn and deteriorate under the influence of the abundantly flowing alcohol. Hecto's wild side starts to emerge, as he can't get enough of the wonderful, old wine. God Bacchus has come to join the party, and who would Hecto be to exclude this old, fun-loving fella! Louder and louder become his comments, and increasingly uninhibited become his actions and words. His entourage also behaves in increasingly despicable ways, like a herd of barbarians tearing the flesh from the bones with their teeth rather than using the silverware dedicated for distinguished dining, roaring and grunting their reactions to the performances as if animals have come together. Chalices are filled to the overflowing, with much of the precious liquid running from their mouths and beards. So bad is their influence that many Lucanians of weak character begin to imitate their behavior, competing to be the biggest animal of them all and see who can shock the refined and sensitive person the most with their lower-self nature and bodily sounds. A brotherhood of the lowest common denominator is being formed, excluding and ridiculing everyone who is unwilling to join this decadent behavior. Soon Hecto, the leader, begins to flirt with maidservants of all kinds who try to pursue their tasks of keeping everyone fed and entertained. Quickly, he turns into an embarrassing stain on King Eurylochos' table, disrupting the gentle peace with his crude and demeaning remarks, getting all offended when a certain maid doesn't respond in the ways he expects and is accustomed to, degrading them by comparing them in unfavorable ways to the maids of Neapolis who — according to him — seem to be willing to surrender to his every whim and lustful demands, and finally he begins to even unstress and call certain individuals bad, derogatory names whom he considers behind the enemy lines of his continuous attacks and battles, in house, and on the battlefield he evidently has not fully left behind, even for the occasion of attending to matters of the heart!

Indirali can't stand the presence of these disrespectful guests anymore. Hecto is completely out of line, but because he is the guest of honor, everyone tries to please him and forgive him for any kind of rude behavior. King Eurylochos certainly feels in a bind. Impatiently he waits for the performances to come to an end and to legitimately call off the festivities. Very soon, however, he can't endure the subtle offenses against his authority and office as a king anymore, which Hecto keeps indirectly hurling at him persistently and way too abundantly, and so Eurylochos attempts to end the day with another thank-you speech. But the guests don't want to be stopped yet; they're having too much fun at the moment. Loudly, they continue to interact with each other as if King Eurylochos does not exist until, at some point, strategically, Hecto pretends to hear the King and take pity on his plight by relaying the King's message to his buddies, who all laugh roaringly, then continue to fall over the remaining meat dishes and wine, of which they just can't get enough. King Eurylochos is close to losing his temper. The next efficient means to end the festivities is to engage his guards and have the drunken guests escorted to their chambers, but he hesitates to go that far, afraid of how Hecto might react, drunken and aggressive as he is right now. And so the King keeps sitting at the table for a while longer, his wife and daughter silent and withdrawn, hoping for the torture to be over rather sooner than later. And over and over again, Hecto bellows out his insulting jokes, even directing them indirectly towards the royal parents and their daughter. He wonders out loud whether Indirali has it in her to give birth to several strong boys or whether she will embarrass him with her infertility. And upon noticing her nonreactive and stoic face, he tries to put her down and embarrass her as maybe being frigid and he will have difficulties getting his pleasures from her. This remark, thank God, crossed the line for Eurylochos. Offended and determined, he stands up and orders the guards to keep watching over his guests until they are ready to be brought to their quarters. The Royal Family, however, has had enough of this and is withdrawing early. He indicates to Hecto that he has transgressed the royal etiquette and made the King of Lucania a laughing stock. This seems to sober the Prince of Neapolis up a bit, and with an air of played regret, he mischievously lays the blame on the King for providing such seductive dancers right under their hungering eyes and explains that he and his men have been on the battlefield for too long and must have forgotten how to behave around women. He continues to argue for his case by taking much credit for the fact that his army has been protecting the borders and that Lucania can be grateful for their services.

King Eurylochos acknowledges Hecto's line of reasoning with a brief nod, then bids his guests a good night. With dignity, he indicates to his wife and daughter to accompany him from the hall. His ministers and courtiers follow the Royal Family out of the hall, leaving the unwelcome guests to their own rambunctious behavior and wild, orgy-like company.

If King Eurylochos hadn't already made up his mind in regard to his daughter's marital fate, he certainly would have changed his mind after this insulting visit. But in a way, it also has its good side, for now he is certain that he made the right choice, and Indirali will certainly be better off with anyone but this ill-behaved jerk of a man, who couldn't even hide his aggressive, demeaning side for the sake of making a good first impression on his future wife and in-laws. Preferably, he would like to call off tomorrow's Sports Games he has arranged to coincide with Hecto's stay, and which the King thought would please and satisfy his guest's competitive, fight-spirited character. At this moment, all he wishes is for Hecto to leave and save him and his family from another one of these humiliations. But unfortunately, Hecto is Neapolis' future king, and as such, King Eurylochos owes him a spectacular visit and thus finds himself unable to renege on the sporting event he already announced to the world. With a pinch in his heart, he wishes everyone a good night and retreats to his chambers for recuperation and reflection.

Indirali, however, feels like everything went pretty well, in an ultimate kind of way, with Hecto displaying very vividly why he just can't be a match for her refined and peaceful nature and King Eurylochos, therefore, having nothing to regret when he sends her on her soul quest and journey.

CHAPTER 16

*U*nderwater World King Hadores and his wife, Queen Lilliane, have a hard time saying good-bye to their son knowing he is leaving to voluntarily submit himself to a life-endangering journey from which they are not sure he will return. They asked him to give them another day to get accustomed to the idea that he just sprang on them and take the time to enjoy a relaxing day with his family and friends. The parents want to be sure Loriolan has thought his trip through as much as possible and is armed with the necessary knowledge and equipment to ensure maximum success of his mission. This day would also give everyone dear to him a chance to lovingly say good-bye and wish him well on his life's journey!

And so Loriolan finds himself surrounded by his loved ones, being the talk of the day and the center of everyone's attention. For a while, Torilander, Chekilian, and the Royal Family are having fun playing games in the water garden, enjoying placing the fist-sized, pearl-white pebble stones onto the patterned marble ground in unique geometric fashions that follow the intellectual concepts of the game, meant to draw on the players' creativity, inventiveness, and humor. The laughter and mutual admiration for one's craftiness and solution orientation, however, begin to trigger Loriolan's melancholy at some point. He certainly will miss these get-togethers and the supportive warmth and spirit of his parents and sister. He can already feel the pain of their absence in his life, but the truth is that until he is united with Indirali, even his family's love for him doesn't seem to fulfill him in the absolute sense anymore. It's as if he can't reach to the deepest levels of fulfillment, fun, and joy anymore, and all the games and fun things that previously provided him with much happiness now seem to fall short in enlivening the kind of bliss he only experienced with Indirali so far. He needs to have her by his side if ever he wants to feel whole and truly happy again, able to innocently and playfully enjoy days like this one, surrounded by his loving family and connecting with them through play and laughter. Nothing, he realizes, feels the same anymore since he met Indirali and since he experienced the infinite scope of breathtaking emotions she is able to evoke in his heart and soul. This is why he has to leave as soon as possible lest he feel compromised and diminished in his ability to feel fulfilled and carefree again! He has to overcome the demons of his deepest fears and master any challenges on his way to unification and marital bliss with his one and only true love, Indirali! He smiles at pronouncing her name in his mind. Her name sounds like purest love itself, vibrating and flowing in the highest bliss realms he could ever endeavor to ascend to and unite with!

Lost in his thoughts, Loriolan has separated from the lively group, standing quietly leaning against a pillar and overlooking the expanse of the beautiful water garden that boasts an infinite array of the most colorful, exotic little fish swarms and saturated green and purplish plant life this part of the underwater ocean is known to harbor. The sunlight shines scintillatingly through the water, illuminating the garden with a golden-hued luminescence that in itself seems to add to Loriolan's reflective mood and to the mysterious beckoning he feels in his soul to leave the life of a protected prince behind for the sake of proving his manhood and mastery over the water and fire elements, thus gaining access to the heavenly realms and winning Indirali's hand in marriage! Such are his longing thoughts and feelings when his father approaches him from behind, lays his hand on his shoulder, and begins to address him.

"I know you will be successful, my son! You are the descendant of a line of heroic and wise water rulers, and you have shown tremendous courage already. Whenever one of our subjects is in need, there is no hesitation: you are just there to help, no matter what the consequences! In this way you are a true king to your people, always putting other people's needs before your own!" he reminds and lauds Loriolan. "Nevertheless, I would be lying if I could just so easily go along with your decision. Naturally, I would like my son around, see his happy face, and turn my scepter over to him without having to fear he might not return from the very depths of our ocean. Because not many have undertaken such a journey, son, and there isn't any record of how many have returned from those dangerously high pressure depths either!" He frowns, staring questioningly into the light-flooded space in front of them.

Loriolan looks at him: "It will all work out, Father! Where there is true love, there is a way! You always taught me to be my most authentic self and to give my attention to those things that truly matter in the end. You have taught me well, and now it is time for me to go prove what I am made of. I will reach the Heavens, and I will bring Indirali back with me as my wife in body and spirit, and there will be a wedding the likes of which the two worlds of the water and land have never seen!" he promises, trying to give his father a smile of deepest conviction. "Indirali is my happiness, Father, and she is the future queen of our kingdom!"

King Hadores swallows his choking feeling, and then the two mermen hug as if to seal the deal with their love and respect for each other. Lovingly, the King blesses his son and expresses his highest hopes for the success of his mission.

The remainder of the day is spent with Loriolan filling his family in on Rachtan's guidance for his trip, and his family trying to give him sound advice, with Loriolan reassuring them that he will be careful and alert every step of the way. It eases the Royal Parents' hearts to learn that not only Torilander but also his brother Chekilian will accompany their son on his daring, adventuresome quest. The brothers wouldn't want to be separated from each other for any length of time, nor do they want their best friend, Loriolan, to be exposed to possible danger without the trio lending their support to one another.

Throughout the afternoon, the friends receive help in assembling packages consisting of essential equipment and utensils, including a good amount of freshly prepared algae-herb cookies, known for their high nutritional value and long-lasting energy content. Later in the afternoon, Torilander and Chekilian's parents check in on the departure-bound youngsters, and their hearts, also, are heavy from sadness and fear of losing their children to the unknown. Their mother especially has a hard time letting Chekilian go since he is still young of age, but her son can't be talked out of it; he feels very strongly about supporting Loriolan on his meaningful quest. King Hadores implores the two brothers to not unnecessarily risk their lives but to return immediately back home once the going gets too rough or impossible for them. He says that as much as he appreciates their friendship to his son, it ultimately is his journey, and there is no gain in them losing their lives over this. And only after they promise to heed his advice does he feel comfortable letting them go along.

Queen Lilliane takes Loriolan aside and, in a moment of heartfelt specialness, hands him the wedding ring of her mother, the former queen of the kingdom of Adriatica, as a gift for his wife-to-be from the female lineage of his ancestors. With tears in her eyes, she implores him to return back to her, because she would not know how to survive without having him in her life anymore. Loriolan thanks his mother with a loving hug, his heart overflowing with gratitude for everything she has done for him and for the blessing she bestows on him for his difficult trip.

The idea is to leave quietly and without disturbing anyone's sleep in the very early morning hours before anyone in the palace usually wakes up. That is why everyone wants to say good-bye now, taking their time with him and getting to the point where they can let go of him, the hope of Azuris' future, and the King and Queen's son. When Arilene gets her turn to say good-bye, she is almost unable to stay the course. Her tears are running down her cheeks uncontrollably, and Loriolan has to take her into his arms and try to comfort her as best he can. He recommends she herself visit Rachtan, to find valuable advice on how to deal with the situation and to receive solace whenever fear would overcome her. It also would be a nice opportunity to get more closely acquainted with Rachtan's apprentice, the young man with whom she feels this special deep bond, and let the chips fall where they may to see whether the Divine wants them to ultimately be together.

This thought sparks Arilene's courage, interest, and curiosity again, and all of a sudden, her brother's departure does not seem so overwhelmingly painful to her anymore. Both hug warmly, then release each other to pursue their own romantic love interests.

Torilander and Chekilian look at Loriolan with both apprehension and adventure spirit in their eyes. Soon they will learn how far they will be able to accompany Loriolan on his life-transforming quest and how far their friendship will allow them to risk their lives for him, if necessary.

The evening gradually fades into the melancholic dark of the night. The inhabitants of the palace have never before been so wary about Azuris' future. Everyone wishes the Prince a successful trip and safe return, then releases him to his own adventure and tribulations.

CHAPTER 17

*I*t is still dark when Loriolan leaves the palace with his two buddies. The Queen Mother has woken from her restless sleep to bid her son farewell. Sad, she stands at the palace entrance to give her son one last hug before he descends the stairs and disappears into the dark. Loriolan waves her good-bye and encouragingly assures her that he will be back soon and for her not to worry. She smiles faintly and then gradually disappears out of his sight.

The three mermen look at each other: their goal is to get to the North Pole and from there find a way into the inner worlds of the planet. Somewhere between the upper world and the underworld they hope to find Velvetia, the atmospheric Ring Guardian of the Underworlds. According to the map Loriolan received from Rachtan, they have to swim around a large landmass, called the Iberian Peninsula, and from there just move continuously up towards the North until they arrive at the lands of mist and ice. The thought of this gives the mermen a chill already, but fortunately they brought some wax-like, fatty salve with which to cover their bodies thoroughly to protect them from the anticipated bitter cold. Their mothers also reminded them of taking woven kelp sweaters along to prevent freezing to death. For now, however, all that is required is to swim, swim, and swim. Miles upon miles upon miles! They agree to take frequent short breaks to recover from the effort and to sleep for a few hours at night. They also agree on a certain sound frequency they intend to call each other on in case they should get separated for any reason. Everyone burns the layout of the map into his brain, and then they begin their long journey through the Tyrrhenian Sea, towards the island of Sardo.

All three of them have been taking sports lessons from their swim master Telechon for many years. He taught them all the styles and techniques of advanced water movement, from the short-breath, extreme force, rhythmic push and eel-like dive to the long, deep-breath, and relaxed soft movement swim.

Loriolan and his friends have mastered them all, enabling them to adjust to any strength of water currents and to any underwater terrain, whether it be smooth and expansive or rugged and full of obstacles. Telechon challenged them to many marathons around the Tyrrhenian Sea, helping them to develop enormous strength and endurance and showing them many tricks on how to avoid or confront many of the underwater dangers and hostile predators. The little group feels adequately prepared and now dashes along the Gulf of Salerno to meet their next goal on the map, the underwater terrain south of the island of Sardo.

Many ships used to roam the Gulf when it was still safe to entertain trade with the islands to the west, but now the sea feels quite empty and under the spell of Poseidon, the lesson-teaching God who is ready to strike at any moment and overthrow any attempt of the human world to enrich each other through trade across the seas. To add leverage to his punishing actions, Poseidon has been engaging the help of Hephaistos, the God of fire and volcanoes, to make sure an arrogant mankind would stay subdued by fear and reverence towards the Gods. However, Loriolan ponders, the underwater terrains of the Mediterranean Sea have undergone major changes as well because of Hephaistos's fire-and-rock spitting volcanic eruptions and massive rockslides, to the point of turning the Sea into a caldera itself with volcanic openings and vents all around. Several deep basins have become the home to many different water tribes that find the brewing volcanic activities actually energizing and nourishing for their lively spirits and communities. At certain spots, however, the seabed has torn open so deep that diving down into increasingly denser areas has become life threatening even to the mer-folks themselves. One has therefore learned to settle along, within and on the underwater mountains that occasionally rise to uncanny heights even above the water surface. The oceanic population sure has had a relatively easy time adapting to Hephaistos's transformational impacts, often withdrawing to subtler levels of existence, to the ethereal realms of refined yet vital life force vibrations, there dancing and enjoying each other's company for as long as Hephaistos makes it his business to restructure the oceanic world with his explosive outbursts, but for the human race it seems to be a much more serious affair altogether. So far,

Loriolan and his fellow mer-citizens of the Underwater Worlds have not cared much for this human predicament that messes with their landmass, kills them under the heat and sulphuric gases of the volcanic eruptions, whenever they occur, and through Poseidon's stormy activities impedes their world considerably in its networking and commercial efforts, but since meeting Indirali, Loriolan has developed a different stance towards their plight, wanting to end this senseless war between the two worlds and regain the peace and prosperity of the most ancient of people. Impatient with the situation, he swims with all the force he has, hoping to arrive at his destination rather sooner than later.

A deep, all-encompassing silence envelops them as they swim in close proximity to each other in the endless seeming waters. Occasionally they glance at each other, as if to reassure themselves that they are still in each other's company and that everyone is still accounted for. Sometimes an underwater marvel catches their eye, and they make sure to share it with one another, sometimes smilingly pointing at it or just looking at their partners with wide-open eyes, expressing their surprise and pleasure. Thus the hours pass by, and the swimmers slowly feel tiredness overcoming their bodies. They decide to rest for a while in the protection of a rocky overhang. The group assembles and reports to each other on the many fascinating impressions they just gathered along the way, comparing their experiences and then taking a short doze, comfortably huddled against ferns that gently engulf them and add to their regeneration.

And so the journey continues, with many new and wondrous water landscapes opening up to them, and many unfamiliar but, nevertheless, beautiful fish and water creature varieties boggling their minds as to their colorful and abundant existence. The journey has already begun to open their minds to let the new and unfamiliar in and continues to lure them into even vaster spaces of the unknown. Soon they swim through the ruins of a sunken city that humans must have inhabited a long time ago. It feels eerie to behold the broken-down remnants of what must once have been a thriving center of aliveness and great architectural beauty. The fleeting nature of life comes to mind, and the three swimmers silently leave this human moratorium of past grandeur behind, ready to overcome any death inclination along their way towards the realms of eternal life. It is quite a pleasure, however, for them to flit through the neighboring underwater kingdoms and occasionally come across members of those kingdoms — mer-people, who, after learning about their goal and journey, wish them well and continue to go about their business. Many impressive and fascinating temples and palaces grace the underwater cities, which Loriolan and his friends espy from the distance. Those buildings tower majestically above the other city dwelling places and often sparkle beautifully in the sunlit waters. And even though the group of travelers would like to visit and get to know these fine cities, they know not to get distracted from their path lest valuable time might be lost and the accomplishment of their goal moved into the distant future. But they vow that after their mission is accomplished to return to some of these remarkable cities and strike a bond with their rulers to establish a greater network of peace- and culture-minded mer-civilizations. It must surely be an exciting endeavor to exchange cultural values and artworks, and Loriolan can already see Indirali overtaking a crucial and venerated role in advancing the oceanic worlds to their highest potential and realization in regard to these life-enhancing influences. The thought about her keeps him going and triggers his innermost resources and best effort in getting to the shores of Sardo.

CHAPTER 18

The day of Lucania's much celebrated Sports Games has finally arrived! King Eurylochos deliberately scheduled it to coincide with Hecto's visit, and his citizens are filled with anticipation and excitement. Lucania's declared champions are nervous to demonstrate the results of their intensive training, to not only impress their King today but to hopefully instill confidence in the hearts of Lucania's citizens that their athletes will bring back any or all of the coveted awards from the upcoming Nemean Games, one of the four Panhellenic Games that take place in a four-year cycle — the calendar period of the so-called Olympiad — throughout the Greek world and of which the Olympic Games are the most renowned, as they take place at Olympia, the city of the Gods. And even though today's Sports Games are a subordinate event to the official Greek Panhellenic Games, most Lucanians have been looking forward to this special event in their calendar for most of the year. As during the official Games, competitors and delegates from faraway destinations arrive in order to participate in the peaceful and religious programs the Games are known and loved for. It fills every heart with a sense of solidarity and unity to come together and admire one another's good sportsmanship in an atmosphere of peace for which all cross-border adversities are temporarily put on hold. In today's uncertain and difficult times the Games have become even more important, allowing aching hearts to find solace in an oasis of fun and purpose, reminding people of their original happiness they once shared with one another and across borders. Many know from their own history that the Panhellenic Games were initiated to unite mankind with the Gods in a spirit of friendship and awe of their superhuman strengths and abilities they amply demonstrated during the Games. Thus setting high standards of accomplishment, the Gods left a great gift to mankind before retiring to the top of Mount Olympos, prompting humans to aspire towards physical perfection, which was inevitably linked to spiritual development. Back then, it seemed, the most powerful Gods were also the most loving and benevolent ones, a synchronicity that unfortunately can hardly be found in the Gods of present anymore that still seem to possess any degree of interest in the human race. Nevertheless, the Games are a reminder of the glorious days of old when the Gods dwelled among mankind, inspiring every individual to unfold his potential and be his best. And in this spirit, Lucania's athletes have been training incessantly throughout the many months, and the population takes great pride in having their kingdom host the events that attract viewers from all over the kingdom and from neighboring kingdoms and city-states as well that have sent their competitors. To keep up the spirit of friendship and peaceful competition, Lucania welcomes its neighbors with a cornucopia of offered sports competitions in various fields, allowing the participants to compete with each other in a generously laid out arena, with thousands of viewers from several tiers able to cheer them on and applaud their accomplishments. In return, Lucania's athletes are invited to compete at the Sports Games of several neighboring kingdoms at various dates throughout the year and Olympiad as well, thus able to stay in practice and good shape, able to continuously demonstrate their prowess, physical strength, and endurance. The athletes are relatively young, with most being around the peak of their lives' performance, and several having distinguished themselves over time as celebrated champions that have earned the honor to participate in any of the four Panhellenic Games that each occur every year in a cycle of four years at their city of origin. The fans love their champions and greet them jubilantly any time they appear in public.

Yes, King Eurylochos intentionally arranged the date of the Sports Games to coincide with Hecto's visit and betrothal ceremony. And with Hecto being a successful army general used to doing battle on the field, Eurylochos thought it appropriate for these two events to coincide so as to offer Hecto an entertaining display of physical prowess and agility as a pompous and exciting way to end the festivities. And he was right: Hecto has been talking about the Sports Games the moment he set foot in the palace, wondering about who might win in certain disciplines and heralding his own kingdom's athletes as if they are the best there are. His competitive spirit loves the idea of a showdown between the kingdoms, and his fight-loving nature would like to see everyone other than his own people defeated and put to shame. With some trepidation, King Eurylochos is looking forward to the event; after yesterday's offensive behavior of his guests, however, he is not sure whether it was a good idea after all to have Hecto among the guests of honor at this — for Lucania — most precious sporting event.

The torch is lit to signal the start of the Games. The torchbearer runs up the northern center stairs to hold the flame up for King Eurylochos' approval, then swerves to the side to allow the Priestess of Zeus to step forward and call upon the Father of the Gods to bless the upcoming Games. Her words of prayer and dedication are to ensure peace among the audience members as well as good sportsmanship among all the participating athletes. She dedicates the Games to the Gods and asks for Divine influx of power, justice, and honor for all competitors. Then the priest choir performs a short anthem to honor the Gods, and the fanfare begins to herald the competitors who, one by one, enter the arena from the main gate at the eastern end.

The athletes assemble in the center area of the arena, and, led by the priestess, the crowd begins to greet them with another anthem that specifically honors the King and Queen of Lucania as well as the kingdom of Lucania as being the host of the present Spring Sports Games. The atmosphere is rife with anticipation and excitement when King Eurylochos finally stands up, all thousands of eyes directed at him, to raise his hand as the final signal for the commencement of the Games. The athletes appear very focused and slightly nervous before taking their respective positions in the areas of their chosen events.

The Games start, and the audience begins to follow every move of their champion of interest, exhibiting supportive or dismissive reactions as demonstrations of their chosen loyalties, either wishing a certain athlete success or condemning him. Soon the whole coliseum begins to sound off every time an athletic feat has been accomplished, much to the distraction and discouragement of other competitors. The crowd feels like a judging agent that needs to be overcome or ignored by certain frowned-upon athletes if focus is to be maintained and success secured, while in other cases, the crowd becomes a main motivating force that magically helps to transport a champion beyond his physical limits to achieve superhuman success in his athletic endeavors.

Hecto follows the happenings with great interest and loud comments. The men of his entourage roar even louder than he does, making it very clear to everyone on what side they are. Sometimes they stand up and utter their disappointment into the crowd with vehement shouts of dismay, frantically gesticulating their offense and, occasionally, when a Campanian athlete takes the lead in a certain event with his performance, they gleefully dance around their seats, toasting with their wine chalices to more of these gratifying feats that make their chests swell with pride and arrogance.

The Royal Family and ministers of Lucania observe their guests' behavior with mixed feelings, especially after yesterday's embarrassing slip-up that has cut a rift between the parties because of their obvious, inherently different natures and understanding of royal etiquette. But the people deserve this grandiose spectacle, especially in today's uncertain and deprived social atmosphere. And so the Royal Family watches the Games graciously, clapping their hands when an athlete has just outdone himself, no matter what kingdom he is from, and kindly cheering those on who could do better, given their past records.

The sequence and attention goes from relay race, hurdle race, to marathon race, from long jump to high jump, from javelin throwing, shot put, hammer throwing, to discus throwing, and, last but not least, the competition in archery and gladiator fighting, of which the latter seems to trigger the roughest, most brutal survival instincts the spectators secretly harbor. Watching a man beat up another man isn't just entertainment of the most gratifying nature for an unfulfilled and hurting soul; it seems to be almost as liberating to his repressed soul as therapy is for a suicidal person. Watching allows these brutal survival instincts to be unleashed from the depth of their collective subconscious minds at any imaginary enemy from among the competitors in order to rid the repressed and hurting souls of their pent-up stresses and negative emotions, which they otherwise have a hard time releasing in a safe manner in their regimented daily lives for fear of punishment.

At some point, Hecto decides to get more closely involved in the gladiator fights, wanting to make sure his kingdom comes out the winner on all accounts if he can help it. With a gesticulation of his hand, he indicates to King Eurylochos that he is ready to join the ranks of the competitors himself and that the King would be wise to heed his request. King Eurylochos swallows his surprise, then nods his agreement. Hecto jumps over several rows of seats to place himself onto the main staircase, right in front of Indirali, whose blessing he seems to request. He holds his long spear towards her, expecting her to fasten her scarf onto the top of the weapon. He wants to impress his future wife and show off their bond to the excited crowd. Indirali looks at her father with surprise and confusion. But he indicates for her to go along and comply with Hecto's request. And so she sadly gives away her beautiful, silken, light-blue scarf she received from Loriolan as a gift, silently wishing for Hecto to not besmirch her honor and to hopefully behave himself and not cause any more of these embarrassing scenes with which he already maneuvered himself into her father's disgrace. With a broad smile, Hecto retracts the spear and, under loud jubilations from the crowd, shows off the scarf to everyone like a victory trophy that has just been handed to him from the highest judge, and which is supposed to magically guarantee his success on the battlefield.

Then he throws himself into the wrestling matches. Several of his men follow him when he invites them with a nod. He can use all the cheers and support he can get, he reasons, and immediately the gladiator ring opens up to him, providing him on the spot with one of Lucania's finest, strongest fighters. The rule is to fight the opponent to the ground until he is unable to get up again. Unlike the practices of several other kingdoms, Lucania frowns on fights to the death, especially when the fights are part of the Sports Games. But even at court, King Eurylochos detests such deadly displays of force and brutality and has banned them from being staged anywhere in the kingdom. He has become an idol to the citizens for his support of peaceful sports and entertainment, and most Lucanian citizens love this trait in their King.

But today the Games seem to derail and spin out of King Eurylochos' control. Hecto gets beaten up badly, and his ego can't take such humiliation, not in front of so many onlookers, and especially foreigners. His opponent has him lying on his back in a relatively short time, and Hecto has to experience the most terrible defeat he could ever have imagined for himself at a public occasion like this. And so, out of his cowardly heart, after his opponent lets up on him and moves to the edge of the ring circle, Hecto gets up, somewhat dizzy from the head blows he incurred, his mouth bleeding, pulls his dagger he hid underneath his pants and throws the weapon right into the winner's back. — The crowd stops cheering, and a total silence engulfs the coliseum as everyone tries to grasp what just happened. King Eurylochos can't believe his eyes: one of his best men has just been stabbed in the most underhanded and cowardly way possible by his supposed future son-in-law, the son of his neighboring kingdom's king. A cloud of shame and growing anger fills the coliseum, and Lucania's citizens begin to cry out for revenge.

Quickly, King Eurylochos gives orders to escort Hecto and his band out of the arena, unencumbered by the masses. He is to be brought to his quarters for his own safety and watched over until he is ready to leave in the very early morning hours of the next day. Guards also carry the deeply wounded wrestler out, trying to get him medical attention and save his life. King Eurylochos steps forward on the balcony and, with a loud voice thundering throughout the arena, announces that justice will be done, but for now the Games should continue for everyone's sake, lest one unfortunate incident would render the efforts of so many futile and wasted. Fortunately, the crowd loves their King and, with all the good will they can muster, begin to put their attention back on the sportsmen, who had taken a break from their activities to witness the shocking event.

And so the Games continue, with a stain on the whole event, but quickly the excitement takes over again, and soon the winners have distinguished themselves against their competitors, causing the crowd to applaud with overwhelming pride and gratitude for the excellent entertainment they enjoyed. The Judge of the Games, the Hellanodikis, announces the names of the winners, placing palm branches into their hands while the crowd continues to cheer their heroes, throwing flowers at them to express their enthusiasm over their champions' fantastic victories and gratifyingly seeing them getting the red ribbons of victory tied around their heads and hands.

In order to satisfy his important guest, King Eurylochos had planned to stage the official award ceremony right after the announcement of the winners instead of at a later hour as is customary, knowing that Hecto would have wanted to see the winners from among his countrymen honored before leaving on the morning after the Games. But even though he had to be removed from the stadium and at the moment is shamefully amiss and intensely hated by everyone, the celebratory procedures must go on according to the new program. All the good will and national pride, therefore, is oriented towards the winner of the Games. Loudly announcing his name, his father's name, and his homeland, the Hellanodikis solemnly places the sacred olive tree wreath on the head of the ultimate winner, he who excelled in the most events with the highest scores and honors. Then the fanfares blare the victory hymn to the rhythmic applause of the frolicking audience. The joyous noise, however, subsides suddenly as the awe-inspiring, statuesque figure of the High Priestess appears on the temple podium, ready to solemnly revere God Zeus and his fellow Gods and Goddesses in her prayers of gratitude, strongly asking them for peace to continue to reign over the kingdom and its neighbors, to protect everyone present until they all meet again under joyous circumstances, and to also bless their kingdom's athletes, who are expected to compete at the next Sports Games held in Apulia in only four months' time. The crowd applauds the speech wholeheartedly. Then many begin to bow their heads in reverence as they see their ruler with his queen and princess daughter retreating, followed by Lucania's ministers, friendly waving their people good-bye.

All in all, the Royal Family and high court officials consider the Games a success and are happy with the outcome: many Lucanian athletes were able to win a palm branch for themselves, making their countrymen proud and cheery on account of their widespread successes in various fields of performance. In the end, the atmosphere in the coliseum is jolly and cheerful, and everyone has a hard time saying good-bye to one another, to the Royal Couple, and to the athletes they won't see competing in their own kingdom for another year. With life having assumed great harshness over the last years, caused by general impoverishment and lack of opportunities, the average citizen is not keen on returning back to his dreary life and waiting another long stretch until the next joyous collective event can distract him from his overwhelming challenges and problems. With a sense of displeasure, most citizens finally get up and empty the coliseum through the main gate.

As soon as he is out of the crowd's sight, King Eurylochos informs himself immediately of the attacked man's condition. He is told that the man is still in critical condition but that the doctor is hopeful he can save the man's life. That comforts the King to some extent, because if the man dies, the relationship to his supposed son-in-law would be damaged to a quite large extent, because at the end of the day, Hecto's unconscionable, despicable behavior defied Eurylochos' ruling that no man is supposed to die during the annually held Games, and especially not in such a malevolent and treacherous way. He feels he needs to confront Hecto on his behavior and let him know that he violated and transgressed one of Lucania's most important rules in regard to its Sports Games.

But when the King enters Hecto's chamber, his guest greets him like a ranting maniac, loudly and impertinently complaining how much he hates being held captive at his host's behest. He accuses Eurylochos for cutting his fight short and for imprisoning him and his men in their quarters as if they were criminals. King Eurylochos tries to appease him at first, but when Hecto continues to aggressively accuse his host of all sorts of unwarranted allegations, the King starts to raise his voice and put the obstinate guy into his place, telling him that he is a guest at his court and was treated like royalty, and the least he can expect of Hecto is that he behaves like a nobleman. He makes it clear to Hecto that he violated the peace of the Games and that his people want to see justice done to the man who treacherously tried to murder one of their beloved wrestling heroes, very likely disappointed that the future husband of their king's daughter turns out to be such a cowardly perpetrator. And Hecto should be grateful for the King's spontaneous wise action to remove him from the field as quickly and as unharmed as possible, lest he would fall prey to a lynch-like attack from the mob on his life.

That viewpoint sobers Hecto up a bit. But not for long! A moment later he continues to argue for the validity of his action, justifying that he is the Prince of Neapolis, a man of noble descent and, on top of that, a war hero who can hardly find his equal. King Eurylochos needs to repress a laugh, considering that this self-proclaimed war hero has just been humiliatingly defeated by one of his men; this wannabe hero still dares to rub his supposedly superior fighting skills in the King's face, thinking he can get away with it! But the King is not in the mood for arguing and quarreling, and he certainly sees no gain in displeasing his guest more than is necessary. And so he just explains to Hecto that because of his underhanded deed and the impact it had on his people, the palace of Lucania reserves the right to annul the betrothal should the attacked man die. He suggests that Hecto pray the man lives if he wants to ever win the respect of his kingdom and especially the heart of his daughter, who incidentally believes in peace more than she does in fighting. This point gets Hecto going even more. With words of insult and taken offense he justifies that war and killings are necessary means in today's world with hostile armies intruding on the lives of the innocent and gullible at heart. It is thanks to men like him that peace can ultimately be secured, selfless warriors who see it their God-given duty to defend the weak and meek that otherwise would fall prey to those immoral, ruthless enemy forces, who — because of their rotten character — deserve no mercy and should just all be killed and gotten rid of.

Hecto could have gone on and on, but King Eurylochos cuts him short and reiterates that in order for the betrothal to still be considered, the injured man has to survive. Curtly, he thanks Hecto for his visit and wishes him a safe journey home to Neapolis. He also extends his well-meaning regards to Hecto's parents and hopes that peace and good will between the kingdoms can continue to exist, no matter what the outcome of the situation is. Hecto, however, sees this condition for his betrothal as an affront to his integrity and honor. He indicates that if the betrothal would ever be cancelled, the possibility of war would arise between their kingdoms, and King Eurylochos better watch out, or he just might jeopardize his people's wellbeing in the short and the long run!

This threat is more than King Eurylochos wants to handle at the moment. His honor prohibits him to demean himself any further in front of Hecto, and so he begins to leave the chamber with his guards, but not before snatching Indirali's scarf from Hecto's bed, throwing him a glance to indicate it was never his to begin with and he certainly hasn't done it justice. He walks out of the chamber with a dignified stride, glad to not look back anymore and glad that his daughter has her heart set on someone else, someone who deserves her more than this idiot of a man does.

CHAPTER 19

Hecto, accompanied by his brigade, leaves before dawn, like a thief and thug trying to escape his judgment day before anyone can stop him. King Eurylochos is informed of Hecto's departure while the brigade is just getting ready to march out the gateway of the palace court, needing the King's approval to have the gate opened for them. With a wave of his hand, King Eurylochos signals his guards to allow Hecto to leave, for he wishes nothing more than for this questionable character to be out of everyone's presence when Lucania awakes. The King puts his robe on and looks out the window to watch the soldiers on their horses disappear through the gate one by one. With a heavy heart, he sits down in his armchair, deeply reflecting on the possibilities of his country's future, now that Hecto has left with a grudge in his heart.

After breakfast, Eurylochos invites his wife and daughter to a walk in the garden, wanting to discuss Indirali's journey and fate and deciding on how to go about sending her off in the most supportive and prepared way possible. Indirali appreciates her parents' love and care and welcomes them putting their combined attention on her imminent departure. She is still trying to get over her shock and dismay about Hecto's behavior and gives off an exclamation of joy when her father returns Loriolan's precious scarf to her, which she was forced to relinquish to Hecto much against her will. As the three of them stroll along the idyllic, winding garden path, the King takes the opportunity to apologize to his wife and daughter for thinking that Hecto could ever have been a match for their beloved daughter, and how glad he is that he was able to see Hecto's true side come out in this unfortunate incident that injured one of their champion wrestlers to the point where his life is now in God's hands. He says that he is now absolutely certain that he doesn't want anything to do with this man, let alone have him as a son-in-law. The challenge though is to disentangle their affairs from one another, which will require diplomacy and something advantageous to offer to the palace of Neapolis, because Hecto could easily react in his usual aggressive way when threatened in his ego pride and false sense of honor, and take the annulment of the betrothal as a welcome trigger to start an unwarranted war. Eurylochos hopes that the King of Neapolis, Hecto's father, is a more reasonable and equanimous man who will look through his son's vanity and pettiness of reasoning and will continue to engage in peace talks, as well as in commercial and cultural trade between the kingdoms. But then Eurylochos gestures with his hand as if to say to heck with it now; he assures his family that he will take care of business and he will make sure that no one will have to compromise and that everything will work out in the end. His wife nestles against his shoulder, a smile of contentment on her face, knowing she can trust her husband if he says it will all work out and have a good end, and she hopes this is especially true for their daughter.

"Father," Indirali reminds him, "don't discount what my infinite love for Loriolan can accomplish in regard to all these state affairs. Our love will challenge the destructive curse Poseidon cast on us humans and will force him to retract it!" She looks very sure of herself, and a spark of hope glints in her father's eye. He leads them to the outdoor basilica he built for his wife when they got married, as a token of his undying love for her. They all sit on the upholstered benches, enjoying the green, lush garden sights, the many colorful flowers that accentuate the healthy green, and the singing of the many frolicking birds that enjoy the garden as much as they do, with the fresh spring breezes gently caressing their hair and faces as if to signal a positive change is ahead, whispering into their ears that good tidings are approaching and happiness and lightness will abound again in the palace and land. Smilingly, the parents begin to inquire about Indirali's first meeting with her apparent first true love, Loriolan.

Indirali is happy to share with her parents her most intimate memories of the greatest experience of her young adulthood, recounting every startlingly magnificent moment the two lovers have triggered in each other so far and the infinite depths of the loving feelings she has known ever since. She tells them about his royal origin and his refined nature and behavior, and about the way they both resonate harmoniously with each other on any level imaginable. Eurylochos and

Penelope look at each other: can it be their daughter has found what they have been fortunate enough to feel and share since they met many years back? Only that she shares these precious, once in a lifetime feelings of true, deep, passionate love with a merman? Life has its oddities, but this fact seems to top them all! How in the world, the parents wonder out loud, are they going to overcome these enormous gaps in their ability to live together, lead a married life, and have children like any other couple does? They don't seem to be able to wrap their heads around this impossible seeming challenge. But Indirali cannot be swayed. Where there is true love, there must be a way! she insists. Even if Loriolan and she will have to conquer the deepest hell and the highest Heavens, they are intent upon shrinking the content and the polarities of time and space and karma to an absolute nothingness, transcending the worlds, and uniting in body, mind, and spirit as a couple united by the Divine Source Itself!

The parents look at each other again, wondering whether to dismiss Indirali's notions and convictions of triumph over the odds as some wishful thinking that will render her ultimately disappointed and alone or whether to take her seriously in her thinking and reasoning, allowing her to go on her life quest and prove herself right in all her assumptions and aspirations. After holding this look of wonder and puzzlement for a while, they both recognize that true love is the most powerful force there is in the universe, and they better not discard what it might be able to accomplish when two true lovers set their will and mind to it. And so they look back at their daughter, fully convinced that she not only deserves her chance, but also that, as her parents, they owe their full support to her undertaking, and that if she succeeds, it will mean a peace for their kingdom no other truce between the kingdoms has so far been able to accomplish. They embrace their daughter, one after the other, and wish her well in her efforts, assuring her of their absolute trust in her and that their persisting prayers will always be with her, no matter where she may be and how long she may be gone. Of course they hope she will return back to them rather sooner than later, but they understand that she will only return once she succeeds in her mission, and for that she has their complete blessing.

Indirali is touched by her parents' love, a tear of sadness in regard to the looming departure showing in her eye, and gives them both a group hug to convey her gratitude for their enlightened attitude and change of heart.

Then the parents go into the specifics of her intended journey. They want to know whether she knows where to go from here. Indirali reveals to them that Loriolan recommended they both see the wisest person they can find, on land and in water, to receive the most helpful advice anyone can give them as to how to tackle the task and proceed with their mission. Based on Torilander's and Hedna's accounts to her, she tells her parents about Loriolan's encounter with Rachtan, the Underwater King's spiritual advisor, and all the helpful wisdom he imparted to Loriolan, giving him enough confidence to set out on his journey. She looks at her parents with eyes that betray her subtle worry and caring love for her beloved merman, and the parents can't help but feel for her situation that surely must cause her much pain for as long as she is separated from her lover, uncertain of his fate and wellbeing, both trying to meet the other in the Heavens, since the Earth tries to keep them apart. With compassion in his voice, King Eurylochos suggests Indirali see the High Priestess of the temple and get her advice on how to transcend into the Heavens in the most rapid and efficient way.

Indirali agrees to see her but admits she has her eye set on a wise Oracle the father of one of her servants knows from his past to be a woman of high integrity, wisdom, and magical healing powers.

Eurylochos and Penelope wonder who that woman is that they have not heard of her. Indirali explains she lives in the depths of the forests outside of Atina and that she shuns the so-called civilized societies as if they were a collective, cancerous being that wreaks havoc on Nature and the human nature itself, but people seek her out because of her enormous healing powers and world-transcending wisdom, and this is why the Princess thinks this Oracle would be the ideal starting point for her mission.

The royal parents are impressed with their daughter's research into the matter, and with a smile of relief and lightness, they continue to stroll along the path, past the beautiful, tranquil lake Indirali knows she will miss, and the many decorative flower beds and bushes that all have begun to bud and blossom, with butterflies dancing around them and, in the early morning sun, all turning the garden into the most beautiful, scintillating spectacle anyone can behold throughout the year!

And deep within the parents' chests, an unknown pride is welling up, for their daughter has passed her coming of age threshold and has masterfully convinced them of her maturity and wisdom, with which she intends to overcome challenges only the Gods themselves are able to master!

Who knows, King Eurylochos finds himself wondering as if under a magic spell, if she can succeed in such a staggering adventure of superhuman proportions, then he might be able to rule his country without having to resort to weapons and war, and his son might be able to return to the palace without having to ever risk his life again in the futility and horrors of defensive warfare and can, instead, in time assume his rightful office of the future ruling king of Lucania and follow in the footsteps of his peace-loving father, who — as he might have to admit — just learned a valuable lesson from his daughter on how there are no compromises when it comes to true peace or true love. Only a heart of innocence and purity can live in peace, he realizes, and when the heart gets compromised and stained with the pain and blood of victims, peace becomes an impossible, elusive state, often throwing the person right back into the battle from which it seems he cannot ever escape unless he is willing and able to face his abysmal wrongdoings, and humbly ask for forgiveness from the Creator of all human lives and of the beautiful living Nature on which war wreaks incredible havoc.

With a smile of contentment, the King enjoys this last beautiful outing with his family before he allows his daughter to leave and risk her life for the most liberating and ultimate journey any human soul can pursue.

CHAPTER 20

In the afternoon of the same day, Indirali and her parents visit the High Priestess of the Temple of Aphrodite. The King wants to make sure his daughter receives all the guidance and advice his spiritual elite can provide, hoping quietly that somehow it will be possible for her to go through a spiritual training period in the temple that might magically grant her access to the heavenly realms she seeks to gain. Because on some level he resists the idea to send his daughter into the unknown, into a world he has learned does not always treat kindness with kindness, but actually takes advantage of and often persecutes those who have an open, innocent heart and not the physical strength to defend their delicate nature. He hates the thought some thug might creep up on her and try to subdue and force her to his lower-self biddings. He could not forgive himself if anything of this nature would befall her on her quest, but since she is so intent on leaving, he owes it to everyone to ascertain whether or not the solution might be right under their noses already, here in the temple of Aphrodite, the Goddess of Love, whom they have always turned to with their pleas for protection, wisdom, guidance, and provision. Aphrodite has been the Matroness of his people for many eons and has proven over and over that she listens to prayers and that she grants those who approach her with deepest reverence and a pure heart the fulfillment of their wishes. If there is so much suffering and destitution in his kingdom, then it is because he and most of his people, including even his priests and priestesses, have become less vigilant in their prayers and trust in the Goddess and have deviated from the peace-loving ways of old for the sake of adjusting to the fears and pressures of the present times. They have allowed the lower traits of the human nature to take over and pollute the collective atmosphere that has kingdoms turning against each other and the Gods turning away from the human world. A vicious spiral of hopelessness and violence has begun to engulf the nations, and it has become almost impossible to resist this negative development and survive outside of its annihilating grip. But today, as his daughter is getting ready to start on her life-changing mission, King Eurylochos deems it appropriate that he himself come into the presence of the Goddess and ask her for much-needed guidance on all his matters, personal and state.

Ascending the low and broadly laid out white marble staircase, the Royal Family members hold their heads high, as priests line up on both sides to bow their heads and welcome them to the sanctuary beyond any worldly concerns and problems. The temple hall is filled with the refined, intoxicating incense smells of rose, stephanotis, frankincense, myrrh, and musk, immediately lifting their spirits and inducing a mood of Divine reverence and elevation. Tall, ornamented pillars grace the hall in colonnades of sacred geometric patterns, and impressive, larger-than-life statues of the twelve Main Olympian Gods and Goddesses flank the sides of the mystically lit, spacious interior naos, reminding the visitor of the indescribable and infinite spaces beyond human perception and knowledge.

Agathe, the High Priestess of this temple, dedicated to Goddess Aphrodite, stands at the altar and solemnly recites prayers and ritual verses of the Divine, ancient texts of Hellenistic lore, invoking the Goddess's presence for the sake of deep communion with her worshippers and followers. Priests are lined up on either side of the altar to lend their deep, resounding voices to the recitations, thus enlivening the atmosphere with the resonance fields of the Divine Essence that seems to stream abundantly from the inner realms. The Goddess Statue towers above the richly decorated altar, inducing a veneration in her temple visitors that has led to a life of devotion and worship. The hall vibrates with aliveness and tender sweetness, and the Royal Family realizes yet again how precious these temple visits are and how they wish they could bathe in these uplifting frequencies at all times.

Respectfully, Indirali and her parents take a seat on the velvety cushions laid out on the temple floor, reverently listening to Agathe reciting the wisdoms of their starry origins and universal importance. A beautiful temple dancer with two male consorts appear from the right hand portico, and a soft, rhythmic, yet highly melodious music sets in, with harp, lyre, flutes, and drums filling the temple hall's atmosphere with a trance-like vibration that seems to become one with the dancers, gently spreading over all who attend the ceremony. The dance begins to express the beauty and depths of the Divine spheres and exudes the power to draw the viewers into a transcendental world of great magic and awe. The movements become more alluring and fascinating with every moment, and a delicious ecstasy enraptures the collective mind. Unresistingly, the visitors fall into a trance that allows them to perceive the inner worlds and higher interconnections of the worlds. While in this trance, they behold truths and visions of enormous beauty and wealth, impressions so profound and refined they cannot be brought to the surface of their conscious awareness lest the Royal Family members would leave their bodies right now to join the celestial worlds, unwilling to reduce their eternal essence to fit into the smallness of their individual bodies and into the limitations of their individual identities. But then Agathe jolts them out of their trance, raising her voice to invoke the Goddess to tend to matters of political and marital importance and to please bless the lives of the King and Queen of Lucania and the lives of their children as well. The High Priestess asks the Goddess for her increased attention and good will and for special protection, guidance, and provision for the ruling family during times of great collective distress and general uncertainty. She requests the Goddess will always show the way with the enormous bright light of her infinite wisdom and will take care of the mounting problems of the kingdom with the infinite love of her deeply compassionate, immortal heart.

Touched to tears, Indirali stares at the tall Goddess Statue in front of her and begins to interact with Aphrodite in a personal prayer of her own. She confides her love of Loriolan, the merman, to the Goddess, who herself was born from the sea, and how the two lovers can't stop thinking about each other ever since they met under auspicious circumstances at the shores of the sea less than a moon cycle ago, where Cupid's arrow of true love struck them both at the same time and made them fall hopelessly in love. She implores the Goddess to help them both to overcome the impossible odds of their born natures and to point them in the direction of their unified salvation in the Heavens of eternal love. Ever since Indirali was a child, she loved coming to the temple and looking at this most beautiful image of a statue of the superior Goddess of Love, feeling this special bond and deep understanding of her essence, and right now, she feels, she needs this loving, compassionate understanding and support of the Goddess of Love in her life more than ever before! So deep and heartfelt is her prayer that the tears keep rolling down her cheeks as she loses herself in thoughts and feelings of the Divine compassion and mercy, which alone seem to have the power to lead her to the life she longs for and to the love her heart truly feels at one with.

And then, all of a sudden, Indirali can hardly believe her eyes that are wet from her tears: she sees the Goddess Statue opening her light-filled eyes to her, and with an overwhelming outpouring of purest, Divine love, Aphrodite addresses her longing child: "Come!" she says. "Come to the Oracle and meet me on Mount Olympos to receive the answers and help you seek!" And with that, her eyes close again, and the life force Indirali felt pouring from the statue begins to recede. Indirali is stunned and immediately begins to contemplate the meaning of the Goddess's invitation. Did she mean the Oracle of Atina? Is she to follow her first lead and not dwell in the temple for too long? But then the priests indicate for the Royal Family to perform their votive offerings and to step closer and lay their gifts on the altar for the Goddess to take pleasure in their venerations. Indirali is happy to offer to the Goddess of her heart the huge bouquet of colorful, nice scenting flowers she earlier picked in the garden, allowing her own longing heart to flow in surrender and devotion to her Matroness. The Queen has brought a cornucopia of the sweetest tasting fruits, and the King brought a big, beautifully shimmering shell filled to the overflowing with precious gems and stones, which he knows the Goddess favors and delights in: rose quartz, jade, aquamarine, emeralds and more. He also brought his best and oldest wine for the libation he hopes will please the Goddess very much.

With a nod of appreciation, the High Priestess acknowledges the offerings to Aphrodite and begins the libation ceremony, pouring from the precious wine and holding the cup up for the Goddess's taste and approval. A toast is expressed, exalting the Goddess to superior status in all of Lucania's lives, thanking her for her superhuman patience and immeasurable support in all of their worldly undertakings, and making their hopes and wishes known to her, the Divine expression of love, to bestow peace to the troubled and unconditional love to the desperate and aggressive. May Lucania recover from its present state of defeat, and may it prosper once again like it did in times of old and ancient.

The High Priestess kneels and prostrates herself, demonstrating her deep devotion and veneration to the Goddess who seems to fully own her heart and soul.

The priests follow her example, as does the Royal Family. Indirali feels like dissolving in the presence of the Divine, and her heart receives a sense of rejuvenation from this most expanding experience only the Divine is able to trigger in a soul.

After a long time of deep inner communion with the Goddess, Agathe stands up and indicates the conclusion of the ceremony. She asks the guards of the Royal Family to wait outside the temple, then invites the Royal Family to follow her and the priests into the catacombs adjoining the temple to convene in the golden assembly hall for the requested meeting between the Royals and the spiritual elite of Lucania.

CHAPTER 21

$\mathcal{L}$ed by the High Priestess and her clergy, the Royal Family descends a flight of stairs and follows along a torch-lit hallway. Guards make way whenever the group passes through an arched gateway or a crossing, and Indirali wonders what secrets and mysteries lie beyond the many doors they walk by. She knows the priests take care of the deceased, embalming the rich who can afford their corpses to be impregnated with oils and thus rendered indestructible and lasting, ready to be ritually laid to rest in a fancy sarcophagus and family tomb. The priesthood is also known for their good-smelling balms and ointments they produce from their gardens, highly aromatic products they create from mood-enhancing and medicinal herbs and oils, which the Royal Family has been enjoying for various purposes for as long as Indirali can remember. She also knows that young novices are constantly being trained in the many disciplines that constitute temple life and that the priesthood enjoys a vibrant musical and dance educational program that enables them to enrich any ceremony, celebration, or any other event with an array of exciting and inspiring artistic contributions that Lucania's citizens have enjoyed since time immemorial. However, Indirali ponders for a moment, it seems that for some unfortunate reason these sacred and festive performances have become less available to the average citizen than to the financial and political elite.

Finally, the group arrives at a tall entrance door, which the guards open to allow the priests and their visitors to enter. A couple of guards lead the way and then take their positions on either side of the priests' thrones. A blinding light reflects off the richly decorated, golden assembly hall, with precious jewels of all kinds, like turquoise, rose quartz, jade, rubies, and emerald stones sparkling from pillars, grand vases, thrones, and other accessories decorating the walls and ceiling of this most opulent, impressive hall. The marble floor is held in the most beautiful pearl white, with soft patterns of sand and golden accents, and tall amethyst geodes convey a deep, resounding healing and purification influence on the atmosphere that can hardly be ignored — that's how strong the transcendental dimensions seem to be present in this room — and above all this material splendor, a delicate rose and frankincense scent lingers in the air, welcoming the guests into the gentle embrace of the Goddess who heads the temple from the inner worlds of the Most High.

The King and Queen take their seats across from the row of cathedrae reserved for the priests, indicating for Indirali to sit next to her father. Demurely, she obeys their wish and waits for the conversation to commence. The opulent atmosphere of this hall makes Indirali almost feel insignificant and stands — in her opinion — in sharp contrast to the poverty she knows most of Lucania's people are experiencing during these harsh and testing times. In her uninformed mind, she does not know how to reconcile these drastic differences in the distribution of Lucania's wealth and, therefore, sees it as her duty to let her father, the ruling King of Lucania, and the spiritual priesthood do the explaining and advising on all matters of political and economic importance.

After a short introduction, the High Priestess yields the floor to King Eurylochos to explain his reason for calling this meeting between the two most influential parties of the kingdom. In swift words, Eurylochos recalls the unfortunate incident of the previous day, conveying to the priests how this event has changed his family's attitude towards the idea of uniting the Palace of Neapolis with the Palace of Lucania through the marriage of their children. He says the shameful and disgraceful character Hecto displayed throughout his visit appalls him and that Eurylochos, as a father, cannot with a good conscience justify such an unseemly marital match between his daughter and this warhorse of a man anymore. He has, therefore, decided to allow his daughter to marry the man of her choice, who happens to be a merman from the oceans of Poseidon.

The High Priestess lifts her brow in slight antagonism. But Eurylochos is not ready to have her thwart his thought process and speech. He says it took him by surprise at first as well, but after listening to his daughter's heart and reasoning, he now has come to a place of acceptance and agreement with her desire and has since begun to try to find a way that would enable her to follow in the footsteps of the heroes and heroines of ancient times, whose heroic adventures and accomplishments are portrayed in the tales of Ancient Greece. According to those tales, the union between individuals of the water and land races is possible for as long as their hearts and souls cleanse themselves of any impurities and fears that bind them to the limitations of their respective worlds and races. If such immense purification is achieved, through the overcoming of inner and outer obstacles, then nothing stands in the way of unification between such odds-defying couple anymore. The Gods of Heaven can't withhold their blessings from these courageous souls and will not only congratulate the couple on its superhuman accomplishment but also announce this divinely arranged marriage to all the worlds to have this pioneering act of selfless, eternal love celebrated in the way it deserves. Such a daring and inspiring act of loving unification must surely have the Heavens and Earth rejoice with a happiness that knows no bounds, because two mortal souls have returned to their supernatural state of immortality, becoming one, and love has conquered all obstacles in its way, thus reigning supreme in the eternal realms of bliss. Such elevation and fatherly pride emanate from King Eurylochos' words that the priests sit speechless for a while, stunned at the boldness of his thinking and the extreme love and care he demonstrates for his daughter's fate.

Finally, the High Priestess responds to his daring suggestions, basically wondering how on earth Indirali would go about such required self-transformation without having to spend the remainder of her days in the rigorous spiritual training programs that have even her most highly evolved priests sweating under their challenges for most of their lives. She says she agrees with the assessment of Hecto's character and would like nothing more than for this badly behaved influence to be banned from Lucania's destiny for good, but she has her hesitations when it comes to the political fate between the kingdoms should the planned marriage fail to come about.

Her concern prompts the King to go into the ramifications should Indirali and Loriolan, her merman lover, succeed in their mission. Poseidon's curse could be lifted once and for all, he ascertains, and not only trade with overseas destinations could be taken up again, but as a result peace will also be restored between the kingdoms and countries, which would all profit and prosper from these fortunate developments. A man not lacking in his basic needs is not prone to fight another man, especially when Lucania is the harbinger of good news and the cause for peace with the powerful God of the Seas.

Agathe nods gingerly. This part of their plan sounds glorious and promising, but what about the feasibility of Indirali's self-transformational journey, she wonders out loud, and what if this quest takes her several lifetimes to accomplish, and she won't ever return to her parents and to her life as the Princess of Lucania in general? Who knows how long it took the heroes of ancient times to accomplish their superhuman feats and how many of the ones that set out on such daring adventure have ultimately succeeded in their mission and have actually returned to the lives they left behind? Is the King of Lucania ready to accept and allow the Princess to spend however long it takes her to not only reach this most elusive of all goals but also overcome the stringent life and death tests and tribulations along the way so she might ultimately succeed in her mission? Because if she falls short even just an inch, then space, time, and karma will continue to limit and haunt her, and she might get absorbed into the cosmic void until she is ready to reincarnate into another lifetime on Earth, unbeknownst to her present parents, who will mourn their daughter's loss.

Queen Penelope throws her husband a look of fright and concern. She never thought of it this way. What if Agathe is right in her reasoning? As a mother, Penelope cannot bear the thought of losing her precious, beloved daughter to the fangs of the unknown, from which her child might never return. But her husband lays his hand on hers, and with eyes streaming with confidence, he assures her that such an uncanny fate would surely not befall their daughter, and to trust that the Goddess must have had her reasons to send her son Cupid to thrust the arrow of true love into both their hearts, and that Aphrodite, the all-knowing and all-powerful Goddess, must definitely have a great and all-encompassing plan that will enable their daughter to live a love beyond all human perceptions and confinements as a shining ideal for their people, encouraging them to strive for higher and loftier goals than the normal citizen dares to dream of, especially now, during these dire circumstances of collective hardship. His wise and kindhearted eyes implore his wife to trust in higher providence and in the surpassing love of their Goddess. He says that Indirali's love for her merman feels infinitely deep and special and has melted the ice around his own heart that has kept him from supporting her happiness in the first place. But now he sees the errors of his ways and has resolved to entrust not only his daughter's fate to the Goddess of pure, unadulterated love, but the fate of their kingdom as well, for there is no purpose to life if love cannot be experienced in all its limitless splendor and warmth.

Penelope agrees, and gratefully she squeezes his hand as if to say he just expressed her own deepest feelings about the matter and that she also wouldn't be fulfilled at all and wouldn't want to live for too long if love would not reign in all aspects of their lives.

This heartfelt realization prompts Indirali to recount her wondrous, magical experience from just a moment ago in the temple that had the Goddess Aphrodite open her eyes and speak to her clearly and lovingly, inviting her to go to the Oracle and to meet Aphrodite on Mount Olympos, the dwelling place of the Main Gods.

Indirali's parents exclaim their joyous surprise, thankful to the Goddess for having confirmed the feelings within their own chests and putting to rest any hesitations they might still have had in regard to the journey their daughter is embarking on, which, in the meantime, seems inevitable even to them as much as it seems also risky to her life. But if Indirali is ready to take the risk, then her parents will not stand in the way anymore. With eyes of inner wonder, they resign to their fate and let the Goddess take it from here.

Agathe, however, does not completely share their sentiment and evaluation of the situation. With words of caution and warnings and supported by the High Priest by her side, she expresses the potential pitfalls Indirali could get caught in as well as the many temptations she could be entrapped by along her lengthy path, since such a deeply life-changing journey will surely trigger her deepest issues and will confront her with the strongest demons of her own psyche and of the collective subconscious of the world she tries to overcome and outgrow. Just the thought of having a girl like her, who grew up strongly protected and deeply loved by her parents, walk alone for many miles into the wilderness of human vices and lower-self traits is quite disconcerting, since her destiny as a descendant of the Royal Family should make her parents want to ensure she is safe and will apply herself towards the betterment of the kingdom's present situation.

   This argumentation, however, doesn't sit well with the King, who has already made up his mind on the matter. With a spark of boldness and annoyance in his eye, he addresses the High Priestess, the spiritual leader of the temple of Lucania. He expresses his dismay in regard to her compromised stance that seems to demonstrate — especially in the light of the Goddess Herself inviting Indirali during the ceremony — a rather non-devotional heart and fear-driven soul that seem to trust more in appearances of the status quo than in the wise arrangements of their Matron Goddess, whose certainly superior and well-organized plan might not look very plausible and clear to the limited mind right now but will in the long run most likely prove to be infinitely more encompassing and powerfully supportive and improving of Lucania's fate than the High Priestess allows herself to realize at this moment.

   With an air of feigned surrender and resignation, Agathe signals her concurrence with the intentions she does not fully understand nor tries to at this time. If their mind is already made up, she injects, then why come to her for advice at all?

   The King looks at her as if ready for a battle of wills. But then he deems it wise to keep her on his good side. In his mind, however, he realizes that Agathe and the priests are far from understanding the delicate nuances of the issue at hand and that he will most likely not receive her support on disentangling his daughter's fate from the alliance with Neapolis, which so far seemed to be the only possible solution to Lucania's many pressing problems. He feels the High Priestess's inner resistance to the idea that Indirali's love for Loriolan could perhaps become the driving force and means to win Poseidon's good will back and have humanity prosper as a result of it. He realizes that the High Priestess probably feels diminished in her own role as a spiritual advisor and guide since Indirali plans to find spiritual guidance at the Oracle, which will involve pursuing her life quest outside the temple halls, the very place the High Priestess commands over. But Eurylochos doesn't want to consider the High Priestess's ego pride when it comes to his darling daughter's wellbeing. And so he deems it wise to keep her at arm's length from now on and to not disclose anything specific about the Oracle, to basically end the conversation as lightly as possible. He explains that he owed it to his daughter and to his wife to find out whether the temple would be the place that could help their child reach the inner realms she needs to ascend to in order to unite with her beloved. And they were right to come, for Indirali received the Goddess's invitation, and the parents thus their reassurance, but it seems that now Indirali must go to the Oracle and not stay in the temple for any training.

Agathe lowers her gaze, hit by his words. But then she flares up in his face, declaring that spiritual enlightenment is not reached in just a few days, or even in just a year's time, but is a goal most seekers spend their whole lifetime or even several lifetimes on trying to attain, and who is to say that Indirali has it in her to accomplish what most of her priests have not achieved after many hard years of inner work and meditation. And even if Indirali feels ready for such a life-and-death journey, who might this Oracle be, Agathe wonders out loud, that she thinks she can send Indirali in the right direction that will surely guarantee the success of her mission and not have her wandering in the inner and outer labyrinths of her own lost mind and desperate feelings?

Shocked by the intensity of her outburst, the Royal Family looks at each other as if to regroup. Then King Eurylochos takes the lead again, putting the High Priestess in her place, reminding her to give respect and credibility to the fact that Aphrodite spoke to his daughter with a clear message. He says he sees no true foundation for the Priestess's antagonistic talk and asks her to rather bless Indirali for her life quest, and to please keep her good fortune and success in her prayers at all times. Then he tells Agathe that he doesn't know the Oracle yet but that he trusts Aphrodite's guidance on it and that they will try to find her as quickly as possible so Indirali can get on with her journey. In the meantime, he would appreciate the temple's discretion on this very delicate matter and that for the sake of peace for all Lucanians, the priesthood should not disclose anything that was just said to anyone outside the temple walls.

The High Priestess gives her word to that, and with a sense of relative discontentment, the parties accompany each other out, pretending to be on the same side of things, glad, however, to be able to part ways for now and each return to the duties they know best.

CHAPTER 22

It is time for a rest now, as Loriolan and his friends have been swimming all day long and Chekilian has begun to slowly fall behind. Loriolan is amazed, however, at the young teenage boy's strength that has kept him going for hundreds of miles already. But all of them can use a good, long break now to refresh their bodies and souls; it has been a long, arduous journey so far, and they are still over a hundred miles away from their first water mark, the island of Sardo. If they continue at the pace they have been going, their final goal seems tremendously far away right now, and Loriolan can't help but begin to wonder whether they will all be able to physically make it there within a reasonable time. This thought feels too overwhelming in the state he is in right now, exhausted, tired, and hungry, and so he postpones thinking about their further journey until a later point in time. For now, the group is looking for a comfortable resting place, preferably within a green meadow of Chaetomorpha algae, of which there seems plenty around. They soon find a good piece of the softest green surrounding a large, old rock formation that seems to exude a heartfelt invitation to the tired travelers. With a sigh of relief, the threesome sink onto the bed and immediately fall into a comatose sleep.

Loriolan dreams about his beloved Indirali, the girl of his dreams! She playfully teases him as she laughingly tries to escape his arms, arms that want to hold and embrace her with all the love he has. Her laughter is infectious, and he can't help but smile as well, but as much as he tries to catch her and make her his own, she keeps escaping, all the while clapping her hands as if enjoying this seemingly endless game that has him increasingly desperate and hurting for her. At some point she seems to be shouting at him: "Hey, what's with you? Can't you get the ball for us?"

This doesn't make any sense. Startled, Loriolan comes to his senses. A pretty girl stands in front of him, looking down on him with a smile. "You don't want to hear me, do you?"

Loriolan clears his throat. Who … Where …? It takes him a moment to realize he has been dreaming, and Indirali wasn't really with him after all, but this girl is. Impatient with his slow reaction, she shows him a golden ball and repeats her question from before: "Can't you be a gentleman and throw us back our ball?" Then she realizes there are two more of these mermen, resting blissfully beside the rock, impertinently oblivious to her and her female companion's presence and their request, which they had imploringly shouted many times to Loriolan from the distance, and who looked to them as if he was just caught up in his thoughts, looking dreamily into the watery sky the way he did. "I see," she picks up her scolding, "there are three of you! And none of you has the courtesy to heed and respond to our request. Instead, you made us come over here all this way! Nice gentlemen you are!"

The other girl pokes her gently in her side and, with a giggle, indicates that the two other mermen appear to be fast asleep. This evokes a great sense of puzzlement in the girls, especially since it is still early in the day. With a question mark on her face, the girl turns back to face Loriolan. "You are not from around here, are you?"

Loriolan wipes his eyes, then looks at the girls more clearly and awake. They are young mermaids, with long, pink and pastel-green hair flowing around them in the water, their beautiful, sparkling eyes full of wonder and puzzlement. The first girl has her arm placed on her waist, the second one supporting her stance from behind her with the same bodily expression, both hoping to get an answer out of this obdurate seeming guy.

"No, we are not!" Loriolan responds. "We've come a long way and have still an even longer way ahead of us. So now that you have gotten your ball back, maybe you can let us continue with our well-deserved and much-needed rest." With a concerned look at the mermen sleeping next to him, he asks the girls with a subdued voice to not create an even greater fuss and stir but to let the boys sleep, lest they won't get the recuperation they need to continue their long journey.

The girls seem a bit offended by this polite put-down, but once their curiosity is raised, there is no turning back from the objects of their curiosity. And so they quietly sit down next to Loriolan and away from the other sleepyheads and kindly begin to whisper to continue their conversation with him. They say that their Princess is a very generous person, and if he and his two companions would like to come and join her in her pleasure palace, then she might offer them her chariot to bring them across the ocean floor in the speediest way possible. This way, they could rest in comfortable beds, enjoy nice company for a while, great food and drink, and have some entertainment and then be off and arrive at their goal most certainly sooner than if they were to swim the distance. How does this sound to his tired ears, they wonder?

Loriolan has to give this invitation some thought. The offer seems to have its advantages and disadvantages. He is not particularly interested in being distracted from his path, but if it means speeding up their journey, then it could maybe be a good thing in the end.

"Of course we would like to come!" Torilander asserts, having just woken from his sleep and, upon hearing the girls, felt like he is in Heaven.

Chekilian comes to his senses as well, waking up to the enticing, good news that seems to make its round through the little group like a spreading wildfire.

"Of course, you can all come and bask in the generous atmosphere and company our Princess naturally provides to all her magnificent guests and playmates!" The girls laugh and have a good time. It's always nice to pick up some cool guys and present them to their Princess, who, incidentally, seems to look for her ideal mate from among her many guests and visitors.

And so the plan is sealed! Loriolan feels somewhat thrown off his guard, but the group has made up its mind, and if he resists, he might have a hard time with his two companions from here on out. And if he is honest with himself, he could also use a good time out to recuperate from the strain of the past days, especially when a chariot possibly awaits them at the end of their visit! And so the mermen shoulder their backpacks and begin to follow the mermaids to the light-filled spheres of the Princess's pleasure palace.

They must not have seen how close they were to this royal summer palace nor must have felt its bubbling atmosphere — that's how tired and overcome with exhaustion their bodies and souls are! The girls have torn them out of their deep sleep, and now the three tumble after the quirky girls, who seem to think they captured a great catch for their Princess's pleasure.

A field of remarkable light infusions from above opens up in front of them, a few small geysers shoot up from the seabed, and playful dolphins dance around them as if in an ecstatic trance; colorful pebble stones all over the ground enliven the atmosphere, beautiful, exotic plants fill the water expanse, and a multitude of sea flowers hang from scintillatingly colored rocks, ocean trees, coral reefs, and giant shells; playful fish, turtles, and sea stars roam dreamily around the mystical feeling garden of leisure and pleasure. From afar, beautiful crystalline laughter is heard, a girl with magnetic charm expressing her jubilant joy for everyone else's delight to behold and to hear. The mermen become more and more entranced and fascinated by the vibes they inhale and imbibe to the overflowing, their aching bodies ready to relax and bathe in the rays of goodness and jubilant joy! They follow the two girls as if in a dream; everything feels surrealistic and out of this world. Now the pink-haired beauty turns to give them the good news: they are entering the pleasure palace of Rhode, the darling daughter of the Ocean God Poseidon!

Loriolan gulps down his surprise. Who would have thought they are in such high company? With an increased sense of wakefulness, he tries to look and feel his best lest he give a terrible first impression to the daughter of such an important God! His two friends, also, give him a look of surprise; everyone is jolted into a higher state of wakefulness.

Impressively decorated watermen guards boasting gold-shimmering skin of their naked upper bodies let the group of five enter the palace without much ado. They follow a winding alley path past incredible marvels and deepest wonders into the interior of the pleasure garden. Loriolan can't shake a feeling of trance-like inundation of foreign but pleasurable impressions and has a hard time staying focused and alert to the present moment with all its challenges, twists, and turns.

He wonders how his journey could have brought him to this splendid place when all he wanted was to find a way to finally and ultimately unite with his beloved Indirali, the woman his heart belongs to for all eternity!

And then they enter the inner circle of the garden. A flock of beautiful mermaids and mermen leisurely stand and sit around the green grass, most of them holding a chalice of wine in their hands. And at the center of all the happenings, Princess Rhode is having a blast of a time and bubbling over with Divine delight as she is rhythmically thrown from a trampoline into the air by two strong-looking, young, and handsome mermen holding the ends of it in their hands like a big elastic skin. Her vibrancy and bounce are breathtaking, and her luminous, lavender-colored, long hair follows her every move in waves of bright shining light, magically changing shades during the rhythmic throws, darker in color when falling down and the Princess going inward, and lighter while she is flying upward and bursting out of herself with shouts of ecstasy and joy, her whole appearance iridescently and phosphorescently glittering in the water that seems to wondrously part on her move upwards and then push her down to help her gain renewed momentum. Grace and support of Nature seem to come naturally to her, and the energy she exudes feels exuberant and infectious. So bright is her laughter that she mesmerizes everyone with her overflowing delight, causing them to marvel at her intense beauty and her ability to enormously raise everyone's capacity to enjoy and forget themselves in the glory of the present moment!

Stunned, the three travelers take their positions among the onlookers, trying to catch a glimpse of the incredible life joy they see displayed in such a leisurely fashion. The Princess giggles and laughs; her shouts of joy travel to the upper realms and seem to have established a channel of bliss and ecstasy of her own, much to the soul nourishment and delight of her surrounding audience. Loriolan rubs his eyes, again, for he does not know how to place this experience in the greater context of his journey. It feels so good to bathe in the joys of highest bliss, and the Princess seems to be absolutely absorbed in these Divine feelings, as if her individuality has vanished to give rise to a pure bundle of joy and innocent playfulness, but deep within, Loriolan still feels the subtle and clear impulse that he is on treacherous ground and his journey might have come to a decisive point, somehow.

And then the Princess decides to jump! And how far and high her jump is! Everyone 'oooh's and 'aaah's at her feisty feat, clapping their hands to express their awe and admiration for such incredible accomplishment. Because it seems no one else can come close to the magnitude of her jump; no one else has yet accomplished what she did in that she established a connection to the all-powerful source of the Divine — her father being a great model of these elevated states — and then used this inner-found power to thrust it into her natural law-defying jump that has everyone shaking their heads in wonder.

The Princess lands safely on her tail, still laughing heartily, happy with her renewed top performance that has her unequalled even among the strongest and most athletic of mermen. Then she beholds Loriolan and his friends, her eyes sparkling at them as if to tease them with her incredible beauty. And because she has never seen these handsome strangers before, she challenges them to a competitive jump of their own. Cheerily she wonders who from among the three will dare to trump her jump, for she would like nothing more than to meet such a special man. Torilander and Chekilian immediately look at Loriolan, who would like nothing more than to find a quiet niche right now and be left to himself and to his feelings for Indirali. But the Princess has picked up on who among those three strangers is the leader and, most likely, the strongest of them as well. With a loving smile, she entices Loriolan to show her and everyone else what he is made of, and to prove her wrong in thinking that no mortal can beat her in her game. So innocent and longing appear her beautiful blue eyes that Loriolan can't resist her wish and, tired as he feels, allows himself to be placed on the trampoline skin.

The two mermen begin to throw him up high, over and over again, and Loriolan feels wonderfully transformed by this experience as the rhythmic throws conjure an incredible lightness and ecstasy in him; his aura and extended body begin to open to the spheres of Heaven, the place he wants to meet her so much, his Indirali, his heart and soul! Tears form in his eyes as he feels so close to her, and an overwhelming bliss begins to spread in him, drowning his pain out and fulfilling him with vibrations and waves of infinite magnificence and joy! His heart and soul begin to laugh, and soon his voice exclaims his ecstatic feelings in full force and power! His delight becomes infectious to everyone, and the Princess takes heed because here is someone who enjoys life and love as much as she does!

And then he jumps! Or rather, the force he conjured from within jumps! The Heavens jump, he and Indirali jump, the whole world stands by and jubilates in the unification of the happiest couple under the stars! Loriolan is dissolved in the bliss of his higher knowing. Never has he felt as close to his beloved since their separation under the light of the last full moon than right now, and this beautiful feeling of unified ecstasy now flows into his jump, the jump into the unknown, the jump of his lifetime that has him surrender his all to the unavoidable fact that Indirali awaits at the other end of time, and space, and love! Infinite love, infinite everything! He jumps for his love, and to his love! He jumps to unite with Indirali!

The jump is the highest and farthest, the most powerful jump in the history of Rhode's young life! Everyone ceases their clapping as the meaning of this begins to dawn on them. The Princess looks startled, almost beaten, and to clap right now would mean to show disrespect for her feelings. And so everyone waits for the Princess to recover from the shock of having found her equal or, even more than that, her victor!

But she quickly finds back to her usual gay composure, and with the clapping of hands of a true fan and admirer, she welcomes Loriolan back in their midst, showering him with her curiosity and deep interest as to who he is and where he is from. Loriolan can hardly keep up with the questions that pour from her mouth, and confused, he tries to locate his two friends, who have been forgotten somewhere in the crowd. Energetically, Loriolan tries to push his way free to unite with his buddies, but the crowd answers to the Princess, and she wishes him to stay put. Only after she obtained answers from him does she eventually concede and give the order for the crowd to part to let Torilander and Chekilian rejoin with their princely friend, who all of a sudden has become the target of great attention and admiration. Silently, the two travel companions walk up to Loriolan to stand by his side, wondering where this turn of events and Rhode's sparked interest in the Prince would lead them all.

CHAPTER 23

*R*hode likes to travel to the Tyrrhenian Sea whenever her parents allow her to and whenever it strikes her fancy. Her father's present main palace is located in the Aegean Sea and always swirls and bustles with political emissaries and social events. It is challenging for her to sometimes feel special and at ease with all these important matters on which her parents put most of their attention rather than on her. But she is her father's darling, and he can't ever say no to her many unique and extraordinary wishes. Unlike her brother Triton and her younger sister Benthesikyme, Rhode enjoys spending time out of and far away from the main palace of her parents, defining the notion of love and laughter anew with an entourage of enthusiastic admirers of her stunning beauty and intelligence. So special is Poseidon's firstborn daughter that it is often rumored only the Sun God Helios would be able to shine next to her radiant beauty without losing face, equanimity, and poise.

But now someone else has managed to outshine her sense of victory over the laws of gravity and karma! The Princess has to settle into this strange and new feeling of having come across a charismatic merman who seems to be even more connected to the Divine Source to which she herself feels so close. Everything in her wants this fascinating young stranger, who, for some reason, doesn't seem as captivated by her as everyone else is. And so she lures him to take a seat on her palace terrace overlooking the vast expanse of her deliciously beautiful, light-filled garden full of opulent plant life, precious articles, and exotic living creatures. Her entourage continues to surround her and Loriolan, holding the two at the center of their attention and behaving as if they were one living organism, following her every demand and expressing their delight and fun in any way she prompts them. So magnetic are her charm and wit that even the sea stars can't stay away from her but rather flock to her, eager to adorn her statuesque figure and sprinkling themselves abundantly on her shining, waving hair, like stars blinking in the purple night skies for the admirers of the universal mysteries to breathtakingly behold.

A beautiful maiden pours a crystal clear liquid into a chalice, then hands it as per the Princess's request to Loriolan. Loriolan indicates he is not thirsty for a drink he does not know the effects of, and Rhode takes it upon herself to explain to him the wonderfully elevating feelings this special Nectar of the Gods will trigger in him if only he gives it a chance. Everyone from the round confirms her comment, and the maiden serves Torilander and Chekilian with a chalice as well. Chekilian is thirsty, and if the drink revives his tired bones and spirit, then all the better. With a few gulps, he pours the drink down his throat, then wipes his mouth cheerfully. This prompts Torilander to do the same, as he also is tired of being tired and would like nothing more than to be accepted into the round and uplifted by everyone's good mood!

Only Loriolan sits with his chalice, undecided. Something in him tells him this is not the greatest idea. But the crowd keeps cheering him on, and soon Torilander and Chekilian join in. They say it is a harmless drink, and all they feel is tremendously good from it. That does it! The price to not drink, it seems, is worse now than to follow the crowd's promptings and experience it for himself. He certainly doesn't want to come across as a party pooper. And so he takes a few sips, then pours the fresh and sweet-tasting liquid down his throat as heartily as everyone else.

But as soon as he tastes the last drop of this mysterious liquid, a strange elevation begins to overcome him, transporting him out of his normal mind and into the vast void of a higher trance beyond human perceptions. A great sense of vulnerability spreads in him as he tries to stay in mastery of his self, but the liquid seems to have dissolved his sense of identity completely, and all of a sudden, he hears himself talking to the Princess as if he is a completely different person. Her questions make him want to answer her with all his heart, catapulting her interests to the highest possible status, as he begins to forget and neglect his friends and mission, all the while just trying to please his newfound mistress, who seems to be able to read his mind and shower him with all of her attention. So great is her charm and attraction to him that Loriolan begins to lose himself in her essence, becoming the slave to her biddings and a hopeless romantic in regard to her feminine beauty!

And so the hours pass by without Loriolan coming back to his good senses. The drink seems to have washed away any sense of tiredness — and feeling no need to sleep at all, the hours of fun and entertainment could go on forever if it were up to the three newcomers, who seem to have found great, incredible pleasure in the gardens of pleasure, thus considerably augmenting the happiness of the Princess of the Oceans! Fun games are being played, lovers chase each other in heartfelt pursuits, and laughter and joy abound as if the Gods are intent on dwelling in this pleasure palace with all the infinite bliss they embody and radiate! Time seems to stand still, and the fun and joy seem to find no end! Everyone becomes happier and merrier as time flies by, and the Princess succeeds in insinuating herself into Loriolan's good graces, conquering his mind with every minute of her breathtaking presence. Soon she invites him to her private chambers, indicating how lucky he is to have impressed her with his higher connections, and his integrity and honor of heart and soul; then the two of them disappear from everyone else's sight, and Torilander and Chekilian see their friend no more.

Behind closed doors, however, a dance of love forbidden begins, with Rhode playfully and seductively advancing her essence towards him and Loriolan as playfully and innocently retracting his essence from her, making her even more hungry for him, in fact causing her soul to scream with unfulfilled pleasure as this hard core of a man keeps eluding her crafty and masterfully romantic and passionate advances towards him. As much as Loriolan feels he wants to please his temptress, on some level he knows this whole scenario isn't right, and he just can't give in to her charms and desires. At some point, the catch and run game doesn't do it for Rhode anymore, and with an exclamation of her frustration, she orders Loriolan to succumb to her libido and stop playing games with her. She looks at him with anguish, ready to thrust her hot body onto his irresistibly attractive torso, hoping his manhood will do the rest and find the way into her innermost feminine secrets and wonders.

Loriolan, however, watches her magic spinning its way into his mind and body, relaxing him below the threshold of conscious awareness and hypnotically trying to force him to surrender to her overly powerful intent and desire. Circle upon circle of her enchanting energy waves come at him, each limiting his free will and weakening his ability to think for himself. He feels entrapped in her web of charming manipulation, wondering how to lift his spirit back up, above the subconscious level, to take the reigns of his life back from her and avoid having to compromise his alignment with the Divine vocation and love he feels so strongly anchored in with all his being and essence.

Rhode is startled, to say the least, as her most powerful love spells seem to not work on him at all, and his manhood stays passive and indifferent to her overwhelming beauty. 'How can this be?' she asks herself. Never has she come across such a phenomenon that a mortal man could resist the onslaught of her feminine allurements and defy her irresistible charms the way in which this mysterious stranger seems capable. Scanning her options in her mind, she either continues to force herself on him and risks making a total fool of herself, or she tactfully retracts right now, hoping she can still salvage her self-respect after this complete failure of a seduction! Because what is a love act without the man performing his most essential part in it, she realizes.

And so she decides for the latter option and begins to lessen her magical grip on his soul, allowing him to gradually come back to his senses so she at least can find out why this elusive beau has defied her like no other man has. Desperately uttering mantras in her mind to help calm down her steamy hot libido, she resigns herself to her fate as a first-time reject, turning her face away from him in order to not show him any more of her disappointment and hurt than he has already seen.

Loriolan shakes his head as if to rid himself of a tremendous fog that had enveloped him for the last several hours since he drank the offered Nectar of the Gods. How weird he can't remember much, and where are his friends? he asks out loud, then looks around to explore what situation life thrust him into during his mind's absence — his first clear thought, dedicated to the friends he lost somewhere along the way!

"They are fine!" Rhode appeases his puzzlement. "They are probably having a more splendid time than we are!" she adds with suppressed frustration.

That makes Loriolan take a better look at her. The vibrant, full-of-life kind of look has vanished from her countenance, and a melancholic vulnerability seems to have engulfed her delicate essence. And then it dawns on him: she tried to seduce him with her magic drink and spell, and he wasn't able to comply with her passion and wishes. Warmly, he tries to make her understand that it has nothing to do with her but everything to do with him. After trying to build up her jaded self-confidence with compliments on her surpassing beauty and inner light, he begins to explain why he disappointed her generous romantic interest in him. He tells her about how he met Indirali, with Cupid's arrow hitting them both at the same time, causing them to realize that they are everything for each other, and that she is his one and only true love. He emphasizes how this meeting has changed his life forever and describes how Indirali and he have decided to take the heroes of ancient times as their model and, in like way, are now pursuing the unification of their souls and lives by overcoming any and all obstacles in their way. This includes Indirali's planned marriage to a dislikable war-hero, a desperate attempt of her father to help solve his kingdom's problems that are primarily caused by Poseidon's curse on the human world. All these obstacles, therefore, now require Loriolan and Indirali to go against impossible odds and overcome them one by one, with him working through the water and fire elemental hindrances, and Indirali mastering the earth and air elemental spheres, ascending from the Earth to meet the spirits of the sky, intent on mastering the ethereal realm, as he also intends, from where they both can finally enter the Heavens and meet up with each other! He says he can't wait to be completely and lastingly united with her and that every hour he can't be in her presence feels like unbearable pain in his soul.

Rhode can't help but stare him directly into his eyes. What merman undertakes such a long, arduous journey just to be with an Earth woman? She has a hard time believing that he would prefer an Earth woman over being with her, the princess daughter of the Ocean God Poseidon! Doesn't he know what super-worldly privileges he could enjoy should he choose to accept her as his companion and lover?

Loriolan picks up on her disbelief and continues to stretch her understanding even more, by revealing to her that he is ready to encounter the darkest, most dangerous monsters of the deep, if only he will be able to see his Indirali on the other side of the long, dark tunnel of separation.

Rhode feels hit by this inconsiderate remark. How much does he need to put her down by elevating this Earth woman above her in such extreme fashion! Does he not see how humiliating this whole situation already is for her! Why does he continue to rub his eternal love feelings for some other woman into her already hurting wounds! How much does he expect Rhode to put up with his nonsense talk! She is about to explode into his face when the pain and sadness in his own eyes cause her to withdraw her attacking energy. Deflated, she sits across from him, the veils of her canopy bed softly undulating in the drafty currents, prompting her to surrender to an unearthly compassion with his impossible seeming situation.

"Why don't you forget about her and stay with me!" she wishes. "My father loves me so much that I think I could ask of him to retract the curse on humanity, if this would make you happy!" She obviously tries not to get the full point of Loriolan's dilemma. "As my husband, you would have unsurpassed powers and resources that you could use for any good cause you saw fit! You could do many great deeds for the oceanic worlds as well as for the worlds on land, if you so chose!" Temptingly, she looks into his eyes, as if trying to uncover and please his deepest needs.

Surprise shows in Loriolan's face. Did she say 'husband'? What deep feelings has he triggered in her beautiful heart that she gives herself so fully to him after such a short time of knowing him? he wonders. Is he to assume that her feelings for him are real? — And then a strange puzzlement sets in that has his mind spinning and spinning in an attempt to find its proper orientation and direction. Such great opportunity and powers are all of a sudden open to him? Poseidon, the mighty, fear-inducing, powerful beyond measure, supernatural God of the twelve Olympian Main Gods could be his father-in-law? What cruel game is life playing on him here! Like a thin veil ready to tear apart before his eyes, his present reality tries to burst into a new reality full of mind-boggling promises and supernatural potential to effect tremendous, welcome changes in all the worlds he knows! Loriolan scratches his head. He has to think this through for a minute; such a grandiose offer doesn't come along every day, heck not even in eons!

He looks at Rhode, who silently holds her breath for fear of disturbing and disrupting his delicate thought process, fervently hoping for a favorable answer emerging from the depths of his heart to sweep her off her tail and make her his own, in body, mind, and spirit! And Loriolan's heart speaks: Indirali! — His heart and soul and body cry out her name as if they are about to drown, trying to hold on to her image as if holding onto a lifeline. Suddenly, Loriolan feels the futility of this kind of wishful thinking and sees that he could never love Rhode the way he loves Indirali. Because nothing compares to the woman of his heart, nothing compares to Indirali! Her name makes his heart sing and float in the Heavens of bliss. No other princess, no other Goddess can take this special place in his heart! Who has he been trying to kid! A deep restlessness begins to overtake him, as he realizes there is no escaping this all-encompassing truth of his life, and that he better get on his way again if he wants to find lasting happiness and union with his other half, which happens to be Indirali, the most beautiful woman of all women, in water and on land! At least for him! A tear begins to form, and he humbly lowers his gaze.

For some unexplainable reason, Rhode's heart melts upon feeling his stance of faithfulness to his Indirali. Wondrously, she feels selflessness surfacing and feels the urge to comfort him, bandage his wounds with tender words of compassion: "You are quite a catch, Loriolan!" she concedes. "This Indirali of yours is a very lucky woman, you know. Not only are you willing to overcome whatever dangerous monsters along the way just so you can be with her, but you also withstand the most beautiful temptress this side of the ocean has ever seen, namely me!" She laughs to lighten the atmosphere, which has been too darkish and sad for too long now, very unlike her normally happy and cheerful disposition.

Loriolan smiles back at her. Rhode seems to be a fine, decent young mermaid after all, he finds, and who knows, maybe they can at least be friends. Who knows, Indirali might even like her.

"I guess it's hard for me to take a 'No' from someone I tried to give my heart and body to," she continues. "All I know from my parents and upbringing is complete fulfillment of all my dearest desires and wishes. To be rejected has so far not been on the plate for me. But I guess there is a first time for everything!" She tries to be upbeat about her rejection.

"It's hard to believe that there is not someone special in your life who arouses more than just temporary pleasure in you," he wonders out loud. "I bet there are hundreds of suitors who would love nothing more than to make you happy on a constant basis! Even from among the crowd outside your chamber!"

She takes a moment to respond. "It's not the quantity of suitors, Loriolan, it's the quality of a man! That's what I seem to have been subconsciously looking for without fully understanding it until this moment. You just made me realize it! Someone like you, a man who knows how to stay loyal to the woman of his heart, no matter how strong the temptations are that come his way! I bet it was your love for Indirali that motivated you to jump farther and higher than anyone else from among the many friends and guests I've entertained over the years! I wish I could be the motivational and inspirational force behind a man's strength and power, and good deeds! I tell you, nothing is more attractive to a woman than if her man sees only her and elevates her to the only Goddess he has eyes for. I guess this is what attracted me to you before I even knew your heart is set on someone else. You just exude this fantastic focus and single-mindedness! One thing is sure now, I want my future husband to display such incorruptible faithfulness as you have demonstrated, even under the bombardment of the magic spells and my irresistible love and charm!" Her eyes glow with a newfound passion she has not known so far.

"There is one God, Loriolan, who has been pursuing me for quite a long time and who has not wavered in his love and attention towards me for as long as I can remember. But being immortal and, therefore, having infinite time at his disposal, he pursued other love interests way before I was born into this beautiful body and incarnation, which fact cautioned me to not throw myself right into his arms when he first indicated his love for me to my parents. Instead, I let him wait and prove his undying devotion to me throughout all these many years while I heartily pursued the joys of singlehood and willful excursions into non-committed relationships to develop — what I considered — my sense of independence and equality with him. Much to his credit and proof of his transcendental maturity, he patiently waits for my attention to grace him, perseveringly offering his undying love and care to me no matter how childish and impetuous I behave around him, and even though I have repeatedly shown only indifference and evasion towards him. His name is Helios, and he is our Sun God!" she laughs. "One would think he is a great catch as well, being immortal and, therefore, eternally young and handsome, so far up in the skies and all, but I guess I wasn't ready for such high commitment and too immature to take his persistent love seriously." She pauses her thought process, reflecting on the deepest issues of the heart. "But maybe I'm ready now?!" she ponders. "Maybe all it took was for someone like you to shake me up and make me realize what I truly want: a faithful heart who sees in me the Goddess that I am and reflects back at me the splendor of my being and world! Because — and this might come as a surprise to you — both Helios and I know that we are eternal soulmates for one another, but when we both pursued other love interests in the recent centuries of human history, all we really did was to give in to our lower-self urgings, losing ourselves in the decadence of the progressing spiritual night right into the fragmentation of our once unified soul essence into myriads of lower, weaker soul elements that we tried desperately to recover and merge with our love, hoping to bring them back into the unity and power we once knew and expressed in the golden times. I'm not proud of this weakness of mine nor do I like to see it reflected back to me through the unfaithful actions of my eternal lover; in fact, in this regard we are no better than the humans who adore us and who continuously and irritatingly project their own shortcomings onto us Gods and Goddesses, as if trying to justify their immoral behavior and life-debilitating tendencies by attributing them to us and thus making them look desirable and morally acceptable."

Rhode takes another look at Loriolan, the man who withstood her allurements with such grace and inner determination, and it feels to her as if a fresh wind just gave her the new outlook on life she was secretly craving to get to but felt mysteriously unable to accomplish on her own until this very moment. It required a steadfast and loyal heart like his to put her back into her good senses and let her see reason within her own eternal love affair with the Sun God Helios. Because deep in her heart, she began to miss the nobility and incredible bliss two lovers experience when they know to the depth of their souls that they are meant for each other, to love and hold sacred their other half for all of eternity, able to absolutely rely on each other's loyalty and purity of character no matter what the temptations and downward trends are that threaten the soul from within and without, to lift them above the mundane and mortal world and allow them to experience the sacredness and bliss of their union once more that knows no boundaries and no comparisons.

"My mother told me that during the presently reigning Iron Age, souls, from one incarnation to another, are splitting into myriads of other, weaker souls," she confides, "thus losing their essence and strength of personality, when during the Golden Age, we were still unified, virtuous, and powerful in ourselves and had only one love partner for all of eternity to be happy with. She said that even we Gods and Goddesses of the Iron Age are but a fragment of who we used to be in the Golden and even Silver Ages and that the Titans our Olympian Gods seemingly vanquished according to human history are, in fact, the more powerful versions of us and our forefathers. They were the whole body and soul, whereas we are just the cells of that body now, cells that call each other different names and which struggle to survive in a hostile environment in which each cell competes for the dwindling resources that are still left for their increasingly desperate appetites for life. And the resources are dwindling because of the overshadowing influence of the Iron Age. And not only is planet Earth becoming less inhabitable, with deserts and natural catastrophes increasing, but the human beings, and any living being for that matter, are becoming more overshadowed as well and are turning into just a fraction of what they used to be in the spiritually lighter seasons on Earth.

And it is this fact that causes humans and the lesser Gods alike to turn into unfaithful, scatterbrained, and starved beings who chase after each other's life energies and possessions, willing to compromise their ethical standards for the sake of gaining another breath of life. It is in this vein that many beings of today can't ever be satisfied with one love partner anymore because, like me, they look in all the wrong directions for another rush of life, another high, another fill of the gaping inner void that extends with every move away from one's own essence. An agonizing spiritual void and emotional emptiness that is the natural outcome of a life lived under the illusions of time and space, and the lost unity of one's own eternal Self! Because, as you might know, in the Golden Age beings were transcendental and unified and existed beyond the perception of time and space most Earth inhabitants of today are entrapped in, in a realm of eternity and infinity, and infinite bliss as well. But ..." she sighs heavily, "unfortunately my father gives in to this fragmentation by whoring around with other women, embarrassing and humiliating not only himself with these transgressions, but mostly my mother at this point, who still yearns for those uplifting and most fulfilling times of the Golden Age when it was natural to be treated with respect, no matter what your gender happened to be. I think I don't want to give in to these self-destructive and fragmenting times and tendencies any more than I already have but rather return to being the one and only eternal beloved to my soulmate, who I essentially and truly am!" A broad happy smile flits across her lips. "What do you think?"

Loriolan smiles serenely at her. "I like what your mother has to say about the Golden Age: I recognize much of it from the legends of old that talk about the Titans and their many super-worldly deeds that we can only dream of anymore. And I think refraining from the mass-conscious tendencies is always a good thing, especially in these degenerative times. So yes, this is a wonderful idea and a most rewarding one for sure. It sounds like Helios came to his senses as well if he waits patiently for you now to accept his love again without him going anywhere else with it anymore. Sounds like he is a good character, and if I were you, I would give him a chance to show even more of his love to you!"

"That's what I thought, but now you confirm it to me!" Her excitement knows no bounds, and with a buoyant jump, she stands up to look out the window. Misty-eyed, she looks into the distance, her heart now all of a sudden directed towards her own eternal lover, the God she spurned for so long because she thought she wanted it all, the full scope and array of love, unaccountable pleasures with any man she fancied, as she dreaded to be fixated and bound to just one man alone for the rest of her life! And if one is eternally young, the rest of one's life looks pretty damn long! But for some reason the dread has vanished, and instead she feels only irresistible charm coming from the idea of belonging to only one man for the rest of all her lifetimes. To explore the depths of their souls together rather than losing herself on the surface level of dead-end relationships and one night stands! Her father — bless his fatherly heart — has not really been a good example of faithfulness and loyalty for her; instead he has been wasting his reproductive energies on women of all kinds, in water, sky, and on earth, much to the dismay and heartbreak of Rhode's sensitive and vulnerable mother, the Nereid Queen Amphitrite. He thinks it demonstrates what a powerful, hot lingam he is and that Rhode's mother should be grateful to have such a coveted stallion by her side. But her mother is anything but happy and fulfilled from it — it's just her unfaithful husband trying to justify his trespasses and affairs. Instead, Amphitrite feels rather abandoned and insignificant, one among many, and has, therefore, inwardly turned away from him, trying to forget her misery by getting distracted in all sorts of social functions. Rhode swore to herself to never let this kind of constant betrayal happen to her and, sorely remembering Helios's womanizing past, has, therefore, either kept the man who loves her dearly at arm's length or has enjoyed the carnal pleasures herself the way her father exemplifies to her. But deep inside, a soul pain has been growing of never finding true, lasting love and, therefore, feeling lost in the oceans of unfulfilling pleasure games and superficial feelings.

Loriolan gives her a caring look. "I'm sorry about the pain your father causes you and your mother," he sympathizes. "I could never do this to my beloved. For me she is the center of my world and universe. To hurt her would feel like hurting myself, and why would I do that?"

"It's because you care! You are sensitive to the finer feelings of a woman. That makes you irresistibly attractive to us females! You don't manipulate a woman into thinking she should be grateful to have an adulterer and womanizer at her side only because he enjoys it that way; instead, you put your lower urges aside and focus on mutually pleasing each other's refined love feelings and higher senses. You see the Divine in your woman, and as a result, she sees the Divine in you too. That's way more appealing and way more considerate and loving to a woman. And ultimately, it's also more rewarding for you as a man! Because a happy woman is way more nourishing and loving to her man and environment!" She lowers her eyes so as to acknowledge that she is not trying to trespass on his feelings for Indirali anymore. "My father provides us with all the amenities of royal life — we don't lack anything materially and socially — but on the inner levels, I grew up with an emptiness and sadness. I can be a very happy child for as long as I don't contemplate the inner truths of my existence, you know! I could have gone on and on and on, making myself and those around me as happy as possible, but then you came along, topped and redirected my thrust for life, and thus burst my bubble of fleeting contentment. And now I don't know whether to thank you or to be cross with you." She smiles at him.

"I would always prefer to build my pleasure palace on a rock, on solid ground, so nothing could ever destroy my happiness," he answers with a sly look. "How about you?"

She thinks for a moment. She guesses he is saying that if he was able to throw her back on herself and her deeper issues as easily as he did, then her happiness does not seem as deep and profound as she has so far been trying so hard to make herself believe, and consequently, it would be wise for her to remedy the situation and try to integrate whatever lesson Loriolan triggered in her, look at it, and deal with it. Which she knows has to do with her ability to love a man steadfastly and with her full heart, and trust that there is a man who will hold her gently, be faithful to her, and take good care of her heart so she can feel safe enough to be able to open it up to him completely, and that she should just forget her father and mother's fate because it doesn't need to apply to her! She can create her own beautiful and elevating destiny!

And so, ultimately, she has to admit that a miracle just happened! Goddess Aphrodite, her secret champion Goddess, has been answering her prayers and has sent an idol of a lover, even if he is not meant for her; nevertheless, he showed her that a man can be faithful to one woman and not fall for any temptation, no matter how strong and powerful! This experience has — magically — reconciled her to the idea that true love does exist during this Iron Age and in this mortal world of ours and that it is worth pursuing and experiencing! Gratefulness wells up in her heart, and with a smile, she contemplates out loud: "You know," she turns to him, "I feel like sharing my regained sense of caring and would from now on like to do a lot of great things! There is an island with my name in the Aegean Sea, the island of Rhode, a monument of Helios's and my love from a time long ago. It is a particularly sunny island, with hardly a day going by in the year when it doesn't have at least several hours of sunshine. The inhabitants are, therefore, predominantly happy and prosperous because the sun tends to lighten the mind and emotions. Many schools for higher learning have been erected to instill enlightenment into the many thirsty souls that come there, and a very fruitful cooperation and mutually beneficial cultural and commercial exchange has been established with the great empire of Egypt. It is a thriving island indeed, but it also has many enviers who attempt to destroy Rhode's beautiful architecture and cultural life and try to seize the land for themselves. I want to rededicate my attention and protection to the islanders' fate and inspire them to new heights of personal achievements and spiritual growth." And upon seeing interest written all over Loriolan's face, she continues to explain: "I felt a little put off recently when the islanders decided to erect a monument in Helios's honor, elevating him to a bombastic status while ignoring the nymph whose name the island bears and who gave birth to the island in the first place. But I guess this is another sign of the Iron Age we find ourselves in, to emphasize the male over the female and revere the male importance in all its splendor while the female contributions and provisions are predominantly taken for granted and go unnoticed." Rhode's head sinks to her chest as she pauses reflectively.

Loriolan looks at her attentively, patiently waiting for her to continue her recount of these most intimate details of her past.

"I see a lot of suffering spreading throughout these Iron Age times," she continues, looking at Loriolan again with a trace of sadness in her eyes, "but women sure have become second to men in most societies of today, sometimes even being put into a position lower than the cattle a man owns. This was not the case throughout the Golden Ages when man and woman were equal in soul and spirit, enjoying the same rights in every worldly expression they decided to get involved in. Anyway, things are different now, and luckily for us Gods and Goddesses, life is still more balanced and harmonious between the genders, thus affording us a lifestyle quite different from that of the more anguished and oppressed human race. But I have to admit that building this enormous statue to honor Helios on the island of Rhode has put me off quite a bit, contributing to me wanting to find my own self-worth and beauty, away from him and without standing in his shadow, so to say. Because it is not just like any other statue, Loriolan; it is an exaggeratingly impressive monument, a colossus, really, so huge that every human beholding it automatically goes to his knees from the grandeur and magnificence it exudes. It is almost intimidating in its size, an expression of human veneration and fear of the Gods." She sighs heavily, "But I have been jealous of the islanders' devotion to my beloved for too long now, and I think it's time for me to wake up and look beyond the human world, to see how steadfastly Helios has kept his loving attention on me, wooing me with a heart way bigger than this earthly world can ever be. I think I'm truly over it now, not the least because of your purehearted devotion to your own eternal lover flame, a purity that has sparked my feminine spirit to trust in the workings of a manly mind and heart again. For that I'm deeply thankful to you, Loriolan, for you rekindled the deeper and finer feelings of my heart." Rhode laughs demurely, lowering her gaze.

Loriolan reaches for her hand to gently express his appreciation for confiding in him. "I understand very well where you are coming from," he points out, "for my beloved Indirali herself is the victim of male oppression. Even though she loves me, she is forced to marry a man she doesn't care for, a man she in fact despises because of his violence and fighting ambitions that greatly contribute to all the social degeneration of our times. This is why we both went on our spiritual journeys, to find each other beyond the dualities and downward tendencies of this mortal world, to finally be able to unite in the Heavens of the Gods and Goddesses, and to become sanctified and unified as the eternal lovers we feel we are for each other." He smiles at Rhode.

Rhode looks up, awestruck at such a time-defying and courageously daring stance. She can't help but see more Divine beauty, purity, and devotion in Loriolan's soul than she has detected even among the Gods of her lineage. How odd she would receive such an invaluable lesson of timeless faithfulness from a mere mortal! Quite embarrassing, actually, were he not so charming about it all! She sighs, trying to rid herself of this slightly embarrassing feeling. Then she continues to explain: "This statue of Helios is actually a miracle of a work! You might have heard about the Colossus of Rhodes, that most impressive of all statues, of God Helios himself, towering near the harbor far above the ground for as high as the eye can see, as if he is to touch his own image in the sky, the humanoid and statuesque God touching his immortal self, the sun globe of his extended radiance and nourishing love for all of life!" She looks up as if in a sweet trance, remembering for a moment the infinitely blissful feelings she and Helios used to share with each other, then gazes back at Loriolan, who supportively acknowledges her newfound inner confidence in regard to her impressive lover.

"It must be odd to see Helios elevated so far above the ground that you provide," he admits. "It seems to be a characteristic of the Iron Age to focus on manly qualities and attributes as something to be given priority, something to admire and strive for as the ideal principle that manages to survive the very same hostile environment it creates in the first place, by its very own nature! Because ruthless ambitions, rough aggressiveness, and crude behaviors are in higher demand throughout a time of social decline and endless wars than they could ever have been during the more blissful and prosperous times of the Golden and Silver Ages, during which enlightened times the genders could easily replace each other, that's how similar their essences were and expressed themselves." He pauses to catch a nod of agreement from his lovely conversation partner.

"My father mentioned to me, on occasion, the teachings he received from Rachtan, his spiritual advisor," Loriolan continues, "and according to him, the beings who inhabited the planet throughout the Golden Age were all of a more androgynous nature, non-aging, and infinitely peaceful and supportive of each other, and respectful of even the least among all the living creatures. I would often dream about such ethereal times, wishing I could one day return to the bliss and grandeur of it!" His eyes become glazed with a deep yearning. Because only in such a spiritually enriched environment can he imagine being unified with Indirali the way he dreams about. Then he looks back at Rhode, who has been intensively listening to every word this exceptional merman has been conveying to her.

"To erect an altar or statue to the Goddess who provides the very foundation for their lives and who gives life in the first place," Loriolan ponders, "a monument of veneration that is as tall and impressive as the one of her male counterpart probably feels redundant and superfluous to the islanders and to most humans of today's world. Sadly, the tendency among the populace is to turn their backs on life and take it for absolutely granted, so granted even that they gladly dispose of it in their many futile wars and oppressions of their fellow humans. But fortunately, we are not humans!" he laughs. "But a race of underwater mer-beings who still think the world of their women, for without our women, we would not be born and nurtured into life, and our hearts would lose their anchorage, making us float aimlessly in the oceans of chaos, illusion, and emptiness. And I truly think you are a fantastically bright and scintillating example of this beautiful and indispensable gender; I think you just have to believe in yourself no matter how immature and ignorant the humans of your island behave towards you. Forgive them, Rhode, for they don't know what they would miss should your support of them stop and their land be taken away from them either by sea-crossing raiders, earthquakes, or whatever other life-threatening virus you would neglect to fend off from their lives and habitat."

Rhode laughs out loud for a second, for Loriolan's words touch her deeply within her soul, and his wisdom seems uncanny and to the point. It truly feels uplifting and heart-warming to have a man address her innermost self instead of focusing on her sensuality or playing into and taking advantage of her status as Poseidon's daughter. Instead, this young, handsome man applauds her dreams and intentions of ensuring the wellbeing and prosperity of her island and conveys to her that he knows she can be successful in anything she puts her heart and mind to; he says he has seen enough of her intelligence and wit to attest to her greatness, and he hopes the people of the island of Rhode will realize what intrinsically important role the water princess plays in their lives, for without her essence, there would be no land to stand on and no protection along the sea routes for the Rhode islanders and their visitors to count on.

How good Loriolan makes her feel about herself! In his presence, all these great ideas seem to come back to life, and as he just stated, she truly feels she can accomplish anything to which she sets her mind! And nothing will sway her from becoming exactly the great Goddess she is predestined to be, at super-radiant Helios's side, the God who has been in love with her for as long as she can remember. Well, if this persistent love doesn't speak for him, then nothing can. With a sigh, she sinks onto the bed, looking gently at Loriolan. "You know, I had this thought, maybe I can help you to get to Indirali even faster by offering you my chariot. What do you think?"

Loriolan exclaims his joy upon hearing her express the coveted offer. "That would be just grand, Rhode! Would you really do that for me?"

"Yes, I think I would," she playfully concedes. "You have been a blessing to me, Loriolan, and the least I can do is to repay you in a manner advantageous for your own goals and aspirations. You are quite a special man, and if I don't help you right now, you might have just lost valuable time on your way to unite with your eternal beloved, right?"

Loriolan stays quiet. He doesn't want to offend her any further, but in truth, he would have liked to be on the way already, far, far away, preferably in the Heavens already with his bride Indirali!

His silence triggers even more of Rhode's tender feelings for his fate and love challenges. "Well, it's yours for the taking. My charioteers will bring you as far as to the Straits of Gibraltar. From then on, you are on your own again! Deal?"

"Deal!" he agrees, shaking her outstretched hand to seal the sweet deal.

CHAPTER 24

*C*ontrary to Loriolan's apprehension, Torilander and Chekilian had a good time in his absence. In fact, he just seemed to have made way for them to become the center of attention. Chekilian sits on a richly decorated bench, a beautiful young maiden standing right next to him, affectionately leaning against the back rest and listening with the others to his excited reports, all the while flirting with him in ways of subtle seduction, well aware of Chekilian's tender, budding manhood that seems to wondrously attract her sweet blossoming, feminine charms. Torilander, however, is encircled by several girls, all vying for his attention that he just won't give them, because what they don't know is that his heart is already taken as well. As soon as he sees Loriolan returning, his countenance lightens up, and he walks towards his friend as if trying to shake off the swarm of girls hanging on him. Loriolan greets him with a smile, for he has good news in regard to their journey.

Princess Rhode greets everyone with an air of victory and lightness. A shadow has just fallen off her soul, and she is intent to let everyone feel that her tête-à-tête with Loriolan was a complete success on all levels. Deeply in love with life, she spins around and in slow motion begins a dance that has everyone of her entourage spellbound and captivated by her uplifting, Divine Source-connecting, spiraling motions. Another influx of highest, purest love and joy begins to enliven the atmosphere, and the group takes a fresh breath of the most refined prana and life energy the water and ether are abundantly suffused with. Rhode begins to sing brightly and melodiously, revering Aphrodite, the Goddess of Love, and then continues to include the Sun God Helios in her venerating hymn, causing several of her flock of servants and guests to cry with touching ecstasy and devotion.

Loriolan, Torilander, and Chekilian stare at her as if beholding the Divine Goddess expressing her innermost beauty and light-filled presence, enlightening the space around her as streams of light radiate from her enraptured countenance, bathing the whole place in the super-worldly light of highest bliss and ecstasy and thus elevating the level of existence for all souls present to celestial places of utter beauty and infinite love. So ecstatic and full of brightest magic is the atmosphere that all souls begin to feel their innermost connection to their Creator, their infinite Source of Origin, to which all long to return, each in their own time, but certainly unite with as soon as they feel able to! Divine Blessings are poured out, and everyone gratefully and humbly accepts their fill of them, then sinks to the ground to come back to their present identity and awareness.

Rhode slowly comes back to the confinements of her mortal self and, transfigured, looks into the round. She takes Loriolan by the hand and shows him off to her people, telling them that here is a man who has shown her how faithfully the heart of a true lover beats, and that the woman of his heart can consider herself fortunate to be able to share such eternal, Divine Love with this hero of a man, and that such a woman must herself also be a heroine and very special, divinely anchored, and highly virtuous to have been able to attract his undying love for her. Then Rhode lifts Loriolan's arm and triumphantly exclaims that she feels fortunate to have met him, and that she has decided to help him and his companions on their extraordinary quest by making her chariot available to them.

The crowd bursts into jubilant applause, for they, too, have felt a deep, wondrous connection to the three travelers, and having learned from Torilander and Chekilian the unique and daring nature of their journey, they can't help but feel a gripping awe of them that best is expressed by a thunderous applause with the capacity to encompass all their collective admiration and support for such a tremendously brave feat!

Loriolan and his two buddies are touched to the core of their hearts and can't decide whether to shrink away from all this loving attention or tough it out with an air of aloofness and serenity, because deep inside, all this love coming at them is triggering an overwhelming amount of sadness as well, for they have to leave this beautiful, fun company behind and confront the unknown and the dangers of the dark and deep! Loriolan turns his head away to hide his emotional state, but the love keeps pouring and coming at him from all sides, making it impossible to ignore and, instead, forcing him to accept it with a grateful heart.

Rhode raises her chalice for another toast, wishing the travelers a safe journey and the successful completion of their mission. Everyone joins in the toast, with chalices clicking against each other, but then stops short as they notice Loriolan is not accepting the chalice someone is holding out for him. With an innocent laugh, Rhode snaps up the chalice and draws close to Loriolan, holding the chalice right under his nose: "No fear, my dear! This magical elixir just enhances whatever you focus your mind on. And since I boast a very strong mind, I took advantage of your weaknesses, trying to subdue you to my romantic interests. But you withstood, and now this elixir will just elevate your own higher aspirations, like most of my companions here are able to enjoy. Besides, …" she teasingly moves the chalice away from him as if to prompt him to chase after it, "the effect of one sip of this precious liquid is equal to several nights of the most recuperative sleep, thus enabling you to feel more rested from your stay with us than if you had taken a week's time out for your recuperation!" She looks at him with resplendent eyes, conveying to him that it would be his loss.

Loriolan swipes the chalice from her hand, smilingly acknowledging that he feels stronger and better than he has in a long time and that her dance has conjured powers from the inner worlds that have him still soaring from its majesty and elevation. And so he thanks her for the toast and drinks from the chalice with great pleasure.

And again, his mind begins to expand beyond his individuality, leaving him stranded in the powerful waves of compassion and love exuding from this extraordinary host and her affectionate entourage. Rhode calls the charioteers and orders them to ready the chariot for departure. Their honored guests are leaving, and all their prayers are going with them.

Every one of these sweet, kind souls wants to be near to the three travelers before they see them no more. Surrounded by maidens and lads who all reach out their hands for a last good-bye wish, Loriolan, Torilander, and Chekilian take their leave, swallowing their tears down in order to not lose themselves in this ocean of love, support, admiration, and compassion.

Then the chariot arrives, the sea horses rearing as they come to a halt. The departing mermen give their last hugs, with Chekilian and the young mermaid for a moment having a heartwrenching time letting go of each other's hand, and then the three turn to the Princess, who stands at some distance on top of the bright, sparkling staircase, overlooking the good-bye spectacle with misty but radiant eyes. Loriolan raises his hand for a final greeting, deep friendship feelings welling in his chest, then mounts the chariot to join his companions.

"I will always love you and Indirali!" the Princess shouts, then whistles to spur on the sea horses. Loriolan looks back at her and sees her blowing kisses after them. Chekilian answers with like gesture, whereas Torilander and Loriolan wave their hands after the departing crowd, which quickly fades into the mist of incredible joys left behind.

The ride is fast and exhilarating, with the sea landscapes flitting by them faster than they can perceive them. Maybe it is still due to the intoxicating drink of which they partook, they assume, or the chariot is just from out of this world! But the impressions of the passing sceneries stay a blur, with occasional big underwater marks flaring up in front of them. Two stunning looking charioteers hold the reigns of the six white sea horse stallions, steering them masterfully around large objects and sufficiently above sea ground level to never run into any obstructing reefs and rocks. And wow! All of a sudden, the chariot takes off from the seabed with enormous speed and lifts out of the water to fly through the sunlit sky, leaving the three travelers stunned and startled, holding their breath at first until getting used to the speed and height of the path taken. At some point, Loriolan thinks he is just able to make out the island of Sardo in the far distance to the right, but then he settles back into letting the ocean pass by him, knowing they are going in the right direction, towards the Straits of Gibraltar, the oceanic passage connecting the Mediterranean Sea with the Atlantic Ocean. Loriolan blinks at the sun, concentric circles of his attention spiraling towards the huge light in the sky, and a deep veneration towards the Sun God, Helios, begins to flow from his heart and soul, as if magnetically drawn out from him, forcing him into a devotional surrender of the deepest magnitude. Loriolan's heart flows endlessly towards the bright shining light, and an inner dialogue of the beauty and importance of eternal love ensues between him and the Sun God. Loriolan hears a voice calling out his name, thanking him for his strength of character and inner purity and for releasing his love from the shadows of doubt and the entrapment through fear and vices to help her see the truth of his feelings for her, and Loriolan, therefore, can count on his help whenever he should be in need.

Loriolan discloses to the Sun God that he intends to meet his eternal beloved in the Heavens of the Divine and that he hopes to meet the Sun God there as well. Helios replies that he looks forward to meeting such a blessed, heroic soul as him and wishes him well on his journey into the light of eternity. He advises Loriolan to not give in to the illusions of fear, hatred, and death but to steer clear of these inferior emotions in order to enter through the vortex of light into the spheres of the immortal souls. He says he wishes Loriolan well and to always count on the light to be more real, more powerful, and much stronger than any illusions born from darkness can ever be; illusions of death and any other form of suffering and negativity won't have a hold over him if he remembers this liberating truth!

Loriolan closes his eyes to integrate Helios's words on the deepest possible level of his soul, all the while rushing through the skies towards the setting sun in the west with what feels like the speed of sound and light to them, dissolving in the rich inner vastness of his infinite soul.

CHAPTER 25

After what seems like just a moment in time, the chariot comes to a swooshing halt, with the sea horses turning sideways, causing a huge water wave to thunder through the Straits of Gibraltar. Crews of ships that dared to cross the Straits feel a storm wave coming at them, toppling several vessels over and causing them to eventually ram into rocks or other ships, resulting in many shipwrecks and much confusion. Anger and frustration grip the seamen crews, with many cursing the Ocean God Poseidon as their hated archenemy and condemned foe while trying to swim or drift to the nearest land mass.

With a cheery laugh, the two charioteers announce the arrival at the promised destination, indicating to the passengers that it is time to get off the chariot and continue on with their journey on their own. Slightly dazed, the three friends dismount the chariot, thank the charioteers for the beautiful and swift ride, and are about ready to sink their bodies into the cool water when the charioteers give them a warning, advising them to take heed of these treacherous waters that are quite narrow at a certain point of the passage and which have sailors and pirates of all kinds roaming these waters in violent pursuits of their own selfish interests. They say that armadas and galleys are frequently seen crossing the two continents and that Poseidon has made this stretch of sea his personal pet project to destroy as many of these ill-intentioned sea-folk as he possibly can, to wipe out the evil and restore peace to the undersea world. They convey that after Poseidon's interest in and dominion over this once thriving seaport-center at the intersection of the Mediterranean Sea and the Atlantic Ocean began to subside under the destructive influences of an endless, agonizing war and under the arrogance and decadence of its residing people, he unleashed natural disasters of such gigantic proportions on the area that they actually sank one of the three major port cities under the water, which was never to be seen again. Having invested much of his time and effort to turn this water crossing into the affluent and prosperous commerce and trade center it had become, considering his trident a proud symbol of his governance over these three splendid cities, Poseidon grew increasingly disappointed with the human race and felt it was time to teach them a lesson or two about losing their gratitude and respect for the one God who cared enough to make a difference in their pitiful lives, and without whom this commercial and cultural haven would have never existed.

The mermen gulp down their surprise. Poseidon seems more awesome and terrifying with every piece of information they receive about him.

At last, the charioteers make the three mermen aware of the fact that a lot of fishing not only for small fish, but also for big fish is going on here, and therefore, they suggest for the three of them to stay within the central currents of the Straits as much as possible and to stay out of any ship's and galley's way, for they make it their sport to go after everything that looks like a good catch for them. "You don't want to end up on someone's food plate," one of the charioteers shouts. Then they wave good-bye, and the chariot lifts off, describing a half circle in the sky before turning towards the darker eastern horizon, vanishing into the dark like a point losing itself in the canvas of an overwhelmingly dark image.

Alarmed, the three mermen sink to the ocean floor, trying to stay as deep down under the water surface as they possibly can, the mentioned warning of possible dangers still ringing in their ears. Carefully looking around to gauge the waters for any evidence of danger, they move forward with slow motion. They decide that it is wise to swim through the Straits as straightforwardly as possible without trying to find a resting place, which none of them feels a need for anyway, still feeling pumped up by the magical drink Rhode gifted them. And so they move forward, mile upon mile, occasionally witnessing parts of destroyed ships either lying on the ocean floor or still sinking slowly to the ground. They also perceive groups of human individuals paddling to not drown, struggling to hold on to drifting wood, trying to float on the broken pieces and boards closer to the safety of the land or hoping to be fished out by one of their peer ships that was fortunate enough to escape the annihilating force of the tsunami wave. The three mermen feel trepidation observing the anguish all around them and have a hard time acknowledging that their chariot has caused so much damage to the sea people, and as much as they liked spending time with Rhode and her entourage, they also don't understand how Poseidon could be so unforgiving as to punish so many innocent people with his mighty oceanic wrath and storms. And the more they see shipwrecked people trying to frantically save their lives, the more they are overcome by a bad conscience and a growing sense of guilt. Quietly they glide through the waters, trying to swim around and look the other way any time another misfortune presents itself in their way.

But then a familiar sound of great anguish finds its way to their ears, prompting them all to stand still and try to locate the source of this whining and screaming of much inner torture. And like a bolt, it dawns on them: a dolphin is screaming out in anguish, for it was caught by raiders of the sea and oceans. The three mermen look at each other, puzzled as to what to do next. Should they ignore the cry for help and leave one of their underwater friends captured in the hands of thieves and murderers, or should they do the right thing and go after whoever dares to disrupt the peace of the oceans in the cruel and dispassionate fashion that they display? A moment of indecisiveness leaves them tarrying in a state of paralysis. The charioteers warned them explicitly to stay deep below the surface and get through the Straits as quickly and invisibly as possible, but who has the heart to leave a friend to his certain death? With a sigh of deepest concern, they all simultaneously turn towards the source of all this anguish and, slowly at first, begin to quickly increase their speed with which they rush to the victim's rescue, hoping it is not too late to still save a member of one of their favorite and friendliest species from his demise.

On their way to the captured dolphin, they have to apply increasingly sophisticated tactics to evade the many humans that roam the waters either still on ship or stranded in the waters. Soon they espy the big vessel that has a large net dragging behind its rear end, full of fish of all sizes and with a young dolphin trapped in it, fidgeting amongst the prey that he obviously had tried to free in the first place, much to his own misfortune. Now the net is being reeled in, and the seamen are trying to haul the fish onto the ship's deck, laughing heartily at the unusual and great catch they were fortunate enough to garner from the ocean as a trophy in addition to all the small fish they usually bring home.

The mermen look at each other, disgusted with the scene, and begin to thrust themselves with full force onto the net, trying to tear it apart, all pulling together to create a hole big enough for the dolphin and the fish to escape. But the fishermen are a vigilant pack, and when they notice their net being tampered with by what looks like a bunch of fishtailed men, without hesitating, they begin to thrust their spears and harpoons full force at them. The dolphin and most of the fish escape, but Torilander gets hit by a harpoon that penetrates deep into his tail, causing the wound to bleed all over the place. Loriolan and Chekilian duck as the weapons keep coming at them. Another net is thrown out, catching Torilander in it. He is unable to free himself, and the pain causes him to collapse into a semicoma. Lifeless, he lies in the net, his body all rolled up and curved by the momentum. The fishermen hastily reel him in, doing everything in their power to not let this one escape as well. Loriolan and Chekilian swim up as soon as the spear throws lessen in frequency and intensity, eager and ready to help Torilander, trying hard to tear the net apart again and keep encouraging their unconscious companion. But the fishermen are fierce, and every available man has come to join the effort; spears and harpoons continue to be thrown, and soon the net is lifted onto the deck, revealing a fishtailed man, something none of the fishermen has ever laid eyes on before. They agree that this is a special catch and that they will receive quite a good amount of gold coins for it. Happy with their day's work — they caught several nets full of fish and now this fortunate catch — they decide to immediately return to shore and get this specimen the kind of help it needs to recover from its injuries so it can be sold off at a phenomenal price to the highest bidder, and better be worth every penny of it!

In the interior of the ship, the slaves are whipped to stay in tune with the beat of the drummer, who increasingly raises the speed of his drum beats per minute to collectively achieve a faster speed for the vessel, because today the captain of the vessel, Alexandro De Gonzales, slave trader and fisherman, is eager to get ashore and take care of a bit of unusual business.

Loriolan and Chekilian feel forced to stay underwater since the spears — and now also arrows — are still targeting them, forcing them to stay at a safe distance, causing them to desperately try and follow the ship that annoyingly keeps gaining momentum with every minute, leaving the two mermen breathless from all this shock and stress. The thought they could lose Torilander to these harsh sea-folk is more than they can bear, and with all the power they have they race after the ship, desperately trying to figure out a plan to still rescue their beloved friend and brother from the evil clutches of these cruel predators.

The ship enters the Phoenician harbor of Tange, lowers and fastens its anchor, and spills out its captain, crew members, and finally its chained slaves, to pursue business on land and get ready for the next morning, another day of hunting and fishing the beasts of the sea. Captain Alexandro is quite satisfied with himself today! He has heard of these mermen but has never seen one; until now he actually thought they were just a myth, and to finally have caught one makes his arrogant chest swell with incredible pride. He can't wait to see the faces of his business competitors, all ruffians themselves, who will be easily impressed with this kind of lucky prey! He hopes that the merman will be okay for tomorrow's slave market, where he intends to impress the nobility of the city and make them compete with each other for such a remarkable half animal. He grins broadly at this lucrative idea and quickens his gait to get to the tavern and boast about his booty.

Loriolan and Chekilian witness the still unconscious Torilander being carried onto land and wheeled away in a cart by a few strong men. Their hearts sink in agony and pain as their beloved friend and brother vanishes in front of their eyes without them being able to help him! Tears roll down their cheeks as they try to hide out behind other anchored vessels, intent on watching every move that's going on around the cursed vessel whose crew injured and kidnapped their brother. Chekilian bends over with pain, ready to collapse into a coma himself. Loriolan tries to stay strong for the both of them, but even he feels like caving in and giving up. Into what hopeless situation has life thrust them all of a sudden? One minute they dwell in bliss land and the next minute they are trying to hold on to life, having to watch their brother being hurt and torn away from them in front of their eyes. Both mermen need to take a moment to weep and mourn and to digest what just happened to them. Their threesome has all of a sudden been reduced to a twosome. That was not the plan! Loriolan feels at total odds with the Gods right now. He feels he doesn't want to go on without his friend. There is no purpose to life if you lose a loved one, your best friend! Why does life have to be so cruel?

And so the two of them cry their soul out behind the protective shield of a vessel. But then someone espies their presence and shouts across the harbor for others to detect what he just beheld. The mermen rapidly escape into the open sea, trying to hold on to whatever little meaning life still has for them.

Finally they stop, leaning against an old rock as if to conjure up its powers, desperately trying to find any help and support available to them. The two mermen can hardly look each other into the eye. Loriolan feels terribly responsible for Torilander's cruel fate, for if it weren't for his stupid quest, his dearest friend would still be by his side, the buddy he has known since childhood, since forever! Chekilian is hardly able to utter a word, that's how numb he is from pain. And so they spend what seems like an eternity in hell, waiting for the night to advance so they can return to the harbor without being seen so easily. But the emotional abyss is so endlessly deep that neither one of them can comfort the other; a dark cloud has descended on them with no end to the all-devouring darkness in sight. They just hope that by some miracle the seamen will cast Torilander back into the sea, giving him back his freedom, his right to exist in the playful, innocent ways they all have known and taken for granted for so long!

Wrestling with the decision for the right timing for their swim back to the world of horror, torn between wanting to find out about Torilander's fate and seeing whether they can still help him, and the dangerous fact that the humans' curiosity and search for the other two mermen might still be going on in the harbor — now that they know there still are two more of these water beings out in the sea, and probably close by, as they presumably would want to be close to their injured and captured friend — all these contradicting reasons feel like a paralyzing burden on their souls right now. But at some point, they can't remain still any longer and carefully begin to approach the harbor area where, to their relief, the hustle and bustle has died off to a large extent. Quietly, they swim towards the marina, trying to distinguish in the dark where any possible danger could still be lurking. They decide to try and find a more agreeable human being who could hopefully be won over to their side by offering him any of their humble possessions, like Loriolan's dagger, for example, which he regrettably couldn't pull from his backpack in time to cut through the thick net that dragged Torilander's collapsed body away at the end. But if this dagger could now buy them a piece of information or even any kind of help from a human, then it would have at least served some purpose in this horrendous misadventure. With a slight glimmer of hope, the two of them cower anxiously underneath the posts of a dock, scanning intently through the dark in the hope of some luck.

After what seems like an eternity, a young man draws closer, sweeping the dirt off the boards of the dock and into the water. Chekilian looks at Loriolan as if to indicate this guy might be worth a try. Loriolan nods, then quietly whistles for the man. It takes a few whistles, but then the young worker stops to look around, wondering about the sounds he just heard. Loriolan makes himself known in an even stronger way, calling out for the man to take a look down at the water. Which he does! And to his surprise, he sees two men in the water who seem to want something from him.

"Hey, what's up?" he inquires, a bit confused as to why they are trying to hide.

"A big calamity just happened to our brother!" Loriolan conveys. "He was caught at sea, injured by a spear, and dragged onto land. And now we don't know where he is!" Despair rings from his voice, as Loriolan tries to enlist this man's help. "We were hoping you could help us!"

"Why? Are you wanted criminals or something?" the lad asks, taking a few steps backwards.

"Not at all!" Loriolan continues. "We just can't get on land!" He shows his tail, which the man has a hard time making out in the dark. But once he sees it, he lets out a shout of surprise. Loriolan asks him to hush up, lest he attract attention that could cost them their lives, as it might already have for their brother.

The man regains his composure, then draws closer to take a better look at these strange creatures. "Are you the kind of mermen that our legends are made of?" he wonders out loud. "That would be awesome! I bet whoever caught your brother will make a bunch of money on the market with a mystical creature like you!" He seems to enjoy this realization, but when he notices Loriolan's and Chekilian's stern and somber faces, he immediately shuts up.

"We need to find out what they intend to do with our brother and whether there is any way to rescue him from his captors!" Loriolan's eyes express pain and hope, causing the young man to take some interest in their plight.

"What's in it for me?" he asks, holding his hand out, as if to collect his payment upfront.

Loriolan holds up his dagger, a gift from his father, richly decorated with aquamarine and crystals. The man takes a good look at it, then tries to take it. Loriolan, however, withdraws it: "First tell us what you can do for us!" he implores.

The man looks at him, puzzled. Then he thinks for a moment and suggests: "I could go to the tavern 'Joys of Pan' and listen to what the captain of the last incoming ship has to disperse to all the other drunkards. That would be a good start, don't you think?" And upon seeing Loriolan and Chekilian's helpless faces, he trumpets loudly: "Or I could just call right now and have someone catch you and sell you off as well. You would make a good profit! And I would probably get a few coins off you as well!" He stares at them with a face expressing teasing and blackmail at the same time.

The mermen ask him to please stay quiet and make him understand that they would be long gone before anyone could lay their eyes on them, and then he would stand there as a liar. That seems to shut the young man up once more. With an air of generous concession, he comes closer to convey his acceptance of the deal. "Okay, so I go and find out what I can for you guys, and then I get this dagger, right?"

Loriolan nods: "Right!"

"Well, then let me see what I can do!" the guy says, then turns to walk off the dock.

"And don't try to trick us!" Chekilian shouts after him, not in the mood for more treacherous behavior. "We'll wait somewhere else, and if we see anyone but you approaching, you won't see us at all anymore!"

"Understood!" With a grin on his face, the guy turns around and waves his hand.

The two mermen shrug their shoulders. They have no other choice but to trust this man they randomly picked. That's all they are able to do at this moment. Their limitations in regard to being able to function on land have never been as much of a problem as right now. They curse the fact that there even are two worlds that exclude each other's races from crossing into each other's native sphere, and they curse the captain and his crew from the ship that destroyed their wellbeing in such a nasty and underhanded way. Who do these kinds of people think they are capturing creatures from the sea for their consumption and sport! What cruel hearts and minds go after innocent, helpless beings, kill them, and devour them like carnivores, unable to notice the pain they cause and unable to experience the interconnectedness of all living beings and phenomena, which ultimately is just an expression of their own extended self?

"These numskulls don't even realize that they shoot themselves in their own chests, and cut off their own heads by inflicting it on others," Loriolan states, agitated. "Time gives them the illusion that violating behavior doesn't matter and that they can get away with any destructive behavior, killing life and being killed by it in the end, only because their ignorance forbids them to see beyond the limitations of their own perceptions, unaware that retribution comes unavoidably to those who earned it but who don't necessarily like to expect and count on it, sometimes being impacted in puzzling ways within either the present lifetime or in the afterlife or the next life. But what they sow, they harvest, and what they try to avoid, they certainly will have to face!" He lowers his gaze, weeping silently. "But what does this realization help right now! The moment seems to belong to the most unscrupulous and to the most selfish!"

Chekilian touches his shoulder, a gentle sign of his solidarity. Loriolan quickly clasps his hand on Chekilian's, trying to hold on to his loving gesture as if deeply grateful for his forgiveness and continued love for him, even in the face of having jeopardized and lost Chekilian's brother in this whole mad quest on which he lured them. Both feel close to crying, and both try hard to not be overcome by deepest grief.

They decide to move to another area, trying to be patient and wait it out against all their inner pain and futile promptings to do more than they are capable of doing. After what seems like an eternally long time, sometime after midnight, it seems, the young man returns. He whistles softly, and the two mermen gingerly approach from their hideout.

"Okay, so this is the story!" the man begins to speak. "Captain Alexandro De Gonzales, a ruthless old sea bear, just boasted to all the traders and drunkards in the tavern about his unusual catch today. Everyone had a hard time believing him, but he told them they will see with their own eyes at tomorrow's slave market what he has a hard time describing, because until he caught that fish of a man, he also didn't believe that such a mystical creature still exists in these waters anymore." The young man goes on to tell the mermen that their brother was the talk of the tavern, and word is quickly spreading around the whole city that tomorrow's slave trade will have a unicum up for auction, and whosoever wants to be his proud owner better be there with a full pouch. He says that Alexandro already received several offers for the merman, provided that the captain was telling the truth and not exaggerating to make himself important, like he is known to do to some extent. "But …" the young man laughs, "I know he is right, because here you are!" He points at them as if to assure himself that mystical creatures like these really exist, and he is lucky to have seen them with his own eyes.

"Yeah, yeah," Loriolan has heard enough of this sensationalistic talk and asks the man whether he was able to find out where their brother might be held and, if so, whether he can think of a way to get in and free him. The man shakes his head to both questions. He says that the captain has a group of guards that resembles an army in itself, watching over his prey, livestock, and slaves. In his opinion, it would be best for the two mermen to disappear from the harbor before the first light hits because everyone else is now aware of their existence and would like nothing more than to find and capture them as well.

That outlook feels pretty damn miserable and bleak for the mermen, who have a hard time resigning themselves to the possibility that they might never see their friend and brother again. So overwhelming is the pain written on their faces that the young man finally feels his heart protesting against his own indifference he has shown so far. With a changed tone of voice that reveals his upwelling sympathy, he begins to unload his own feelings of unease about the fate of the city of Tange since the days the giant Antaeus laid the foundation to it, and the hero Heracles left the area to fight against evil in other countries and city-states, like Arcadia, Crete, Corinth, and so forth. The lad lowers his head as he reflects on a sore event in the city's history: "Even though Heracles succumbed to Goddess Hera's black magical influence over him and killed his own wife and children in a fit of madness, he still had a good influence on this whole area and was an icon for peace and justice."

Loriolan and Chekilian look at him aghast. Who could kill his own wife and children and still be regarded as a hero?

The young man picks up on their puzzlement and continues to explain: "The power of the chief Goddess, Hera, is very strong; she cast a powerful spell on Heracles, as she had resentments towards him, being the illegitimate son of her husband, Zeus, and a mortal woman. Man, that Goddess must have been uncontrollably jealous to go after Heracles the way she did for all his life!" He rolls his eyes. "Anyway, after going into solitude for a while and sleeping in a cave nearby to get all powered up, Heracles began doing his penance, performing twelve supernatural labors he was charged with by his adversary King Eurystheos, Hera's champion, so the story goes. But before he left, Heracles remarried, the widow of Anteaus, to be exact, and their son, Sufax, is actually the one who improved things around here and built most of the city of Tange. But he withdrew from active duty a long time ago, and now the city is ruled by a group of evildoers. Much decadence has been taking over the city since then, with scum like Alexandro catering to the rich and privileged, who like nothing more than exotic distractions from foreign countries, slaves that please their every decadent, lecherous taste that doesn't even stop at the doors of the native young women and men of the city of Tange itself. Young, poor, and pretty women and men aren't safe in the streets anymore, for the decadent pleasure of the rich has usurped the city's wellbeing, causing many to disfigure themselves in a desperate attempt to look less attractive, or to simply leave town to find a life elsewhere.

Loriolan and Chekilian look aghast. What deeply disturbing facts is this man conveying to them here on the eve of their own horrendous misfortune. This news makes them feel even more hopeless and concerned for Torilander. How can they ever leave him to such bottomless evil? They start convulsing under the stress and pain they are under. What hellish place have the Gods placed them in, and how can Torilander ever be saved? Beaten and resigned, Loriolan hands his dagger to the young lad to pay him for his information. But a newfound decency in the man, caused by empathizing with the mermen's pain, prompts him to decline the dagger. "Don't get me wrong," he assures Loriolan, "it's a beautiful piece of art, and I could probably live off the gold I would very likely get for it for quite a long time, but you guys need to probably use it on your further adventures, and I don't want to steal from you more than you have already lost. So keep it!" He looks at them with an air of generosity.

"What's your name?" Loriolan wonders out loud.

"Neleus!" he answers, then begins to slowly walk away to continue the sweeping he had left undone.

"Thank you Neleus," Loriolan shouts after him, "thank you for standing out from among your kind and for showing us grace and mercy. You help us to not completely despair about the human race at this point. We won't forget your friendliness!"

"It's alright!" Neleus responds with a vague smile. "I wish I could have helped you more. But unfortunately, our city is run by evildoers and degenerates! Give me one of those …" he points at their tails, "and I would leave with you right now, if I could. But I have my mother to look after. So, off ye go!" he shouts at them encouragingly. "Don't let yourself be caught! It would be such a shame!"

"May I ask one more thing?" Loriolan asks. "Do you think this dagger could buy us the help of a guard or some other hero-like man who could help us free our brother?"

"I doubt it," Neleus thinks, "most of them are either afraid of Alexandro's vengeance or are corrupt beyond belief. They would take your dagger and still capture you on top of it. There is no loyalty to higher values in this place, just to lower-self urges. Unfortunately!"

"Then at least let us check in with you tomorrow!" Loriolan insists. "Would you please do us the favor and find out whether our brother — his name is Torilander — survived his wound okay, and also who might be buying him on tomorrow's market." This thought makes Loriolan and Chekilian sad beyond measure. Their eyes wet from tears, they look at Neleus imploringly.

Neleus looks at them, wondering about the compassion in his heart that just won't let go of him. "Yeah, I can do that. I will do that! Just meet me here tomorrow, late at night, after the noise has died down and the crowd has gone to sleep. … And by the way, what are your names?"

Loriolan and Chekilian call their names out to him, then thank him from their vulnerable hearts. With a clueless look at each other and with a heavy sigh, they finally glide into the deep water, reluctantly swimming away from the land that holds their precious brother captive, land, to say the truth, they harbor a tremendous amount of resentment against at this very point.

CHAPTER 26

Drowning in the oceans of melancholy, the two mermen lean against a rock and look up through the dark water, wondering whether any God is aware of their plight and suffering and whether anyone of the Great and Powerful Ones would ever care enough to help them.

Loriolan remembers Helios's words to him just a few hours ago and wonders how quickly any kind of blissful feeling can turn around and thrust the unsuspecting, guileless soul into the bottomless pit of utter despair. What an unmerciful ride between gifts of highest bliss and sacrifices of the most terrifying nature, between hope for the highest and loftiest goals a merman can aspire to and the harrowing experience of absolute hopelessness, defeat, and loss! "Why?" his heart cries out, why has this calamity happened to them? So early in their journey, so unpredictably and suddenly, and so hideously sprung on them that all they could do was helplessly watch their brother being hauled away by robbers and life violators, mercilessly left to their feelings of impotence and humiliating powerlessness, unable to come up with a reasonable plan that would make any sense and would have the power to turn the situation around and to their advantage again. But unfortunately, there doesn't seem to be one shred of evidence that such coveted miracle could ever occur. Loriolan feels rage welling up and, with all the strength he has, punches his fist on the rock, as if trying to get someone's attention. Chekilian looks at him from under his wet eyes; sadly, he shakes his head, as if conveying that this rage won't help their situation either. And so the two companions fall into a doze-like sleep, each hurting in their own painful way, writhing and tossing around as if trying to escape the intensity of the feelings this loss causes them.

Whenever he wakes from this restless, nightmarish sleep, Loriolan prays to Poseidon and Helios as if his life depends on it. And slowly, the rage and anguish yield to a feeling of insistence that the Divine Beings must help and need to send their messengers out to create the miracle that Loriolan and Chekilian can't come up with on their own. Help from the highest source of life is required, and Loriolan is intent to bend the All Powerful to his will. But the hours pass, and nothing of any significance happens; instead, the restlessness increases continuously as the day begins to dawn, and a huge emptiness is felt amongst their midst. Torilander's laugh and friendliness is missed by both mermen very deeply, and the pain emerges again full force. Trepidation about what the day and night will bring hangs between them. They feel like swimming up to the harbor, hoping to get a glimpse of Torilander or Neleus or just catching any piece of information that could give them a hint as to whatever fate has befallen Torilander. They just can't stand the thought and feeling of being so far away from their beloved brother, and so they overcome whatever hesitation and little resistance they have towards the idea and carefully begin to approach the harbor.

Ships and galleys go in and out of the port. There is a lot of unloading and loading going on, and a large crowd of traders, porters, and other simple workers are all running around, noisy, busy, and preoccupied. Loriolan and Chekilian find a safe hiding place behind a big, empty sailboat and begin to watch the hustle and bustle with tense eyes and mind, hoping to find an opening that could allow them to somehow find a solution to their problem. But then they see several guards walking up the dock strenuously scanning the waters as if they are looking for something. "They are looking for us!" runs through the mermen's minds. And as quickly and quietly as they can, they sink further down into the water and dive as deeply as possible to escape the sharp, radar-like eyes of the searching guards.

And so the two forlorn souls are forced to tough it out at a far distance from the shore, observing from afar how greedily the guards keep looking for another one of these precious finds so their master can amass more of those precious coins that seem to turn certain humans into abhorrent, selfish monsters.

The day passes by in great anguish for the two lonesome mermen, making them long every single agonizing minute of it for their friend they cannot bring back. At some point, Loriolan considers turning back and enlisting his father's help, but the thought brings terror to his heart. How could he possibly face Torilander's mother at this point, how could he ever explain to anyone how wrong he was to set off on this journey? These thoughts bring tears to his eyes again. Nothing will ever be the same! Instead of returning as a hero, as he so proudly boasted to everyone about, he would return a complete failure, with his head hanging, and his spirit faltered. So, unless he wants his journey to be over and his chance of ultimate happiness destroyed, he shouldn't even consider swimming back and getting everyone all riled up about Torilander's disappearance and the disturbing fact that he might get abused by his perpetrators. With a deep, sharp pain in his heart, Loriolan racks his brain as to what other solution there is to this seemingly dead-end situation.

Chekilian just lies on the ground, his body wrapped around the rock in a fetal position, strangely quiet, disconcertingly quiet as far as Loriolan is concerned. Loriolan starts to worry about him as well. He understands the grief, but in all this grieving, a plan must be devised if they don't want to die here on the spot. He begins to pace around, feverishly running all kinds of scenarios through his mind, but it all boils down to the unavoidable fact that they are mermen who cannot just walk onto land and go rescue Torilander, nor do they possess many valuables with which they could buy any relatively decent man to do their job and try to free Torilander for them. It feels to Loriolan as if this situation just wants to stay unsolvable, and the mercy of the Gods is not raining down on them either. And so it seems that the only alternatives are to either give up and return home to be the freak sensation of all times, the antihero, who will have a hard time winning anyone's respect for his alleged future job as a ruler — if that is even in the cards for him anymore — or to give up their spirits right here on the spot and thus try to atone for the now seeming irresponsibility that brought them into this horrendous situation or, last but not least, to move on if they can still muster the courage and strength after this incredible loss and all the devastating experiences around it. As much as he tries to make up his mind, he falters again and again, as if an evil spirit is trying to squash the life out of him completely. Loriolan sinks to the ground and falls into a fetal position himself, trying to hold on to his sanity and locate a glimmer of hope within himself, as faint and as weak as it might be, for right now all he feels is the desire to die and be done with all the pain and suffering. How he longs for someone strong to swim up to him right now and assure him that all will be well and that Torilander will be with them once more. He prays fervently that Torilander is being taken good care of and that he will be released and set free as quickly as possible! Loriolan's mind begins to drift in and out of realities. He can't decide which reality feels more nightmarish, his dreams or his wakeful state; all he feels is the urge to escape and forget!

After what seems like an eternity in purgatory hell, Loriolan is woken by Chekilian. He indicates that it is time to swim to the harbor and meet Neleus. With a jolt, Loriolan sits up, rubs his eyes, and nods his agreement. And again, the two of them begin their silent approach to the docks, painfully aware of every move they make so as to not cause any splashes and attract any unwanted attention from anyone.

Soon they hear Neleus's familiar voice quietly calling out their names. Loriolan and Chekilian assure themselves that Neleus is indeed alone, then come out from behind the ship where they were hiding. Neleus greets them with an apologetic and worrisome look. "I'm afraid I don't have good news for you guys. I'm sorry to say this, but your brother has been sold off to the King of Carthage, one of the wealthiest and most influential rulers of the Phoenician Empire. This bargain was arranged even throughout last night, without Torilander appearing on the slave market today, simply because your kind seems to cause quite a stir among our kind, making us wonder and guess about your species and way of life, and the mer-kingdom you all must come from!" He pauses reflectively, then continues: "He is being brought, as we speak, eastward on the Mediterranean Sea shore bordering our large continent, to the city of Carthage, a city many of us poor souls here can only dream about because of its unimaginable splendor and riches."

"What will they do to him?" Chekilian asks, upset. "Will they put him into an arena for everyone to look at, or what?"

"I really don't know what the King will do with him, but from all the choices, I think Torilander is in luck to have found a more intelligent and sophisticated owner, who probably will let him be himself more than other rather decadent and selfish owners might have allowed him to be."

The mermen still aren't pleased with the situation. The idea of owning another living being just sounds strange and arrogant to them, especially when it is the member of a different race.

"How are they taking him, by water, or by land?" Loriolan inquires.

"That I'm not sure of," Neleus responds. "I was only able to get so much information out of one of the guards without making him suspicious as to why I'm so curious. I'm sure they must treat him like a rare treasure and guard him well. But I would assume they took him by ship; nevertheless, to try to locate him at this point is like looking for a needle in a haystack. The guard says that one of the King's tradesmen happened to be in town on royal business when he heard Alexandro boasting about his unique catch, and the deal was sealed quickly, to everyone's satisfaction."

"He is being transported back all the way to the East!" Loriolan gives off a sigh of frustration. "That's all the way back to where we came from, and then some more!" He holds his hand to his head, as if trying to not faint from this bad news and the futility of it all. Chekilian looks at him with an empty look. What does this mean for them now? Are they to go back all the way and forget about Loriolan's journey? And how would they make it into the King's palace anyway? Should they go home and enlist everyone's help? But what can King Hadores possibly affect in the end; how in the world would he free Chekilian's brother from a human stronghold? For hundreds of years, the mer-kingdoms have not communicated with the human world anymore, and Poseidon's condemning curse on them has not helped their contact and cooperation amongst each other at all on top of that.

With a raise of their hands, the two mermen take their leave from Neleus, thanking him again for being their eyes and ears on land, then head out into the deep waters, ready to recoup and come up with a workable plan.

Chapter 27

*C*owering next to their chosen rock, Chekilian and Loriolan discuss their limited options, none of which are sounding good or are making them feel as enthusiastic about life as they felt at the very beginning of their journey when Torilander was still with them, supporting them with his quiet, serene, and strong way and heart. To stay and simply die off is not an option anymore now that they know the fate of Torilander, and at the least, they should try to let his parents know where his harsh, unjust fate has placed him, leaving it up to them to decide how to proceed or whether to proceed at all. Loriolan doesn't particularly like this option because this whole disastrous trip and his unfortunate love for a human woman would probably — for the rest of his life — be blamed for this incredible calamity that has put his best friend's life in danger, and if not blamed overtly, then most certainly covertly. Also, he absolutely couldn't live with himself, knowing that his friend gave up his life as a free merman for nothing, suffering his imprisonment for no purpose at all. He remembers how intent Torilander was to come along on this journey, because he deeply believed in Loriolan and in the feelings of true love he harbors for Indirali. It was as if Loriolan's love for Indirali inspired his friend to hold out for his own eternal love, which he seemed to have found in Indirali's maidservant, Hedna. One day, Loriolan was hoping to ask Indirali for Hedna's hand in marriage to Torilander, hoping for the two of them to be as happy as he and Indirali are when they are in each other's company. But what is going to happen to this beautiful picture of their common bright future if neither of the friends make it to the Heavens to meet their lovers, to the transcendental realms from where fulfilling lives are created, and the lovers' victory could win their respective earthly and oceanic worlds over to realizing the long-lasting peace and harmony that have been amiss from their lives for so long? The more Loriolan thinks about giving up, the more he feels compelled to do just the opposite and render their ill-begotten journey as successful as possible in the end. Who knows, maybe he can convince the Gods to free Torilander from his captivity once he enters the Heavens as one who has earned their respect and support by overcoming and mastering his deepest fears and issues along his challenging soul journey. This thought alone seems to have the power to fill Loriolan with much-needed strength and courage. Only when he thinks about moving on, and conquering whatever other dark challenges are in his way to complete mastery over this planet, moving towards the light that shines brightly on those who believe in it, able to free anyone from imposed bondage who retains the willpower and Divine alignment to win out over his adversaries and bad luck, only such kinds of bold and daring thoughts are capable of drawing the deepest motivation out of him and inspire him to become and be the victorious hero he craves so much to be, and thinks he owes it to his best friend to be.

And so, with a faint glimmer of hope flaring up in his vulnerable heart, Loriolan begins to tell Chekilian about his intention, how he wants to set things right, how he wants to honor Torilander by not giving up but rather succeeding in his mission and coming back to free him with the powers of the Gods, and with a body that knows no limitations anymore and that can walk through the doors of the human world, and reach Torilander, no matter where he is, to bring him safely home and thank him for his sacrifice that conjured the deepest willpower in Loriolan, jolting him into wanting to succeed at all costs so he can help his dear friend, who means so much to him.

Chekilian can't help but see the logic in this daring speech. And when Loriolan begins to suggest that he could accompany Chekilian back to Rhode's pleasure palace, where he most certainly could get a ride back home, Torilander's brother just wards off this well-meaning but superfluous suggestion because his mind is made up as well, and he wants to honor his brother by finishing the task they all set out to accomplish together. Who knows, maybe Loriolan is right, and with the Gods on their side, they can accomplish the miracle they don't seem to be able to muster at this very moment, namely to set his beloved brother free.

Loriolan is touched to tears by the loyalty he encounters from his best friend's brother, who also has been his best friend for as long as he can remember.

They both hug, as the thought of being victorious over this hopeless seeming situation fires up their wounded souls quite a bit, and then they begin to swim into the Atlantic Ocean, the sea that will lead them to the North Pole and, from there, into the deep interior of the Earth.

Still hurting from what just happened to them, they try to stay positive while moving ahead, gingerly looking forward to what is to come next and hoping life will treat them gently from now on, even though they already know that they are to confront their deepest fears and doubts along the way into the innermost core of the Earth. And as they swim along the currents, trying to navigate their every effort as intelligently as possible and in harmony with the laws of Nature and the currents, they pray to the Gods for their help and compassion, and for a sign that they made the right decision and are doing the right thing after all.

Soon they approach and behold the underwater ruins of the sunken city of Troy. Having been taught the history and cause of the destruction of one of the wealthiest cities of its time, Loriolan and Chekilian marvel at the uncanny aesthetics of the architecture and the expansive vistas surrounding countless impressive palace- and temple-like buildings, as much as all of this can be discerned from among the mountains of rubble and mud. There was a time, according to mer-people history, when humans and mer-people coexisted peacefully, able to cross over into each other's realms of existence, but this time is long gone, and the respect and reverence humans possessed towards the Sea Gods, and especially towards their main benefactor Poseidon, have unfortunately vanished with it. 'These ruins are just a sad memory now, a mausoleum reminiscent of the most desperate of times in both races' common past,' both mermen ponder melancholically, prompting them to swim faster so as to leave this unfortunate terrain as quickly as possible.

Many miles later, having left the ruins of Troy behind, a group of dolphins joins them. A mother dolphin thanks the mermen kindly for rescuing her baby from the death trap of the human raiders and tells them how they usually try to stay out of the humans' way as much as possible, and that means out of the Straits of Gibraltar altogether, where much human ship traffic is constantly going on. But unfortunately her baby wasn't fully aware of the guile and underhandedness of the fishermen and simply followed his compassionate heart that prompted him to sway from the safe path and follow the net traps, trying to help those caught little fish with which he loves to play and have fun.

Loriolan is happy to see the little dolphin okay and buoyantly jumping around, as if he was never captured and tormented. Speaking to her telepathically, he thanks the dolphin mother for her gratefulness and mentions to her how he and Chekilian lost their brother to these ferocious raiders and that there is nothing they can do about freeing him and getting him back. The dolphins are shocked to hear the bad news. They are greatly concerned about the merman who sacrificed his life for one of their own and begin to show compassion for the mermen's plight. After learning more about Loriolan's journey and goals, they offer their help in getting Loriolan and Chekilian across the Atlantic Ocean, at least to the shores of Britannica, beyond which the water becomes a bit too cold for them. But for several hundreds of miles they are happy to offer their transport services by allowing Chekilian and Loriolan to hold onto their fins and be carried through the waters with much ease and speed. They say this is the least they can do for the two travelers, who sacrificed their beloved travel companion in order to save their own precious baby.

Loriolan sadly smiles at them. The Gods seem to finally have answered their many prayers and have given them a sign of support, some much needed reassurance! What a strange and wondrous journey they are on, full of highest bliss and deepest despair, the whole range of emotions a living being is able to experience, hopefully without losing his sanity throughout it all! With a renewed sense of hope, Loriolan looks forward to what is to come, hoping he will be able to remedy all the problems he caused for Torilander and hoping that there is still a joyous life waiting for everyone at the end of the dark tunnel, a life of absolute fulfillment on all levels and in all of its areas! And so the journey continues, and the two mermen thrust all their courage and love for Torilander into the swimming that carries them closer towards the awaiting challenges, challenges that are to lead them through the darkness of hell and then all the way up into the brightest lights of Heaven.

Chapter 28

The morning mists sparkle gently on the grass and wildflower meadows that pass by Indirali's dreamy eyes, as she cozily sits next to Hedna and across from her father in the royal carriage, pulled by six select stallions from the King's finest breeding stables. Her thoughts drift back to those happy moments in the ocean waters when she would swim with Loriolan to their hearts' delight, feeling this indescribable joy and bliss that only the Gods seem to be able to experience for all of eternity, never having to separate from their eternal beloveds, never having to cross the ocean of abysmal sadness and pain of separation. Feeling misty-eyed herself, Indirali feels the mists of the meadows wondrously reflected in her own eyes and heart. Her longing for unification with her eternal beloved has her heart aching every waking moment, and the fact that she is now finally on her way to meet him in the Heavens of pure joy makes her feel reconciled with their unfortunate situation to some extent.

She actually had planned to leave the palace incognito, clad in simple garments, she and Hedna walking through the country's sites without anyone knowing it is her, the Princess of Lucania, who passes by them on her way to the Oracle of Atina. But her father — bless his caring heart — insisted on accompanying her and taking her in his carriage, persuading her by letting her know he, also, is seeking the Oracle's advice on matters of political and spiritual relevance. He said he was not very happy with the conversation they had with the temple's Priestess and clergy and that he hopes the Oracle can give him much-needed advice and direction for his business as the king and leader of his people, because he feels strangely let down by his own temple. And who is Indirali to refuse such a heartfelt offer to help, because the truth is, the faster she gets to where she wants to be, the better! She actually would like to race into Loriolan's arms right now, if only she could!

They left the palace at morning dawn, Indirali's mother all dissolved into tears but still wishing her child all the best of luck in the world, knowing that Goddess Aphrodite will look out for her beloved daughter as if she were her own and that Indirali will surely succeed in her mission and come back to her victorious! The travelers have been on the road for several hours now and still have a few hours ride ahead of them, with about thirty guards escorting them, and people on the fields and in the towns they pass through joyfully waving after the carriage, for it bears the King's emblem, and everyone loves their King who has managed to keep them out of war, despite threats at the kingdom's borders and much political pressure from the neighboring kingdoms.

Even though Atina is straight to the east from Posidonia, they need to take a detour around the Mount Albernus area, following the Sele River up north, then curving to the east to eventually drive along the Tanager River, which leads all the way down south to the small city of Atina. Not always is the river in plain sight, but others have gone before them and carved out the dirt road to make it a safe passage for those who follow it. But it is a challenge to drive the carriage along such a bumpy dirt road, and often the horses need to trot slowly and carefully to make it through some difficult and mountainous stretches. And so the carriage bounces along the forest path, trying to avoid deep potholes and rocks in order to deliver the precious passengers safely to their destination.

King Eurylochos smiles melancholically at his daughter. What unusual love affair has fate chosen for her, and what strangely challenging path still lies ahead of her?! He finds it hard to let her go off on her own, his fatherly heart unsure of how far his duties and responsibilities extend to her. He wants her to be safe and happy, and if he could, he would go on this journey with her or even do it for her. But he knows this irrational thinking and his fears of losing her to some unknown fate are making him extra careful and vigilant in guaranteeing she has the best start into her adventure that he can possibly provide for her.

Indirali answers with a sublime smile, then turns her head towards the window, as if to say good-bye to him on the soul level. She knows this trip is going to be her true coming-of-age ritual, the adventure that will make her a woman who can face any challenges in life on her own and thus be a tremendous source of support and inspiration to the man she loves and to whom she belongs. And so, it is time to let go of the custody and care of her parents towards her, as dear and as loving as they have always been to her, and no matter how much it hurts all of them to let go of each other in this heartwrenching way. She knows she wants to ultimately have her parents in her life again after she has found her own life's dharma and vocation, but for now they will have to let her go so she can find herself, her strengths and weaknesses, and master her own fears and doubts so she will earn and deserve the respect of the Gods and the everlasting love of her truly beloved, Loriolan, who is so much more than a mere merman — he is the man that will rock her life for all eternity with waves of unending bliss!

The trees are old and majestic, and Indirali feels strangely welcomed by their calm and soothing presence. It's as if they confirm her thoughts and feelings, conveying to her that everything will work out for as long as she trusts in the higher forces of life and for as long as she doesn't give up on her own inner guidance and clarity. These silent ambassadors of the deva kingdom embody goodness and strength, being rooted deeply in the earth, yet stretching their arms and branches into the vastness of the blue skies, a symbol of steadfastness and constancy and of unending life force abundantly flowing from their rich and nourishing auras, generously protecting whomsoever tries to find shelter and comfort under their majestic crowns and branches. Indirali feels deeply encouraged as to her own path, smilingly acknowledging the comforting influence these ancient tree spirits are able to give her. Like them, she wants to become a nourishing influence to her people, able to protect them from any potential harm and able to provide for them anything that is needed to see them continuously growing towards the light and bliss of higher existence.

Occasional rays of the late morning sun flicker through the green branches, brightening her face she holds out to feel the warmth and light of the Sun God, Helios. Having her eyes closed, she beholds a lively scene on the inner levels of her being and world, with fairies and elves dancing in the sunlight, weaving their magic and sparkling energy around the forest flowers and plants. Laughingly the graceful light beings interact with the serene and powerful tree spirits they are fortunate enough to have guarding their peaceful native environment and connecting them with the higher spheres of their common origin. Some of the fairies are aware of Indirali and curiously fly to approach her, hovering in midair, their wings beating lightly, to take a better look at a human who is still able to perceive them with her inner eye. When realizing Indirali's gentle, loving heart, they begin to smilingly interact with her, telling her all about their interesting lives and frequent celebrations with which they like to entertain themselves to everyone's delight. Indirali is enthralled with their joyous existence and would have liked to dwell in their world for a good while longer, but the carriage begins to slow down as the King has ordered to drive up to an inn along the road to rest from the ride and have some food.

Torn out of her inner worlds and interactions, Indirali looks around as if trying to come back to her worldly senses. The King says they are very close to Atina already, and a group of scouts have located a big farmhouse for them whose owner is happy to offer it to the King for the duration of their stay. After they have all had a good meal, he intends to drive to that farmhouse and prepare to meet the Oracle with his daughter. Indirali blinks her eyes; she sure is ready for this auspicious encounter! The inn is located within the deep of the forest, with a stable full of animals of all kinds and a big sign hanging over the entrance door saying, 'To the Old Boar'!

Indirali and Hedna look at each other, hoping the innkeeper won't serve boar meat to them but rather have fruit and some good fresh bread available, like the Princess prefers. This thought, however, makes Indirali realize that soon she won't have the privilege anymore of choosing the kind of food she wants to eat but will have to be content with whatever she can find. Nevertheless, for a long time now she has been objecting to eating animal meat. The thought of partaking of any living animal that has sensory organs and a face is just despicable to her and causes her stomach to convulse. Her infinite compassion for all living beings, whether small or big, mammal or not, prevents her from consuming what someone has killed in order to serve it up to those who are too inconsiderate and insensitive to notice they are hurting and violating a life in order to advance their own. She can never be part of such self-centered viewpoint and world, and for as long as she walks a planet where these life-killing procedures are justified as being okay, she considers herself as living in this world but not being of this world. She will always strive to outgrow the karmic mud that keeps this kind of subdued planet in spiritual ignorance and darkness, caught in the cycles of death and rebirth because of murderous instincts and actions or — in the case of vegetarians — of entrapment by subtle resonances with these realities that has them sharing a world of predators and prey, victimizers and victims. Indirali, therefore, can't wait to gain the powers of the Gods in order to be able to effect true and lasting change in all crucial affairs that can help the people of her and Loriolan's future kingdom to see the life-supporting Divine views and values in all of life, so they may prosper in ways known only throughout the most ancient and most enlightened of times.

The innkeeper and his wife come to greet the high visitors, deeply bowing to show their respect. The King's servants bring the luggage to their rooms, the best ones in the house, while the coachman unharnesses the horses to let them find much-needed rest from the long ride, leading them to the well and letting them feed on a large pile of hay. Several stable boys run to take the horses from the guards to take care of them and ready them for another stretch of their long journey. Relieved, the guards disperse about the property, trying to unwind from the long ride and stretching their limbs and muscles until the meal is prepared. Indirali and Hedna are escorted to their room while the King relaxes in the room across the hall. They agree to meet within the hour and have a good meal prepared for them. Indirali is happy to hear that the innkeeper's daughter has gathered a big bucket full of the most delicious berries and that bread will be fresh and ready for them as well. The King, however, still wants his roast and looks forward to some satisfying meal.

Servant maids immediately begin to bring kettles of hot water to fill the bath for Indirali to relax and unwind from the journey. Hedna arranges their belongings and, as soon as Indirali is ready to step into the bathtub, begins to attend to the wellbeing of her mistress, taking off her precious garment, then her golden headband, combing her long, beautiful hair and then pinning it up to keep it out of the water. This bath is only meant to help Indirali relax and is not a full bath. And so the hour passes quickly, and soon the maid knocks at the door to inform them of the meal waiting for them. Indirali is already in her new pretty garment, her hair nicely fixed, when she invites Hedna to take a quick plunge into the water as well just so she gets the stiffness out of her bones. Gratefully, Hedna removes her dress in a hurry, then splashes into the water to get as much fun and relaxation out of it as is possible in a moment's time. But both of them are ready in plenty of time since the King is not really in a hurry to see his daughter off, and the innkeeper couple deem themselves the luckiest people of the area today, being able to serve the King of the kingdom in their humble abode with the finest food and beverages they can come up with.

The inn is full with the King's guards, with only a few other guests sitting in a corner, respectfully leaving the King and his daughter the space and privacy they deserve. The guards are not their usual selves today while in the presence of the King but rather relinquish their normally more rough and unmannerly behavior to allow a subdued and respectful atmosphere to please the King and his daughter. Guests feeling overwhelmingly surprised that their King has shown up at the doorstep of this modest inn whisper behind their hands, quietly muttering what none dares to say out loud, namely that they can't believe their eyes to see the King so close up front and in such a humble environment as this.

The King and his daughter have an enjoyable time eating their hearty meal, conversing quietly about the remarkable circumstances that led up to this trip and about what they both intend to inquire of the Oracle, whom they hope will be exactly the kind of wise guide they both need for their continued life's journey. So relaxed and at peace is this small Royal Family group that everyone in the inn keeps indirectly staring at them from across the room, enthralled by the simplicity of their behavior and the beauty and nobility of their looks. When the time comes to bid farewell to the departing Royals, every single guest and every single staff member assembles in front of the inn to see their King off with all the love and respect they feel for him.

The guards are ready to take their positions, and Princess Indirali and her maidservant mount the carriage, as does King Eurylochos, only to show his face one more time to friendly wave his good-bye to the hospitable innkeeper family and their guests. Lycus, the innkeeper, thanks the King with another one of his reverent bows and invites him to come back at any time so he can serve him all the best food he has, and says that it has been an honor to serve him and his lovely daughter on this very special day that he will remember for the rest of his life. His wife agrees with him, and then everyone bursts into a triumphant shout of adoration that expresses once more their deep honor and respect for their King.

Then the carriage departs and leaves the little crowd at the inn wondering and excitedly recounting this memorable moment.

CHAPTER 29

The carriage arrives at the farmhouse in the early afternoon hours and is greeted enthusiastically by the owner, who couldn't resist meeting the King in person before joining his family at their neighbor's farmhouse, where they are able to occupy a comfortable little cabin for the time being. Overcome by awe, he leads one of the King's bodyguards around the house and property, hoping the King will find it an adequate accommodation and will be pleased with the moderate amenities. The bodyguard hands the man a richly filled pouch, which is gratefully accepted. The quarters are acceptable, and the King and Princess are led into the best rooms to wash off the dirt of the road and freshen up for their next little trip, which everyone knows will be by foot.

Aeschylus, the man who disclosed the Oracle's existence to Indirali, told the King and Princess that meeting the Oracle is an adventure in itself, as it requires a pure heart and lofty wish to even be able to open the inner gates that shield her paradisiacal dwelling place from the outsider. Many have tried to meet her, but only a few were able to enter into her forest sanctuary, for most go insane trying to penetrate the ring of darkness surrounding her heavenly abode like the hells of Tartarus keeping the uninvited from trespassing into the lightness and joys of the Elysian Fields. On the other hand, he conveyed, the Oracle graciously appears to those who need her healing powers, often materializing from the invisible realms right into that person's home to all of a sudden be ready to lend her helping hand and cure the patient from an incurable condition in just a matter of moments. She would thus only appear to those who turn to her in fervent prayer, willing to put their selfish traits aside and allow the Divine Source to determine whether they are ready and deserving of the Oracle's magical help and powers. Sometimes she even assists those who have been overwhelmed by the negative traits of an oppressive individual, be it losing their house and possessions to his greedy and stealing nature or being subjected to any kind of oppressive and violent behavior from any kind of perpetrator. She is, therefore, also known as a representation of the Goddess Aphrodite, whose far-reaching ability to protect, nourish, and heal has won her many faithful followers, who sometimes come all the way from faraway locations and kingdoms to gain her favors and help.

Upon hearing such wondrous and amazing news, the King was speechless as to his own ignorance about her existence and found it even more important and pressing to meet such an elevated being, who has been existing outside his conscious radar for all these many years within his kingdom, not even that far from the main Grand Palace of his several palatial residences. He found it increasingly timely and necessary to meet the Oracle not just for his daughter's sake but also for the sake of his kingdom's future. If his temple can't steer the spiritual fate of the kingdom in such a way that prosperity and peace are growing and expanding, and if he can't find inner support from his priesthood on crucial matters, then it is time to turn to the Gods directly and receive their support from a source other than the one he has gotten used to and has relied on for too long, it seems. His mind is, therefore, made up, and after some refreshing, he eagerly begins with the preparations for the trip. Suddenly every moment in time counts for him, now that his daughter is inspiring and impressing him with her resolution and willingness to confront whatever it takes to overcome any and all obstacles in her way in order to realize her highest dharma and vocation to unite with her eternal lover. Yes, King Eurylochos is quite speechless at his daughter's transformational influence on him, and even though he doesn't speak about it to anyone — he still needs to come across as the steadfast, most reliable pillar of political responsibility to his kingdom's citizens — inwardly, he is grappling with the importance of his daughter going off on her own self-discovery journey, and him having to decide whether to stay put in the stagnation and looming deterioration of the status quo or to follow her daring example and begin to outgrow the status quo, ready to face his own inner demons that have held him in a prison-like state for too long, hindering him to invite and attract the kind of positive and prosperous destiny he would like his kingdom to have.

Father and daughter meet after an hour of refreshment, ready to set out on their walk they intend to take without anyone else accompanying them, afraid no one else they might bring along would be able to pass through the thick protective layer around the Oracle's abode and might thus go insane for trying. Even if King Eurylochos still has some slight doubts and reservations about the accuracy of Aeschylus' account, he would not want to compromise the mental health of any of his subjects unnecessarily. And so they walk side by side, clad in rustic garments that allow them to cut through the thick underbrush where necessary without having their precious clothes torn from the many thorns and prickles along the way. The King uses a wooden staff to support his gait, fondly remembering his youthful days when he loved to explore the forests and meadows around the palace of his parents. The fresh forest air and the physical movement put him into a good mood, with him deeply inhaling the pine and cedar aromas and feeling like he is finally coming back to his senses after a long time of living like a hermit in his own palace, surrounded by people who never get to see the real him. It feels like a crust of artificiality is falling off him, and a newfound carefree spirit emerges, enjoying wholeheartedly the wonderful company of his daughter and the refreshing atmosphere of the forest. For a moment, he can forget his many burdens and obligations and dedicate himself completely to the happiness and lightness of the moment. Oh, how wonderful life can be, and how restorative to the spirit, mind, and body Nature can be, with its abundance and infinite array of magnificent plant life species as well as many endearing varieties of animals that inhabit and roam the forest to their hearts' content. Frolicking birds and mysterious sounding eagle owls hooting in the distance all add to the wonderfully restorative and enlivening nature of the environment, and the King wishes this walk would never end. The only thing to complete the bliss of this experience would be to have his wife here with them wandering in the woods, as if leaving the sorrows of the world behind and trying to find entrance to the Heavens of a better world. The King is ready to be transformed and wishes nothing more than to return from this experience a changed and better man and ruler, able to turn the fate and negative trends of his kingdom around for the wellbeing of all his people.

Indirali smiles at her father, for she has hardly seen him so carefree and joyful as he is right now. He jokes with her, and they both laugh heartily, and the birds — it seems — laugh and joke with them. A big bubble of bliss forms around them, and it seems as if Nature parts and opens up to them at every step of the way, letting them pass into the deepest interior of the forest without them having to fight their way into it, without fighting their own inner limitations and boundaries, the joy functioning like a key to a higher, more fulfilling reality zone. Already they have come farther than many people have penetrated into the forest before; the trees seem to step out of their way to let them soar on the clouds of happiness towards the celestial dwelling place of the Oracle.

Then they arrive at the stream Aeschylus made them aware of, and which they have to cross if they want to make it to the Oracle. There are natural boulders within the water already, and someone has placed a few bigger rocks between some of them to create a bridge of sorts that allows the hiker to jump from stone to stone in an attempt to make it to the other shore. It looks a bit daunting, but Indirali assures her father she is up for it, and together they begin the crossing, with the King leading the way, then holding his hand out to catch his daughter's hand and help her with her jump and balance. They do fine; only once does Indirali get her foot wet, but she shakes off the water and laughs at her father, indicating there is no harm done. And so they get the job done, arriving safely on the other shore to continue their walk. From here on out, however, the terrain gets wilder and more mountainous. Thick underbrush greets them at every step, and it takes their whole attention and effort to climb the increasingly steeper slope of a mountain. They follow a winding path that often has them wondering where to go next because not many seem to have trodden on it before them. Soon the both of them find themselves out of breath and need to take a break more frequently. But when they turn to look back across the vast landscape underneath them, they can't help but marvel at the beauty and serenity of the area and become increasingly exhilarated by the whole experience.

Soon they reach a plateau that leads them once more into the interior of a forest, only this time the forest is situated in a valley surrounded by high mountains with creeks gushing from them, adding to the rich and lush flora that has both of them amazed and in high spirits. They gradually descend into the valley and into the forest, and for some inexplicable reason, their mood begins to shift with every step down from their hillside vantage point, slowly overshadowing their spirits and making them feel increasingly frustrated with the overwhelming underbrush they have to cut and fight through at every step. The birds have stopped singing or have all disappeared, and in their stead, endless swarms of biting insects have appeared out of nowhere, falling all over their bodies and inflicting painfully itching bites that have them both scratching and cussing incessantly. What seemed funny or elevating a moment ago now just triggers the opposite of their emotional range, rendering them helpless as to how to turn the situation around again. With every step into the interior of the forest, the King and Princess fall prey to their deepest, most negative emotions, starting to make them doubt as to why they have come all the way here in the first place and almost cursing Aeschylus for sending them on this wild-goose chase. Because all that greets them is the harshness of a wild, untamed Nature ready to thwart their efforts at every turn and forcing them to stop in their tracks every time a thorny branch hits them in the face, causing bloody wounds to their faces and tearing their clothes apart so they begin to look like paupers and madmen. Feeling triggered in his sense of fatherly responsibility to protect his daughter from harm of any kind, the King begins to seriously consider turning around and insisting his daughter come with him. But as soon as Indirali hears her father expressing his innermost doubts and frustrations out loud to her, her higher nature kicks in again helping her to remember why she is here in the first place and how her love for Loriolan enables her to walk through any kind of challenge and tribulation along the path, and so she overtly resists the idea, trying to make her father see reason and not jeopardize their chance of meeting the Oracle now that they have come this far. Her adamant speech jolts her father out of his complacency with which he has allowed himself to fall into a negative mindset and become a liability to his daughter rather than a model of courage, persistence, and victory! With a sigh of acknowledgement, he pulls himself together and continues to cut the underbrush with the saber he brought for just this kind of challenging circumstance.

And so the King and Princess continue to fight their way into the forest, step by step moving closer to what they hope is the Oracle's dwelling place, hoping she will come to their rescue rather sooner than later and that the struggle will be over before long. Exhausted and overwhelmed by the challenge, they both collapse at some point. The forest has begun to feel like a dark place, with the trees feeling overly dominating and almost exuding an air of resistance to the intruders they behold. And as they lie on the ground gasping for air and for some light to shine through the darkish wall the tall trees put up, it somehow occurs to them that the trees are beginning to encircle them, closing in on them and entrapping them until there is no more room left to breathe, or so it seems. Both are ready to cry out for help; that's how cramped and hopeless they feel at this very moment. All of the King's powers seem good for nothing out here, and in one instant, he understands and feels his true powerlessness in the face of the Divine and of Nature itself.

"Goddess Aphrodite," he begins to pray silently, "please show me the way out of my present overwhelming situation. Show me how I can change the destiny of my kingdom around and how I can bring happiness and prosperity to my people!" So deep and heartfelt is his prayer that tears begin to form in his eyes, blurring his vision and making him feel humbled in the face of his own impotence.

Indirali has a prayer of her own, her heart longing for Loriolan with all its might. With tears in her eyes as well, she keeps imploring the Goddess of Love to give her a chance to demonstrate her deservedness and readiness to do whatever it takes to reach the Heavens of the Eternal Gods, and to meet her, Aphrodite, the superior Goddess of her loving, craving heart, to behold her in all her splendid beauty and radiance, and to receive the guidance she, Indirali, seeks from her, helping her to understand the fabrics and workings of life and enabling her to unite with her one and only true love. Feelings of humility and intense yearning for the Divine stream from her heart and begin to stir the mercy, infinite wisdom, and love Goddess Aphrodite is happy to shower on her most faithful followers and devotees. And like a breath of fresh air and the light of the first morning ray of sunshine, the atmosphere begins to lighten and freshen, as if a magic hand lifted the heavy veil of illusion and its distorting grip on reality to let the infinite bliss and light of the Divine shine through the branches of the ancient trees, to touch their foreheads and open their third eye to the mysteries of life that lie beyond the veils of human erroneous thinking and burdened feeling. As if in a wondrous trance, Indirali and Eurylochos stand up and begin to slowly turn around as an invisible presence seems to look them over while a gentle rain of colorful blossom petals begins to sprinkle on the two stunned visitors, and quiet whispers prompt them to turn their heads around every time they hear another murmur flitting by.

And then the circle of trees begins to fade into a bright light that outshines everything to the fullest. So blinded are the two seekers that they have to close their eyes, occasionally blinking to try to adjust to the light intensity that has them spinning and dissolving their essence in the brightest light either of them has ever beheld. Soft, celestially beautiful music and an angelic choir resound, lifting Indirali and her father into the higher-frequency spheres of the Oracle's dwelling place. And then the light slowly subsides, revealing a huge, friendly-looking tree spirit, who reverently invites them to step closer and enter into the sacred spheres that lie ahead of them. Blossoming trees of various kinds decorate the sides of a long, beautifully winding path, and the skies look invitingly pastel-blue and light, making Indirali and Eurylochos want to float with the playful clouds that seem to drift into the higher Heavens of unearthly beauty and existence.

As far as the eye can see, a supernatural beauty, mild and refreshing climate, and gentle atmosphere welcome them, with lush green and colorful flower meadows enlivening their tired senses, fairies and elves living in the flowers and grass varieties, beautiful trees accentuating the scenery with their majestic or adorable looks, and the birds frolicking to their hearts' content, being present again and eager to impress the doubtful senses of the visitors with another string of life-celebrating, exquisite melodies and twittering sounds.

The tree spirit indicates for them to walk down the path and to see what happens. And so Eurylochos and his graceful daughter begin to walk, marveling at the colorful life that greets them at every turn and wondering when the Oracle is going to surprise them with her much-anticipated presence.

CHAPTER 30

Walking down the path feels like enlivening their higher nature: trust in the Divine workings of life returns, and an incredible sense of aliveness and mind-blowing enthusiasm for life lifts Eurylochos and Indirali up as if spiraling towards the infinity of their own Divine Selves. Incredible beauty surrounds them at every step, and time seems to stand still as the present moment begins to expand beyond its normal boundaries to encompass realities from faraway worlds and dimensions, all merging and melding into one mind-exploding moment that has them gasping for more and more, as if on a mind-transcending trip into the most inner secrets and worlds that any human can ever behold.

And then they behold her! On a hill in front of them, a bright light reveals the transcendent figure of a beautiful young woman, peacefully and serenely looking down on them, acknowledging their presence with a smile that seems to dismantle their outer facades and has them crumble at her feet. Eurylochos feels himself strangely transformed, hardly recognizing his usual self anymore. What wondrous environment has he been piloted into by his daughter and her love for this merman! With eyes of wonder, the two seekers stand still and go to their knees, when a bright, friendly laughter shocks them out of their reverent mode. Several yards behind them, a beautiful woman makes them aware of herself by letting her laughter ring out to their ears and causing them to turn around to focus on her.

"Got you!" she jokes. "Works every time! Like clockwork! The young at heart just love to be surprised!" She spins around her center and her wide fluffy garment flows gently and adorningly with her movement. It seems the wind spirits support her every move, because everything about her is carried by air and seems to float gently in space, as if beholding a gravity-defying miracle in motion. "It keeps them growing and expanding so they become the infinite ocean of bliss that they are!" she exhales like a sweet melody riding atop a fresh spring breeze.

Eurylochos and Indirali yank their heads around to stare back at the hilltop, but the transcendent figure inside the bright light has dissipated, and only the light remains, which also is now slowly subsiding.

"Here I am!" she calls, but in the next moment her voice shouts from a far distance, way behind a group of elm and birch trees, teasing Eurylochos and Indirali with her ability to change position any time she pleases and wills it so. And her visitors have a hard time following her every move, zooming in and out with every new stance she assumes until, at last, she stands right in front of them, smiling at them with a face that radiates pure love and stunning beauty.

"Welcome, Eurylochos!" she nods at him, and he at her. "Welcome Indirali, my child!" she continues. "I have been expecting you. Please follow me to where we can have our conversation! Let's see what other surprises life has in store for you!" And then she magically lifts them up and, on invisible clouds, transports them to a higher-dimensional place that has Eurylochos and his daughter looking down on the earthly scenery as if living in the cloud kingdom of a higher world, with planets they have never seen before surrounding the atmosphere. Everything seems so unfamiliar and mysteriously beautiful that the two of them quickly settle into a feeling of deepest surrender to the powers and wisdom of the Oracle, whom they believe more and more to be a fantastic emanation of the Goddess of Love, Aphrodite herself.

Humbly, father and daughter offer their gifts to the Oracle, who truly strikes them as an angel sent from Heaven. Luminous, sparkling jewels of different saturated colors speak from the heart of the King to demonstrate his appreciation and reverence for the Oracle's willingness to meet. With a Divine smile, the Oracle accepts the offering and integrates the jewels into her head tiara where they transcend into the most splendidly radiating light and effulgence. She also lovingly accepts the beautifully woven silk scarf Indirali had embroidered with soft colored roses and, with a whiff of elegance, throws it around her shoulder to let it gently trail in the warm summer breeze, as if a light-emanating flower path is unraveling in front of their stunned eyes.

"I have seen into your hearts and know why you have come to seek my advice on important matters!" she enlightens them. "Know that you always have a choice as to what option and path you want to take in life, but for as long as you seek the highest guidance possible, you have to be prepared to go the distance in overcoming obstacles in your way and mastering your own inner weaknesses and fears to the point where they dissipate and make way for the miracles you want."

Eurylochos and Indirali feel in agreement with this assessment and are open for further guidance and instruction. The Oracle smiles, and the sun begins to shine more brightly, for two souls have returned to the light, ready to be absorbed into it until there is no shred of darkness left in them anymore. With a wave of her hand, the Oracle conjures up a huge reflecting mirror made of transcendent matter, a holographic shield able to portray back to them the inner workings of their soul, and let them gain insight into the challenges ahead of them.

With an inviting gesture, the Oracle asks Eurylochos to step into the mirror first and to behold his destiny, as it is intertwined and at one with the destiny of his kingdom. With slight hesitation, Eurylochos steps forward, wondering what to expect and whether it was still safe to run from what he might see and maybe not like to know. But his sense of honor and responsibility immediately win out over this shred of evidence of his cowardly nature, and with the heart of a hero, he immerses himself into the mirror to face the unadulterated truth of his life and existence.

As soon as he steps into the unknown, several tunnels of spinning energy open up to him, confusing him as to which direction to take in order to arrive at a destination of his highest choosing. And as he stands there, dumbfounded as to what to do next, it dawns on him that each tunnel triggers different feelings in him, some making him feel good, others bad, and of the good ones, some trigger even higher and more light-filled feelings, whereas others trigger more dull and less vibrant feelings. Of the bad ones, however, some make him feel utterly bad to the point of complete despair and agony, whereas the milder versions of the bad ones allow him to feel more hopeful. Choosing to take a better look at the latter version, he discerns lighter and darker shades of intensity in regard to feelings of compromise and frustration. It actually is a no-brainer for Eurylochos when it comes to choosing the main category of what kind of feelings he prefers to follow. He turns his attention towards the good feeling tunnels.

And as he gauges the ramifications of this choice, he notices, much to his consternation, that he feels torn between the very good feeling tunnel and the average good feeling one, when he should actually be immediately drawn to the highest feeling levels to which he can aspire. When he tries to examine why he feels split-minded about the situation, he realizes that the highest and best choice possible seems to have an emotional burden of its own built into the tunnel path, very much according to the saying that every good thing has its price. It dawns on him that choosing the best possible solution, or tunnel in this case, always brings with it the necessity to work through some heavy load of karma and face subconscious realities and issues that the average person prefers to avoid until a later point in time, and if possible, until another lifetime altogether, hoping that the karmic burden will somehow magically disappear along the way without having to be dealt with. The less vibrant of the good feeling tunnels, however, seems to feel less strenuous, less challenging to the core, allowing some time to relax and take it easy. The goals aren't as lofty and rewarding as the ones that await at the end of the highest feeling tunnels, but they still seem to have enough of a reward waiting at the end of their less brightly lit tunnels as to warrant choosing those lesser ones, lest Eurylochos be completely consumed by the strains and pains of dealing with his whole karmic load all at once, and maybe break down from it and become useless to his people and office.

This fear prompts Eurylochos to choose a less vibrant tunnel from among the better feeling ones, curious to see what's on the other end of it, whether he will feel confirmed in making the right choice, able to be happy with its results, and able to live with them without regrets. Hesitatingly, he takes a step in, feeling righteous for a moment for not being overly ambitious with his choice, wondering what might happen. A strange force field immediately begins to take him over, gradually catapulting him forward through the tunnel that keeps sending images from his past by him, lulling him into a certain receptive mode that has him contemplating his life from a particular angle. He sees past experiences and events running through his mind that all lead up to a feeling that he has done good under the circumstances, and that there is not much he needs to change in order to feel any better than he already does. At some point, however, the tunnel opens up to a light, which he flies through, and lo and behold, once his inner eye adjusts to the light, he sees the most likely future outcome of his lifeline presented to him based on his present — and therefore most comfortable — inclinations and outlook on life.

But how displeased is Eurylochos when he realizes his present comfort zone inclinations all just lead him to an outcome he prefers not to have, namely seeing Indirali heartbrokenly married off to Hecto and both their kingdoms at war with several other kingdoms, if for no other reason than that Hecto likes to do battle, and if there wasn't a reason to convince the world that war is a necessary evil, Hecto would invent one, dragging many innocent and not so innocent people into adversity and war just to please his lust and ambitions. Eurylochos also sees himself a broken man, ready to degenerate into death rather sooner than later, with life not holding much attraction for him since his wife and children all feel heartbroken, and his son — despite his name Athos meaning 'immortal' — loses his life at a young age in the perils of war, thus leaving Lucania to fall into Hecto's greedy hands. Eurylochos shudders from this unwanted outcome and wishes himself back to the crossing to try out another tunnel path.

And the Oracle fulfills his wish; he is granted another choice and instantaneously put into the position where he is able to make one. This time, Eurylochos exerts the extra effort of stepping into a tunnel of greater challenges and hopefully greater rewards as well. The spiraling energy of this tunnel feels quite different, more tense and extreme in its polarities actually. He feels quite elevated at times, then deeply overshadowed, tainted, and pained about not feeling in control of certain problems that force themselves into his life and awareness without much consideration of his feelings and wellbeing. Vulnerable and exposed, Eurylochos flies through the tunnel with a feeling of being victimized by life, just so he can come out and feel in charge again. And he finds that the more he surrenders to life as a teacher, the more generous life treats him when he is on the upswing again. If he, however, chooses to resist the unknown and more powerful life source and life force with all the stubbornness he has and fights it at every step of the way, violating others, and thus violating himself, he quickly finds himself broken and whining, wanting attention from his mother and father to heal his many inflicted wounds that stem from his own ignorance in his actions. And so he learns that obedience and surrender to the Source of Life have their great and much-coveted rewards, allowing him to feel better and greater about himself in the end than when he falters, when he despises the Source of Life by ignorantly elevating the antithesis of life, namely the source of death and emptiness, to assume the place of the Source of Life, and by doing so, he not only distorts the truth of life, revering death and evil as if they were the highest truths known to mankind, but he would also betray himself in the game, burying his soul and love in the sarcophagus of all his lost ideals and broken promises. Eurylochos decides to exude the innocence of an infant, learn like a child, love as passionately as a teenager, express power and courage of an adult, and look through everything with the eyes of a wise old man. Thus transformed, and his ego-edges honed away, the ride becomes more smooth and light, eventually spitting Eurylochos out on the other side of the tunnel into a light that seems brighter and more promising than the one from before.

A new possible future scenario presents itself to him. Eurylochos can't decide whether he likes it or not. A lot has changed for the better, but the end result is still not satisfying enough. Indirali went on her journey and returns victorious with her lover. They marry and reign over their underwater kingdom; peace is restored to the kingdoms of Magna Graecia, and Athos, Eurylochos' son, reigns over Lucania, but … Eurylochos scratches his head, he still is unfulfilled, gets sick soon, and dies early because his contact with Indirali is for some reason sparse, Athos excludes him from his life and business, and even Penelope is wary of him because he has turned into a naysayer, a hopeless person who still sees much wrong in his kingdom without being able to fix it. Decadence and cold-hearted indifference are rampant amongst people of all walks of life, and he feels too weak and defeated to dare to change anything about it anymore. The only accomplishments he can be proud of are that he allowed Indirali to pursue her love and was instrumental in avoiding war between many kingdoms, thus saving Athos's life as well, but beyond all that, an inner emptiness remains, a spiritual vacuum that cannot be filled, and, therefore, he withers into death at a relatively fast rate, and in the meantime observes his people and neighboring kingdoms fall complacent, harsh, and violent in all kinds of interpersonal ways, emotionally oppressing each other, selfishly exploiting life force from the meek and weak, and arrogantly aggrandizing themselves above others and even above the Source of Life itself. Eurylochos turns away in shame. No, this outcome won't do either, he decides. He would rather die now than go through a whole lifetime full of illusions, thinking he is doing his utmost to create the best possible outcome not only for his family but also for his kingdom and for life in general. He wants to save himself from such a waste of a lifetime and asks the Oracle for another chance to make a better choice for himself and for all the souls with whom his life is intertwined.

The Oracle is happy to oblige, for he came to her wanting to find the best and most appropriate path for himself that would allow him to thrust his full motivating power into action so he can accomplish nothing less than a miracle for himself and his loved ones, the miracle of a life fulfilled, a life of no regrets because it aims at the highest ideal any man can want for himself, the Divine choice of a life that renders all of life infinitely enriched and infinitely enjoyable. And without further delay, the Oracle places Eurylochos in front of the opening to the most brightly radiating tunnel, prompting him to take his first daring step onto the path that demands all of him but also delivers all he expects, the path of complete self-transformation that leads to complete spiritual mastery and enlightenment.

Eurylochos is all for it now! Having checked out his lamer, more compromised options, he feels miraculously ready for whatever this most challenging path might ask of him. He realizes the high energy of the tunnel corresponds with the pure impulse that brought him here in the first place, an impulse born from the love he rediscovered for his daughter in the midst of her plight and propelled by the courage he feels running through her veins as she attempts the impossible on her path to ultimate redemption and true love.

Eurylochos steps in and immediately gets absorbed by the vibrations of highest energetic life force, rattling away on his innermost blocks and limitations as if it were a grinding machine, ready to expose his real self underneath the debris and rubble of his accumulated karmic burdens and entrapping mind illusions. Eurylochos begins to sweat and puff under the wearing influences, ready to be boggled out of his mind and catapulted into a higher state of awareness. This path means business, and he is ready to give it his all! Negative thoughts and emotions of all kinds emerge from the depths of his soul, giving him the choice to either strengthen them with his continued attention on them or weaken their charge and influence on him by merely observing them move out of his body and aura, to see them floating away like the clouds in the sky. He tries to stay with the latter option, since this one seems to wash the negative charge out of his bodily system more quickly and more profoundly, whereas if he were to get all riled up about the negativity leaving his body, and even more so if he were to succumb to the illusion that it is caused by anything or anyone outside of himself, and that these entities or circumstances would therefore deserve him lashing out with wrath and anger at them, he would feel strangely weakened and bogged down from it, wondering where to take the strength and motivation from anymore to be able to continue on this demanding path and still believe in the bright light and outcome ahead of him.

But Eurylochos feels sobered up and purified from the disillusionment of his first few choices, and so — having nothing to lose or to regret — he feels ready to face his darkest emotions and most distorted thoughts, hoping he will get through them unscathed and without falling prey to creating even further illusions and negative emotions that continue to uphold the vicious cycles of spiritual entrapment, as he understands now that only a self-referral mind is able to penetrate the thick layers of self-limiting beliefs and karmic burdens, ready to create the unlimited version of his life that comes closest to the Divine ideal of absolute fulfillment and infinite expansion of bliss consciousness. Understanding that he is not only the cause for his suffering but that he also possesses the power to change his destiny any time he wants, in whatever direction he wants, puts him in the position of being the creator of his own lifeline, his own destiny the way he wants it! But for that to happen, he realizes, he has to give it his all; he has to be able to stare death into its eye and defy it for the sake of having more of life, life to the overflowing, and infinite abundance of every good thing!

And so Eurylochos finds himself torn between the impossible odds, trashed to an egoless pulp, chewed up and spit out by the monsters of his subconscious mind, all so his ego pride and futile sense of human arrogance can be reversed and dissolved at the hands of the Divine, stripping him bare-naked to his Divine Essence, the only essence pure enough so as to never having to die or suffer anymore. With transcendental gratefulness, he finally emerges through the brightest light he could ever imagine, into the future possibility of his present lifeline, as the King of Lucania.

This time he sees not only Indirali married happily to Loriolan and commonly reigning over a splendid kingdom that knows no limitations in regard to happiness and fulfillment, but also Athos reigning wisely over Lucania with a loving wife by his side, and both Eurylochos and Penelope are radiantly happy and fulfilled, having mastery over their lives to the point where they determine their time of transitioning to higher dimensions themselves, able to live for as long as they like, and for as long as they wish to be in their children's lives, able to have a wonderfully deep relationship with their children and grandchildren the likes of which was known only during the most splendid of ancient times when man and woman lived to be more than a thousand years old and enjoyed every moment of it to the fullest!

King Eurylochos sees Penelope and himself performing many beautiful and inspiring deeds that go into the archives of history reporting on the royal couple who inspired and helped humanity by their example and good deeds to be the highest best any human being can be, and to pursue the highest goal any human being can pursue — to become the infinite bright light of their innermost Divine Essence so the world may rejoice again in the waves of pure bliss that is man's and woman's Divine birthright and uppermost dharma and vocation.

This is the future vision Eurylochos has been looking for, the reason he came to the Oracle, and with deepest conviction in his chest, he steps back out from the mirror of truth, ready to pursue this brightest of options and ready to implement any and all of the necessary steps, challenges, and lessons learned into his daily life, so he will surely reap the rewards he just beheld, even if it means to humble himself in front of the all-powerful Creator of Life and thrust aside once and for all the illusions of small grandeur, the illusion of being in control of who deserves to be rewarded and who deserves to be punished, of who deserves to live and who deserves to die, and the illusion of death itself.

CHAPTER 31

*E*xcited, Eurylochos reports on his experiences and the final choice he made as a result of going through several different options, only to find that the Oracle knows all about it and was with him within her supermind every step of the way. Humbled, he opens up to her infinite wisdom, allowing her to shed light on the deeper meanings of his realization process, ready for her to enlighten him on what needs to be done in order to achieve and secure the outcome of the life he wants. Because even though he already knows the price of self-transformation has to be paid in order to get to his desired goal, his tunnel experience only gave him a condensed energetic experience about the path and didn't show much of any details on how his path will be unfolding and what kind of manifestations will most likely happen along it.

First of all, the Oracle emphasizes the importance of spiritual transformation within himself, and as a result of that, much improvement will manifest on the outside for the benefit of his whole kingdom. This transformation requires a deep readiness and willingness to face the issues that brought him and his kingdom to the brink of war, as it will also make him realize that he himself created the necessity to consider bad feeling compromises, even in regard to his beloved children's welfare and future.

Eurylochos looks at her with startled, questioning eyes. So far, he thought he had a fulfilling spiritual life, attending temple ceremonies relatively regularly to show his respects and venerate Goddess Aphrodite in the deep ways to which he is accustomed. But the Oracle jolts him out of his complacent attitude, telling him mind-blowing truths about his temple priesthood he never would have imagined but, strangely enough, on a subconscious level, knew and anticipated that this was going on. He is told that however many true Goddess worshippers from among the priesthood are left to uphold the present spiritual power of the temple with their inner purity, in truth they are gradually overcome by the spiritually corrupt influences of the leading priesthood elite that seems to gain abusive power over all spiritual matters in and outside the temple with every passing moment. Thus the priests are becoming the agents for the dark, giving in to the destructive influences of the fast evolving spiritual Winter season. The Oracle tells the dumbfounded king that while pure-hearted souls like he and members of his family can still notice and connect with the true essence of Goddess Aphrodite in her temple, most other worshippers have long lost their inner connection to the Divine Matron and have begun to ignorantly be subjected to and be possessed by abusive discarnate spirits of the lower astral plane, spirits that like to energetically feed off humans and lead them astray, prompting them to act out the lower urges which the discarnate spirit cannot act out by itself for lack of a physical body. Thus many such possessed humans have now become the instruments through which the dark forces located on the lower astral planes are able to unleash their destructive forces on the human world, to sow the seeds of annihilation and have an army of willing, possessed subjects enforce spiritual death upon the world.

To Eurylochos' dismay, he learns that most of his temple priests have succumbed to these disheartening influences, and that Aphrodite's temple is at risk of losing the Goddess's benevolent matronage at any time now. Like many other divinely-steeped Gods and Goddesses, Aphrodite is recoiling from the uninviting scenarios she sees unfolding on planet Earth. The painful truth is that the necessary inner and outer purity of individuals and their environments, as well as the spiritual awareness and mind-transcending peace of mankind, can hardly be felt anymore to warrant the Divine help and attention on our world. She is, however, available to individuals who strive for purity and enlightenment, and has therefore connected with Indirali to such a significant extent as to give her guidance and invite her to meet her in the celestial realms. As for the temple priesthood, however, the Oracle states, the perfect picture his priesthood paints to the public is not real nor are their spiritual powers of any significance compared to what could be possible on the planet at this point in time. She reveals to him some pretty disheartening truths that cause him to reel from their underhanded and perverse nature. According to her recounts, he sees in his mind's eye how in the meantime the majority of the priests and priestesses indulge in sexual pleasures of all kinds, in hidden catacomb quarters specifically equipped for their carnal orgies. She says they go so far as to even take advantage of young men and women from outside the temple, forcing them to participate in their sinful sessions by bribing their parents with a few tokens from their immeasurable wealth they hoard in the deepest chambers of their contradictory compound. This underhanded undertaking accounts for many illegitimate children being born to the thus abused women as well as for the pile of discarded infant skeletons — the unwanted fruits of their sexual interactions — stored in the deepest, most inaccessible underground caves the priests painstakingly guard from public view and awareness. She discloses that the priests are savvy in concocting mind-altering drugs that add to their perverse pleasures by subduing their sexual victims to put up with all sorts of sick and abusive behavior from their perpetrators. He also has to swallow the bitter truth of their political betrayal, as the priesthood not only conducts incognito business with enterprises within the kingdom but also creates profits by leaking delicate information about King Eurylochos' political intentions and strategies to the highest bidders from among foreign rulers and ambassadors. She explains that their wealth is by far greater than that of his royal treasure chamber and that its magnitude could easily solve the kingdom's problems and poverty in one stroke, if righteously and wisely applied.

Upon seeing Eurylochos' shocked face, she cautions him to not confront the temple priesthood too drastically and openly with what was said here but to go about weakening their underhanded and jeopardizing influence in a wise and measured way, lest he risk turning them into his enemies and very likely losing the battle against them. She strongly warns him that the temple enjoys the traditional value of representing the Divine to the people, a fact that cannot be underestimated in its importance and impact on the people when he intends to expose the temple priesthood's corruptions and weaknesses. If he wants to avoid riots and resentments of all kinds coming at him from among his people, he better keep the cleansing act of his temple undercover. If he wants to succeed in extracting the most twisted, evil leaders out of their rotten nest, he has to keep certain facts in mind and apply highly effective tactics that will help avoid the whole situation from erupting in his face before he is ready and powerful enough to deal with it.

She continues to describe that the temple itself was originally dedicated to connecting the people with the Divine Source of Life, with the realm of the Gods and Goddesses, and that it is the priests' vocation to mediate between the world and the Heavens, channeling and embodying spiritual truths and values to their congregation, just as the brain functions as the transmitter of higher frequencies of life force, sending crucial electromagnetic impulses to the rest of the physical body. A corrupt priesthood, however, resembles a brain tumor, a self-destructive fabric that falters in its proper functioning. If the Divine representation is as corrupted as King Eurylochos' priesthood obviously is — and the priesthood of most other kingdoms at this time is as well, to tell him the whole story — it begins to malfunction, growing in self-destructive ways that jeopardize the health and wellbeing of the whole of society, the whole body as a holographic image of the brain or priesthood. Tumor cells behave in irrational, greedy ways, devouring any life in their way, no matter what damage to the overall health they create for the rest of the body; like greedy, vampire-like, and egocentric selves, such cells or people turn against each other in the futile pursuit of amassing chunks of energy and material wealth they crave to absorb and possess, trying to fill their notoriously empty bodies and minds with what they hope will give them what they lack. However, the very fact that they steal life energy from outside sources rather than tapping into their own infinite inner resources shows the extent of their spiritual blindness, since life force streams from the innermost sources. Arrogantly taking life — or dignity — away from another human being or life system, therefore, just activates the unbending law of karma that takes away what was taken, and gives what was given to either harm or support one's own life, depending on the nature of one's actions. It is this spiritual blindness, this irrational outlook on life, and the resulting irrational behavior that constitute the life-destroying tumor or cancer, severing the connection between higher life forces and the brain and the body, between the Divine Source of Life and the priesthood and the kingdom, interrupting the flow of cosmic energy and intelligence as the body or kingdom ceases to be an extension of the brain or priesthood, and the brain or priesthood ceases to be the receptor of higher frequencies and light impulses from the Divine. As a result, these faulty human transmitters and receptors succumb to the self-destructive influences that the belief in lack fosters, competing amongst each other for the seemingly dwindling resources an irrational outlook on life steadfastly believes in, ignorantly eclipsing themselves from the fundamental energy cycle that — according to the ultimate truth — keeps every individual, as all of life, intricately connected to and abundantly provided for by the Divine Source. This ultimately free-will based, yet self-inflicted ignorance and illusory attachment to self-destructive influences causes the individual soul and, in Eurylochos' case, causes his whole temple apparatus to eventually collapse into a shutdown that will separate the spiritual lifeline from its Creator Source, thus eclipsing mortals from the precious, eternal self-sustaining life force and turning the physical expression into the lifeless dust of transient frequencies. This mutually triggered downward spiral of lost life force and growing ignorance begins to overshadow the individual's awareness to such a point that he becomes unable to recognize and apply the unbending, timeless laws of our universe to his advantage, unable to hold onto the fact that life is eternal and benevolent, and instead grasping for evidence that death is inevitable and the sure outcome of a life lived according to lack and spiritual blindness that leaves us powerless and out of control of our own destiny.

The Oracle teaches that life comes from life, and life is eternal. She says that people on this planet have grown accustomed to the idea that death is inevitable, simply because they don't want to undertake the effort to probe to the bottom of this belief, afraid they might have to change their thinking and their ways to create a more life-enhancing outcome for themselves. But whereas Eurylochos has just changed his choice and has accepted a vaster investment of himself on his path, ready to tackle deeper and more challenging issues in order to achieve greater and more fulfilling results in his life, the average human tries to avoid this choice, persistently repressing uncomfortable issues, hoping the karmic burdens will vanish on their own and leave them to the pleasures of life without any consequences, happy to be an empty shell without much inner depth, and eager to rob others of their depth and energy to live the resemblance of a life that leaves them wanting for more and more. The Oracle says that this is the state most priests are in and is the reason why they come up with increasingly dramatic sexual, commercial, and political distortions and betrayals, just so they can continue to be on top of their faltering game, afraid to ever be found out by the public and by any emanation of the Divine, afraid they will fall short of any evaluation of their job performance and character, eager to cover up the tracks of their evildoings so no one can ever tell they exist. This neurotic behavior is the impetus and propellant of the innermost doings of the temple elite, and the devotional image they portray to the public is a cleverly devised deflection, the elegantly and richly decorated, by stately stallions drawn spiritual elite carriage, so to say, that is supposed to deflect from the truth of the real situation.

     Eurylochos feels his senses fading under the weight of these revelations. He would sit down if there were a seat available; soft clouds, however, carry him and his daughter and he doesn't feel a stable support to hold onto, therefore he lets himself sink into the cozy warmth of the enveloping mist. The Oracle points at him with a ray of light shooting from her finger, and immediately he begins to feel better, as if a ray of hope just touched him and helps him stand strong in the midst of all this harrowing news about the very place to which he and his forefathers had entrusted their own and their people's souls and fate. Shame of an extraordinary nature overtakes him as he struggles with an attempt to find the higher meaning in all of this. He is especially distraught to have his daughter witness the uncanny extent of betrayal he just learned of himself, and is concerned about what miserable example of a leader he must demonstrate to her right now. But then the superceding love of the Oracle begins to caress and alleviate his pain, addressing him such with words of great compassion and wisdom:

     "Tell me, oh King of Lucania, what inspiring image impressed itself onto your memory from among all the images of your past that sped by you while you were pursuing your brightest light goal through the last tunnel you chose?" She looks at him encouragingly.

Eurylochos thinks for a moment, then his countenance begins to brighten. "I used to love sitting by the fountain in my parents' country palace, gazing at the water's movements, enraptured by the mysteries of its unending cycles, how the water kept shooting upwards, then spraying its mists that kept collecting in the basin, only to be reborn again in the fountainhead of eternal spring!" His eyes glow with newfound enthusiasm.

"Nice!" she agrees. "You are describing your own role here as the ruler of Lucania. You want to bubble over with life force, ideas, and concepts that enrich and fertilize the minds and lives of all those who depend on you for your strength, guidance, and wisdom. This image captures the essence of your vocation: to be the fountainhead of your body of water, your body of people. You want to be able to endlessly uphold the rising and falling of energies, the inspiration and distribution of your highest ideals and aspirations, to create the loftiest and most rewarding outcomes for any situation you and your kingdom find themselves in at any given moment in time." She pauses to let her words sink deep into his awareness.

A moment later, he looks at her: "I thought I was supposed, and I think I was taught, to rely on the priests for any higher inspiration and for ultimate guidance. But now I feel terribly disappointed and misled." He lowers his gaze.

"It is not an either … or," she explains, "but rather a call to any soul who is able to hear the fine and delicate voice of the Divine to be all that it can be, the most connected, the most inspiring to others, the happiest and the most truthful! If every soul can blossom to its fullest potential, then there is no need to steal, violate, and cheat; there is only reason to celebrate the abundance every soul feels inside and, as a result, sees it manifested in the outside, rejoicing in the fact that as many souls as possible have awoken to this beautiful and enriching truth, able to participate in the joys of others and feeling the deep interconnectedness of life all around them, determined to never ever harm or violate another life again, for it is part of their own infinite and Divine nature." The Oracle radiates her love and compassion like the sun, bathing Nature in the warming rays of life itself, allowing it to grow and prosper to its heart's content. She beams with inner light, and Eurylochos gratefully begins to stand strong in her nourishing presence.

"How then can I begin to turn things around in my temple and for my kingdom?" he wants to know. "Right now it feels quite overwhelming and hopeless. Even if I change my ways, who says it will affect and benefit everyone around me?" Deep worry is written all over his face.

"Infinite powers lie hidden inside each and every soul!" she encourages. "As you tap into those reservoirs, you will find the power to effect change within the dharmic ramifications of your kingdom's destiny. And even if not everyone can respond to your change and calling, you will attract those who can follow you, and together you will create a better nation, a more enlightened kingdom that collectively has turned its primary focus to the infinitely nourishing Source of Life, letting death and misery rot away in the corners of the dark that they belong in. Your example, guidance, and support will fall on rich soil and will begin to sprout and prosper in all those who are ready for positive change and for an abundance that exceeds any expectation, which is all possible because people will have assumed responsibility for themselves, for each other, for their kingdom's wellbeing, and for the health of Nature in general."

King Eurylochos likes what he is hearing! He just needs more details from her, please, he asks. And so she continues, with Eurylochos and Indirali glued to her wisdom-expressing lips. "Elevate the meek and humble of heart and turn your attention and reliance away from those who abuse and take advantage of your trust and support. Find deserving souls who have not disappointed you within this life, light-filled individuals who strike you as trustworthy and devoted to the Divine, and make sure they are initiated by a true master soul into the highest truths of human existence. Find and appoint an enlightened teacher who embodies the wisdom and light of one of the most ancient teachings of the Divine here on Earth and who, therefore, might be merciful and helpful enough to initiate your prospective new priesthood into the art of spiritual growth and physical ascension into the light body man is comprised of. These individuals should be initiated into mind-transcending techniques and learn about righteous behavior that uplifts all of life and creates wellbeing for anyone they come in contact with.

Accept spiritual aspirants who have dedicated most of their lives to spiritual purification and who, therefore, have reached a considerable level of maturity and enlightenment. Place these pure individuals in lead positions and have the purest and most spiritually mature high priestess and high priest head your temple, even if you have to create a new temple altogether." She pauses, assuring herself that both Eurylochos and Indirali are still following her words carefully. Then she continues with her suggestions:

"You can also affirm that such a spiritually enlightened priestess and priest will manifest into your life from seemingly out of nowhere and at any moment in time, whenever you might deem yourself truly and deeply ready to have her and/ or him enter your and your people's lives." The Oracle blinks her eye, spraying an abundance of fairy dust around that has Eurylochos enveloped in a magical light of the most refined ether, thus conveying to him that miracles are bound to happen to souls who truly are ready on all levels of their being and life. Then she continues: "Also, in the bottom catacomb chamber of your temple there is a library of sacred texts that no one has seen for many centuries, and certainly not within your present lifetime, simply because the high priestesses and high priests for many generations have guarded the knowledge of their existence from leaking out to the public, and now even to you, the present worldly ruler of the kingdom. Their hope is that these papyrus rolls will stay forgotten, never to inspire and revolutionize anyone who might find out about their existence and be changed by what he might read in them."

Eurylochos lets out a scream of dismay. This is getting worse and worse, and he feels increasingly foolish for not ever having demanded accountability and transparency from his temple elite. To think that such a treasure of wisdom has been right under his nose for all his life without him ever having been made aware of its existence is more than he can bear. He feels quite furious, to say the least. But the Oracle cautions him to not let anger overcome him when all he needs is a plan and the patience to stick to it. That settles the King down again, and gratefully he continues to listen to what this marvel of a wise woman has to say next.

"Ask Agathe to show you the library. Tell her that extraordinary measures are needed to turn the kingdom's fate around and that you want to find guidance in those wise papyrus rolls that were written by the highest, most enlightened teachers this world has known, all collected and copied from the great library in Alexandria. If she doesn't yield, bring several of your strongest guards just to spook her enough to yank her out of her baseless sense of ownership over this wealth of wisdom, which should actually belong in the hands of those who are able to take on the responsibility of leading the kingdom in all the various and different areas of public life to the most lofty goals that can be achieved. Have your clergy and students study those texts and report back to you with findings that — from time immemorial — are believed to contain the wisdom and power to make a profound difference in anyone's fate who endeavors to live by these enlightened principles. You can, therefore, expect your kingdom's fate, on whatever level or area of life, to greatly benefit from this research and reacquaintance with ancient wisdom and knowledge. Let your people get inspired again by what is possible and by the understanding that there is always a way open to those who refuse to succumb to compromise and to life-destructive behavior." She looks at him and sees the deep impact of her words resounding in his soul. Eurylochos understands, and the seeds of her words are already beginning to sprout in his awareness, as he mulls over problems and challenges and rejoices in the fact that there are solutions available to him that he is going to find and implement for his kingdom's sake.

"Find guidance in those texts on how to initiate as many people of your kingdom into meditation, to quieten the mind and allow it to transcend the confines of their intellectual understanding on a constant, daily basis, connecting them to their own higher, Divine Selves and having the collective effect of transcendental coherence compound and flood the kingdom in waves of harmony and bliss. This will restore the connection to the Divine Source of Life for the kingdom as a whole and for every meditating individual as well, to enjoy and reap the resulting benevolent repercussions. As coherence spreads throughout your kingdom, like the irrigating waters flowing from the well of collective consciousness, it begins to enliven not only the higher nature within each individual, but also the laws of Nature themselves, to have them support life and lift the human spirit with their conducive, harmonious, and prospering influences. Then, Eurylochos, will you have done justice to your office as the King of Lucania, and you will feel fulfilled on all levels of your life, able to transition in your eternal light body to the higher realms without any regrets, and with a smile that supercedes all worldly concerns and pleasures! If you do that, your kingdom will vibrate with perfect health and perfect invincibility and won't be able to be compromised by any outside intruders, nor will it be undermined by any internal enemies, for these destructive energies will be drowned out in the waves of coherence, dissolved, and eliminated, and as a result your country will become an example of wise statesmanship, stable peace, and overflowing abundance in all areas of collective life."

"How do I individually deal with those who don't want to let go of their evil ways but rather keep jeopardizing the wellbeing of others just to suit their corrupt stance in life?" Eurylochos wants to know, because the fear of potential retaliation to his radically new tactics still sits like an indigestible clump in his stomach.

"Once a new, life-enhancing priesthood has been established and the situation is more under control, hard-core perpetrators and manipulators should be publicly tried and sentenced in order to pay for and reflect on their evildoings. In regard to lesser transgressors of spiritual law, pay them a severance and get them out of your life and out of your kingdom. Tempt them to leave your kingdom by voluntarily going into exile, and allow them to build a life at a different location with the severance you gave them, a kind of life that still caters to their evil ways, somewhere where they can continue to vibrate and resonate with the compromise and violation of the laws of Nature the way they are used to and which they have a hard time letting go of," she suggests. "The Divine certainly doesn't want to limit the free will of any soul, even if that soul continues to create suffering for itself and tries to drag other souls down with it into the oblivion and despair that await those who cannot turn their path around when the Divine knocks at their soul's gateway, hoping to be heard and followed."

King Eurylochos looks transfigured. There seems to be a Divine solution for everything, if only he can stay aligned with the Divine Will and persist with applying it in all of his affairs while resisting to compromise any of these precious, benevolent Divine values and solutions. With the Divine backing him up, there is no need to let fear run his affairs and have violence take over like a cancerous organism that strangles the life out of every soul in its way. As Lucania's leader, he owes it to every helpless and impoverished soul to look out for their best interest and be the strongest he can be, the most courageous and the most defiant of any danger of potential retaliation; he is the father of the nation, and as such, he needs to be anchored in the highest truth, willing to live by it at all times! With tears of gratitude and feeling deeply cleansed, he thanks the Oracle for her great wisdom and guidance. He says he will follow her advice and will begin with the change within himself by believing he can do whatever life asks of him, even if it means growing continuously beyond his comfort zone, which obviously is required of him right now, this very moment, knowing that his beloved daughter is getting ready to pursue her own path, no matter how far away from home it will lead her.

The Oracle gifts him with a bright, restoring smile, assuring him that he will succeed in all his intentions and undertakings, for he has realized the enormous importance of having the Divine Source of Life enlivened in himself so he can be the eternal fountainhead for his people, for his family, and for himself, a gift to life and Nature and a model of greatest courage the world of present is seldom able to behold!

Eurylochos smiles back, for now he knows he has everything he needs to effect the change he wanted and nothing to lose that would be worth hanging onto unless it is anchored in highest truth and love.

Both turn their attention to Indirali, who has been intently following the incredible revelations that have turned her father inside out, readying him for the momentous occasion of letting her begin her own journey. With a serene smile, she follows the Oracle's invitation and steps into the mirror of truth, to behold her own destiny the way she wants to see it unfold.

CHAPTER 32

As soon as Indirali sees the tunnels in the mirror of truth opening up to her, she is magnetically pulled to the brightest shining light, the one that pales all other possible paths in comparison. Her heart knows what it wants, and there is no need to contemplate a lesser alternative: she wants the highest goals a human soul can aspire to, for her infinite love for a merman, a man of a different physical nature than hers, ignites a willpower of grandiose proportions and the heart of a most courageous heroine to bridge the gap of their born differences and to prove to the world that love conquers all odds and wins any and all battles. There just is no doubt in her mind at all, and as if in a high frequency trance, she allows herself to be drawn into the tunnel that has her spinning to the tunes of the Divine game of life, Heavens high jubilations, and abysmally deep, melancholic agonies of death: the extreme polarities this path forces her to endure and integrate are explosive in their breakthrough nature, constantly throwing her out of her limitations and closely held beliefs. Indirali tries to let go of any resistance so she may be able to adjust to the high energy charges that try running through her, electromagnetic waves of such strong charge that they threaten to wipe out Indirali's conscious awareness at times. Intuitively she feels that if she resists, the charge will destroy her beyond conscious recuperation, and so she does the only thing that allows her to hold on to any shred of life, which is to surrender, surrender, surrender …

Her nonresistance allows the supercharge of highest, purest life energy to run through her meridians and nervous system without causing damage to her refined energy body, recharging her with the subtle yet most powerful life force frequencies the Divine Source is able to impart on the devoted soul who seeks to outgrow its limitations and boundaries of point value identification. But again and again, the Divine influx of light energy hits up against her inner obstacles and boundaries, causing her body and mind to jolt under the impact and overwhelming purification. Alternatingly, she feels rejuvenated and built up by the energy, only to once again fall deep into the pit of darkest despair and excruciating pain of forceful purification. It is difficult to not stay attached to and identified with the cleared-out material from her subconscious mind because of the overwhelming amount of karmic debris she has kept repressed for many lifetimes, and to not get carried away by the many negative emotions and terrifying visions this cleansing process triggers in her soul. But how wondrously beautiful and elevating are the feelings and sights when she manages to come out of one of those harrowing experiences, and see the light shining stronger in front of her than ever before! It's as if every cleansing act prepares her for an even clearer look at the increasingly more powerful light that awaits her at the end of the tunnel. Feelings of stunning clarity and joy emerge once the mud of her lower self is washed away, and visions of great beauty and sacred geometry present themselves to her awakening third eye, immersing her increasingly in the dimensions of higher-frequency celestial worlds. But these moments of clarity don't remain for very long yet. She knows there is a certain amount of these cleansing acts required for her to be able to meet her strongly desired goal and to be able to dwell in these high frequency, bliss-filled worlds forever! And with her mind resolutely made up, she is intent on toughing it out no matter how difficult the ride is in the meantime!

But at some point she realizes the trip is getting harder and more merciless as time goes on. It seems the breaks between the ups and downs are getting shorter and less recuperative, leaving her increasingly exhausted from the ordeal and longing for it to be over to give her the rest she craves and needs. But life doesn't seem to care for her needs at this point: it's as if an inner voice keeps cheering her on and at other times mocking her intentions and efforts, encouraging her and discouraging her, thus forcing her to choose the side she wants to be on, hold on to, and measure up to. A deep fear begins to build up in her, threatening to jeopardize her every effort, thwarting her at every step, and beginning to foster the illusion that she is risking it all for nothing, that Loriolan can't ever be hers, that love is not worth living for, that there aren't any Gods and Goddesses who ultimately care, that she is absolutely powerless in the face of all the overwhelming evidence, and that death and hopelessness are more real and powerful than life and love can ever be. Why else is the world in the state that it is in, having everyone die after a life of short-lived pleasures and relative suffering and pain? So grave are her thoughts that her will to live begins to dwindle in the face of all the burdensome irrational thoughts and feelings she harbors and finds justification for at every step of the way. A vicious spiral of negativity pulls her down, threatening to implode and short-circuit her energy and render her ineffective on her way into the light of her desired goal, forcing her into resignation, into a darkly spreading agony of devastating proportions, extinguishing what little light and clarity she is still able to perceive, and paralyzing her will to live and her ability to function as a human being. A huge cloud of darkness envelops her, ready to end her life when, out of nowhere, an inspiration prompts her to give it one more try, to keep holding on to life with all the might she has, to not despair and give up but rather believe in her higher self that will most likely come to her rescue if only she continues to believe in it, and to ultimately give the Divine Source of Life the credit of being the most marvelous phenomenon she will most likely ever come across, able and willing to help her out of her dilemma if only she dares to dream again, hope again, and allow the unconditional love and mercy of the Divine to throw her a life anchor, to pull and lift her up into the Heavens from which she is born, ready to integrate her back into the ranks of the blessed ones who dwell in the Heavens for all of eternity.

Indirali lifts her eyes up, tears streaming from her face; of course she is ready to give it another try! She has only been waiting for such blessed opportunity to hear the voice of the Divine address her, encourage her, and show her the way! It was never she who left the path and fell into deepest agony; it was the weakness of many accumulated karmic burdens that threatened to squash the light out of her! But she is over that now, now that the Divine Source has begun to speak to her, and if it is up to Indirali, there is no need to go back into this state of despondency ever again, for her immanent nature is happiness and love, and she longs to be surrounded by beings who live by these values incessantly and permanently. So positive and full of hope is her interconnection with the Divine

Source that the last veils of ignorance and energetic distortions begin to dissolve, freeing her view to encompass the vastness of her being and the unity of all of life! She beholds a light of such super-shining radiance that her eyes feel flooded with an ocean of the highest frequencies any human can behold, prompting her to dissolve her remaining essence in the light that knows no boundaries, and thus bringing her home to the place she never fully left and always longed to return to.

As she steps into the light, it begins to clear and presents her with the vision most likely to happen to her in her glorious future should she in fact undertake this most challenging of all paths, the path of most radical self-transformation and of the dissolution and purification of all the remaining karma from all her earthly lifetimes! Indirali sees herself surrounded by the most illumined beings she can imagine, lovingly interacting with them for the wellbeing of all the souls inhabiting different worlds, including the one she just mastered the life lessons of and thus ascended from, readying her for her return to Earth and for a fulfilling life and mission at the side of her eternal soulmate, the future mer-king of their common king- and queendom of — and the name just comes to her, as if Goddess Aphrodite whispers it into her ear — Aurorazuris! An empire that functions like a light vortex opening to higher dimensions of light-filled living, allowing aspiring souls to travel through the inner dimensions of purification to ultimately unite with their brothers and sisters of the light-filled realms! She sees herself happy and fulfilled, deeply in love with her husband and with life itself, abundantly flowing over in what good she has to give and share with the world, and experiencing the satisfaction of a deep, loving bond among her family and friends, as also between Loriolan's family and friends. There is peace for as far as the view stretches, and citizens of their families' combined kingdoms deem themselves lucky and blessed, for their leaders are of the highest integrity and of far-surpassing wisdom, their compassion enveloping the collective soul as if it were God's beloved child that does not need to want and lack anymore.

Indirali falls to her knees, thanking the Divine Source for lifting her out of her limited being and world and for showing her this most inspirational and most probable outcome of her life's quest, now that her mind is made up to follow her dream and intentions through whatever harsh inner and outer circumstances will present themselves on her way, as long as love eternal awaits her at the end of it, and a peace that surpasses all understanding. She is totally up for it and begins to slowly surrender into the feeling of being pulled back into the Here and Now of the present moment, of stepping back out from the mirror of truth and sharing her vision with two loving souls who can't wait to help her get on with her mission.

CHAPTER 33

*W*ell done!" The Oracle is full of praise and admiration. "You went for your goal straight on and gave it your absolute all! I wish all souls of this planet would not only have it in them, but would also actually act on their God-given ability to penetrate the individual and collective boundaries that choke the higher life force out of their bodies and realities." She smiles serenely: "Maybe one day soon again, when the universal Sun of spiritual Spring floods life on this planet with its rejuvenating, warming rays, the Earth will be turned into the paradisiacal haven it used to be, thus inviting and housing the many frolicking, bliss-exuding races of the deva queendoms that have gradually left the physical reality of this planet throughout the last many centuries, in order to be able to survive and maintain the integrity of their own divinely-suffused natures on higher dimensions of existence during these harsher realities of a dawning spiritual Winter on planet Earth."

Still in an elevated state of highest perception, appreciation and love for life, Indirali looks the Oracle deeply into her radiant eyes, conveying interest in her statement but, at the same time, also some subtle puzzlement, for she in fact had just a little while ago encountered Nature spirits, fairies, and elves in the meadows and woods they passed through with their carriage and whose existence, therefore, is a confirmed fact for her, for she saw them interacting with and enlivening Nature to the delight and soul nourishment of anyone who can feel their benevolent presence.

The Oracle picks up on her inner question, and explains: "Compared to how it used to be during the spiritual Spring season on Earth, the average human lifespan is now much shorter, only a fraction of what it was, limiting the individual remembrance to just fragments of its former capacity, leaving the abundance, wealth, and beauty of innumerable natural expressions in the dark corners of forgetfulness, and with that, the memory of the existence of many different species of Nature spirits has vanished from collective awareness for now. What you see today, my child, is but a tiny fraction of the former glory, of the overflowing cornucopia of distinctive, beautiful plant life, with the Earth now rather resembling a progressively dying body whose soul essence is departing to continue its existence on higher, refined frequency levels of existence, levels that still resonate with the large degree of life force these Nature-bound spirits live and function on. And much like the human soul that leaves the body during the individual's death experience, the physical planetary body also loses its life force and decomposes in its own cosmic time to return to the dust it is made of, devoid of conscious awareness and devoid of the awareness of the devas that once inhabited this level of physical existence with all the beauty and wealth they embody."

Indirali is shocked to hear this truth of growing inner emptiness so bluntly stated as the Oracle just did. With a sense of displeasure, she inwardly reels from this disheartening revelation, trying to find a solution to this distressing condition that seems to be spreading on Earth whether the average inhabitant is consciously aware of it or not. Something in her tells her that she does not want to wait around for this Nature-consuming event to play itself out but that she rather wants to be part of a higher solution that will not only save these many delightful Nature folks from having to withdraw to the inner realms — because of the harmful, polluting human behavior and compromised collective awareness — but will also help enliven human consciousness to embrace and celebrate the Nature spirits as part of their own higher connections to life source.

"Most humans have lost the ability to see and communicate with the Nature spirits and have begun to ignore their needs for the purity of the natural environment and of the inner emotional landscape — individually and collectively — a purity that begets and underlies all outer manifestations," the Oracle reiterates. "Your ability to communicate with these refined, ethereal beings supports you in attuning yourself to the laws of Nature and to the Divine Source of Life that upholds all life expressions. This attunement and surrender to life-enhancing tendencies enables you to keep following the pure impulses of your heart and live your life according to the life-supporting principles that govern and underlie all physical life expressions and all of creation. Thus, moving along the life-affirming spiral of purification and physical ascension, you are magnetically attracted towards the Source of Life, cumulatively diminishing the risk of wandering off and erring from the most direct, royal path of self-transformation that exists and the focus on which, in the end, leads to ultimate self-realization. Your love for life and your respect and compassion for every aspect of it, give you the courage to face any and all challenges on this path and give you the power to overcome them one by one. Thus you outgrow the grasp of the wicked ones, the ones who violate and ravish Nature as they violate and ravish their own kind and nature with an awareness that dims and diminishes with every hurtful act they perform." She slightly touches an ethereal branch, prompting the branch to unfold into myriads of smaller twigs and leaves and then erupt into the most beautiful blossoms Indirali and Eurylochos have ever seen. A transcendental white and pink sea of blossoms unfolds in front of their stunned eyes, awakening the memory of such opulent expressions of blissful, revitalizing, and mesmerizing natural spectacles that once belonged to Earth's population's everyday experiences, an ecstasy of sense-enrapturing scents that once interacted with their fully functional brains, causing them to channel highly potent, cosmic life energies into and throughout their bodies, keeping their life force centers wide open and powerful and allowing them to see and interact with the Nature spirits that weave their energetic magic throughout all of Nature, imparting Divine intelligence and energy into the vast array of expressions of Flora, the Goddess of all plant life.

"Your eternal beloved is mastering the five elements as you are, and being a member of the water race, his focus is especially on the water element as well as on its opposite or complementary element, the fire element, in order to integrate the two polarities with their accompanying characteristics, and if he succeeds in mastering these, he will develop a wholeness that will allow him to meet and unite with you in the abode of the Gods, the transcendental Heavens beyond the fifth element of the ether and akashic realms," the Oracle continues to explain, "leaving you on your journey to primarily master the earth and air elements to form a unified soul with his, beyond the grasp of duality. Because as I understand it, he is to swim the world's oceans — the water element — and penetrate into the interior of the Earth to unite with and transcend through the inner sun — the fire element — whereas you will walk the Earth with all its mountains, forests, and meadows — the earth element — and climb the windswept mountains to befriend and gain the support of the air spirits, the sylphs, and the winds — the air element — to lift you into the Heavens of the unified beings and the Gods."

"Yeah!" Indirali is all ears as her eyes begin to moisten slightly, for Loriolan is home to her soul and heart, and hearing about him tears open the wound of their ongoing separation.

"In order for you to progress on your path of mastery over the earth and air elements, you will want to not only pass through Nature, and in some rough areas probably feel its faltering aspects heavy on your soul — beware to not be overcome by it and falter from this collective karmic burden yourself — but you will also want to find a way to benefit Nature greatly in some special way, helping the Nature spirits to keep functioning and enlivening the earthly natural landscapes for as long as possible," the Oracle suggests wisely. Then her hand moves up, as if to indicate the ascent of Mount Olympos: "Do you have a plan on how to approach the abode of the Gods and Goddesses? Were you given an inspiration, vision, or invitation?"

"Goddess Aphrodite spoke to me in the temple," Indirali reveals. "She asked me to seek your guidance and to come meet her on Mount Olympos, the abode of the Gods and Goddesses." Her eyes betray her joy and pride that the Goddess of Love herself addressed her such, but a subtle nervousness vibrates in her voice as well, prompting the Oracle to take heed of Indirali's most inner needs.

"So you will have to traverse the Adriatic Sea by ship to get to the land of the Illyrians and to Macedonia if you don't want to spend several times the amount of time it would take you to travel by land, along the long curving shoreline, and risk being severely thwarted by a vast area of mountains and wild, unexplored coastal areas along the way." She pauses to await Indirali's reaction.

Indirali nods reflectively, for she has not given it much thought yet, but upon hearing the Oracle's suggestion, she realizes how unprepared in her mind she truly is for this long and arduous journey and adventure. Her two options are to either wander and climb endlessly in the mountains or to traverse the Adriatic Sea by ship, risking to be thwarted by Poseidon, whose curse may prevent her from reaching the Illyrian shore safely. Sweat breaks out on her forehead all of a sudden, and she can't help but feel the urge to faint. She grasps around to find support, only to realize that soft, misty clouds carry her gently and that she is far from falling, and from falling into oblivion. The Oracle is here to help, and none of Indirali's anxiety will change that.

"You will want as much support of Nature as you can possibly get in order to attain your goals, and master the water element along your way by winning the support of the air spirits!" The Oracle sparkles her eyes at Indirali: "Zephyros, the God of the gentle West Wind that brings spring to any region he blows over, is one of my trusted friends and colleagues. You will want him on your side when you cross over to Illyris, for his winds blow to the east, the very direction you want to go. I suggest you conjure up his presence with a magical invocation of your melodious voice, accompanied by some alluring pan-pipe play, then try to win him over to grant your request with something he likes and identifies with, like hauntingly beautiful flute music that will have him joyously dancing to your tunes. If you succeed in evoking his interest in you, enough to show his face, you might approach him with your need for his assistance and ask him to please help you enlist the cooperation of the other Wind Gods to not play into Poseidon's wrath and blow strongly against Zephyros's winds, lest the ship you happen to be on gets tossed around and shipwrecked under the onslaught of stormy winds and waves coming from any and all directions."

Then the Oracle continues to describe how Zephyros's wife, Iris, is a gentle and compassionate Goddess as well, being the Goddess of the Rainbow, the bridge and messenger to all the other Weather Gods, and once won over, would definitely pass on Indirali's request to help her secure a safe passage. Indirali is beside herself upon hearing such a wonderful solution to what looks like the biggest challenge on her quest. The Oracle recommends Indirali captivates the panel of the Wind Gods with an extraordinarily beautiful, ecstatic dance that leaves them spellbound and unable to deny her request, for she will have demonstrated her mastery over the air element with her graceful, ethereal movements and Divine Source-attuned attitude, leaving them to marvel about her inner, deep commitment to highest, Divine values and ways of living. She says that if Zephyros cooperates, Indirali will get to meet Boreas, the North Wind, Notos, the South Wind, and Levantera, the East Wind, along with several other winds that blow from any thinkable direction. The key is to stay calm inside and not let the presence of these powerful Wind Gods throw her off her balance, for they will try, with some being obstinate teasers, and being wildly windy and passionately stormy at heart.

Indirali confirms she understands, but deep inside she feels a nervous anticipation creeping up on her. Her father also looks quite disturbed and worried, for it is not every day that he lets his daughter go off on her own to meet with the powerful Gods of the Weather, and the Gods and Goddesses beyond earthly concerns.

The Oracle, however, drowns out any worrisome thoughts and feelings with her sunlit smile, inviting Indirali cheerfully to entice Zephyros to gently sweep across as many fields and meadows as he possibly can, since his winds help Chloris, the Goddess of flowers and blossoms, to spread her colorful, beautifully smelling garment across the natural landscapes of the human world, thus helping to enliven and strengthen the presence of the fairy and elf kingdom on Earth. She says this would be a nice way of helping planet Earth to feel more healthy and vibrant and to have the spiritual realms be more intertwined with the physical world and realities, allowing for a softer, gentler atmosphere to suffuse the planet. This certainly would contribute to her mastery over the earth element, as a happier Earth will most assuredly release her easily to her higher destiny and destination.

Indirali agrees and hopes she will be able to impress Zephyros enough with her invocation and flute play for him to consider her requests. She had some lessons in flute play as she grew up; her primary instruments, however, are the harp and lyre, and to now have to depend on and excel in her flute play seems a bit daunting to her. But the Oracle assures her that for as long as she thinks only about pouring her heart and soul into her playing, she will do just fine. Then she gives Indirali the magical invocation she is to use to conjure Zephyros's presence and attention, and tells her where to find him at this time of the year, with spring having just begun and his winds being in full demand by all the Nature spirits. She says that it will be a gift from Zephyros if he helps her cross the Adriatic Sea since he has his mouth full to blow just on land alone at this time. But he is a very nice fellow who likes to see the good win, and once he realizes Indirali has a heart for the Nature spirits and that she herself is in love with a Nature spirit of the oceanic world, a merman, he will certainly take heed and will most likely try to help her as best he can, especially when she succeeds in enchanting him through her music with her lovely essence and being.

And again, Indirali appreciates the Oracle's wise words of recommendation and agrees to follow her guidance to the letter. Then the Oracle needs to address a less pleasant subject, namely on how Indirali and Hedna might want to travel in these spiritual Winter times, being women, and especially Indirali being the Princess of Lucania. She thinks it's wise to hide their true identity from anyone they might encounter along their path since a certain breed of less conscious men, who are unable to deeply care and love, would rather give in to their lower-self nature than live by the higher principles of decency, morality, and virtue. She makes Indirali aware of the possibility of being treated unfairly and as less than a man along the path since the male majority dominates the war-prone world of today with their aggressive and sexually-driven ways, making it difficult for women to travel safely alone, unencumbered by man's lower urges. She therefore proposes that Indirali and her maidservant dress like men and thus limit their physical endangerment substantially.

Indirali gulps. Another one of these unforeseen problems she wasn't fully aware of until the Oracle — bless her heart — addressed it for her. Gratefully she nods her head in consent, deeply wondering about the hostile environment through which she and Hedna will be travelling.

Eurylochos feels increasingly restless. He suggests providing Indirali with a carriage and having one or several of his most trusted guards accompany her for most of the way. Both the Oracle and Indirali smile at him, for his heart is in the right place, but they also know that he won't be able to protect her throughout all her travels and that standing up for herself will be required of Indirali if she wants to reach her goal, to demonstrate her growing maturity and mastery over the elements, including and foremost of all, over the human nature itself. Still, she thanks her father for his caring offer and accepts the carriage and one guard. With words of appreciation, she makes his loving heart understand that she will be fine no matter what and that she will make him proud, for she will succeed in her mission and return to help him restore peace in Lucania and the neighboring kingdoms. With tears of joy and sadness, Eurylochos releases his daughter to her own fate, trusting in the Divine plan of life and that goodness and love will prevail in all of their lives.

Then the Oracle directs Indirali's attention towards one more challenging station along her path. She says that the City of Gods at the base of Mount Olympos was once inhabited by enlightened people of all walks of life, philosophers, architects, priests, astronomers, scientists, poets, artists, and more, all wanting to be as close as possible to the Gods and Goddesses of their beliefs, but that nowadays this illumined citizenry has vanished to give way to a pile of wannabes, souls who lost their connection to the Divine Source of Life, and like everywhere else on this Godforsaken planet, the City of Gods has become a conglomeration of lower selves, with several people having turned to black magic to help them stay in control, and lowlifes running the city's social and commercial life, reigning supreme in the many taverns, bathhouses, massage parlors, and brothels that have popped up along the crowd-filled streets for the entertainment of large numbers of visitors, high and low, and for the fulfillment of the insatiable hunger any starving soul feels deep in his chest as the individual desperately tries to distract himself from the fact that he lost contact to the one Source that alone can fulfill the gaping void and agonizing emptiness he feels in his soul.

Eurylochos lets out a sigh of deep dissatisfaction. What hellhole is his beloved girl trying to get herself into? What more disconcerting news will he hear here today? The sweetness and elevation of their meeting place in the clouds stand in sharp contrast to the disturbing and almost vicious prospects to which his daughter will be exposing herself. He knows he should just let her go, supporting her from the inner levels with his positive attitude, but the man and father in him wants to make absolutely sure no harm will befall her, the baby girl he raised to be such a beautiful, graceful, and independent thinking being as she is, hoping that her delicate and refined nature will survive the harshness of a world that often persecutes those who stick out from among the mass-conscious average with their inner light and beauty and who, therefore, are likely to be punished and hammered into mass-average shape by the mob, or eliminated, so the average person can avoid being reminded of his own shortcomings and need not take a shocking look into the mirror of self-reflection, where he risks seeing his compromised spirit, aging face, and faltering soul! — But again, the blissful frequencies the Oracle is radiating begin to drown out his concerns, and one by one, they dissolve as soon as they emerge, leaving nothing but harmony and deep trust in Divine Providence and Its Workings.

Responding to a questioning frown of Indirali, the Oracle begins to explain that the City of Gods is the shadow side of the celestial dwelling place of the Gods and Goddesses, for it represents all the accumulated collective karma that stands in the way of living in unison and harmony with the Divine Ones. She says it is a dividing line between souls of different worlds, keeping the undeserving souls in the worlds they create and resonate with, away from the glory and magnificence they once knew and experienced when they were still able to vibrate and resonate with the purity and unconditional love of the higher realms. She reiterates that only a pure and divinely-surrendered soul, a soul of great purpose and vocation with the single-minded focus of a deeply devoted heart and mind, will be able to penetrate the thicket of lower-self vices, able to not be distracted, tempted, and overcome by the false promises and overwhelming allurements of the most hideous kinds. So treacherous and entrapping are the city's influences over the soul that the inhabitants sincerely believe themselves to still be the chosen ones, thinking they live in accordance with the Divine principles of life but are nonetheless, at any moment's notice, ready to destroy anyone who dares to question or challenge their rotten beliefs, even if the person they feel challenged by does not oppose them overtly, so long as his whole nature rubs them the wrong way and doesn't contribute to making them feel superior.

"Is there any way to circumvent this city altogether?" Indirali wants to know, because by now she does not see any merit in entering this Godforsaken place. But the Oracle points out that this city is the departing point for anyone daring to climb and ascend the mountain. She says there are still some high-minded, good-hearted people strewn around the city, and it's best to quietly affirm to herself that she and Hedna will find someone who can offer them a place to stay while they prepare for their ascent. Otherwise they will be quite exhausted from the journey, with no decent resting place to nurture them for their challenging climb. The Oracle also emphasizes that the negative belt around the base of the mountain has to be penetrated and traversed if she truly wants to meet Aphrodite at the top of the mountain. Otherwise she might end up dead or lost, like many other individuals who tried to reach the top before her and failed for lack of working through the negativity, resisting temptations along the way, or overcoming the obstacles before them, all of which are necessary preparations for the immense purity any persevering aspirant will encounter on the top of the mountain. Only a soul who has purified itself through these tests and tribulations will most likely not be destroyed by the powerful life-force charges the Gods and Goddesses impart on those souls who try to meet them there on top of the world. It is therefore paramount for Indirali to meet, withstand, and overcome all obstacles and temptations in her way with the attitude of a true heroine, courageous, fearless, and daring, steadfastly anchored in her higher values and unconditionally loving attitude towards life. Then the gates of Heaven must surely part and let her through, so she may attain enlightenment and unison with her eternal beloved, her twin soul from all lifetimes, past, present, and future.

Indirali is overcome with emotion. She understands her mission and journey now better than before and can't wait to get on with it. The Oracle gives her last advice to the two travelers, then indicates it is time to leave. With gratitude showing on her face, Indirali falls to her knees to give the Oracle the respect and appreciation she deserves for her overwhelmingly generous and wise guidance. Eurylochos shares the sentiment and falls to his knees as well. They both received what they came here for, and both their hearts are full of appreciation and love as the Oracle blesses them and wishes them well and, with a soft and gentle spinning movement, takes her leave from them, gradually fading with her breathtakingly beautiful world into the mists of glorified realms, leaving the two travelers stranded in the midst of the dark forest they were originally picked up from by the Oracle's guardian and messenger tree spirit.

As if awakening from a most beautiful dream, they rub their eyes, smile at each other, and then begin their walk and descent back to the farmhouse to meet up with their entourage.